HOW WE SEE THE STARS

Tyler Bansil

To anyone that has been under the stars.

Lilith: Day Four

It just dawned on me how little I cared about school. Today I left in the middle of the day, not particularly scared of any sort of authority catching me ditching. By this point, I've ditched class so many times that leaving was nothing more than a two-second decision for me.

Usually, I don't have much of a reason to skip class, other than the fact that I rather watch paint dry than sit in class most days, but today I have *somewhat* of an excuse.

Last night I called my older brother, Taylor, to ask if I could come to visit him in his dorm. If I'm being honest, it was a kind of scary to talk with him over the phone. Even though our physical selves were tens of miles away. I felt like I was somehow isolated in a room with him. My voice wanted to start shaking, but I tried my best to hide that.

He said that I could visit him after his afternoon classes. Those ended at one, so I left my school at twelve to drive to his college a few miles away.

When I arrived at his college, I tried to remember where his dorm was and loosely guided myself there. Taylor went to a community college, so the vibe around there was pretty dead. I got the feeling that every single person that I walked by hated every day of their lives. The college wasn't the cleanest either. There was loud construction everywhere, random litter scattered throughout the campus, and people smoked wherever they pleased. Even though it was a shithole, I was just glad at the fact it got my brother in school and away from where our family lived. I feel bad for admitting such a thing, but he won't read this, and hopefully no one else.

I arrived a little early, mostly out of anxiety. Taylor kept his spare dorm room key under his welcome mat, so I unlocked the door myself. I've only been in his dorm once or twice before. But those times were with the rest of my family. It was harrowing enough to make me take a deep breath before entering.

I set down my backpack and began to look around the room, trying to get a feel for how Taylor lived. Funny enough, his long absence in my life made me forget how he was when we lived in the same room.

Everything and I mean everything, was clean and organized. His bookshelf was organized alphabetically. His bed was made and his floors looked like they were vacuumed less than a week ago. It wasn't just an upstanding-adult-clean; it was a crazy-person clean. It made me think for a moment he was maturing and becoming a normal person, but I had a really hard time thinking that through.

While waiting for him, I picked up a book at random from his shelf. Taylor was into books by famous philosophers or poets. The type of books that instantly make you feel more intelligent and give you more perceptiveness. It stumped me how comprehensive these philosophy books were. I knew all the texts revolved around greater forms of thinking, but I had a hard time grasping everything. I wonder if Taylor even remotely understood this because I didn't really associate him with his intelligence, but to be fair, I barely knew him.

The lock suddenly turned and my heart sank a few inches. Taylor walked in and I became self-conscious of where I was and what I was doing. Once again, I was feeling extremely out of place. Taylor greeted me with a wide, wholesome smile. I tried smiling back, but I couldn't smile properly without it feeling out of place for me. All I did was wave awkwardly. I tried my best to feel comfortable because he's my brother, but too many things felt wrong at once.

The first thing I noticed was his hair. It was brunette like the rest of our family, but for my entire life, I saw him with messy hair. It wasn't exactly a nice look, but you would get used to it after a while. But now, his hair was clean and sharp. He gelled it to make a left part. I didn't even know he had a left part. His physique was so proper and unfamiliar to my eyes.

Taylor wore this business-like outfit to school: Brown dress pants and a button-up shirt. His very apparent skinniness made it seem baggy, even though it was made for the average person. It was weird to see how properly he dressed when he went to community college. Everyone else went to school in what they slept in.

"Uh, how are things, Taylor?" I stood up from his bed. That probably wasn't the best opener, but it was *words,* at least.

It seemed awkward being in the same room as him, let alone having a conversation with him. Keep in mind, this is my own brother with whom I shared a house with for a good half of my life. He'd have to be my guardian if something were to happen to Dad. Yet I can't seem to be normal around him.

"Great. I got a raise at my job, so I can afford things like that book you're reading." He pointed to the book I had in my left hand.

Every time I talk to Taylor, I don't recognize his voice. It's so unfamiliar to my ear that I have to look up to make sure I was talking to the right person. I don't know how to describe it, but I felt like I was talking to someone new whom I've never met.

"I didn't know you had a job." *Or liked reading,* I thought to myself. I put the book back on his shelf.

"Yeah, I work at a music store down the road. The boss likes me a lot, so he gave me a raise." He said proudly.

Taylor was sorting his textbooks on his desk. He aligned them perfectly to the edge of his desk. He seemed to color coordinate them as well.

"That's nice," I commented, with a genuine smile this time.

"Also, check this out." He went into another room, making me hold my breath for a second. "I bought this." He brought an old-looking guitar, either that or the wood was very darkened.

"A guitar?" I questioned.

"Yeah, I bought it a couple of weeks ago. I've been wanting to learn how to play since forever ago!" He sat down with it and stared at it like a kid gawking at a new video game.

"Do you know any songs?" I asked, looking at the guitar instead of him.

"Yeah, I've been practicing this one in my free time."

He started strumming away at the guitar. I could tell it was some country song of some sort. Taylor wasn't much of a singer, but I could hear his quiet humming through the sound of the chords.

I started to silently phase-out and only heard the mere rumor of guitar music rather than it being the main sound.

The way he strummed at his guitar reminded me of my cousin Tess. The slow plucking of the strings to make some sort of melody felt so familiar, but when Taylor did it, it felt so much different. If Taylor knew that it reminded me of Tess, he wouldn't dare touch the guitar.

"Hey, are you okay?" Taylor's concerned voice broke my train of thought. I looked up at him and he looked at me concerningly. I touched my face and a few droplets of water ran down my face. I didn't even notice them. "What's wrong?" Taylor asked. He started to back away a few inches away from me. I wiped off my tears, and I made sure to wipe them hard enough to feel like they never were there.

"Nothing." I started to laugh it off, not something I normally do. "That song started to remind me of Tess. I haven't seen her in a few months. I miss her a lot, y'know?" I lied, and pretty convincingly too, which I was happy about.

"Ahh yeah, you two were always around each other as kids." Taylor looked very uncomfortable but tried his best to look normal. I knew that would make him uncomfortable, so that's why I said it in front of his face. That's something we have in common. We're both bad at hiding our reactive emotions. It reminded me that we lived under the same roof at one point.

Taylor put down the guitar and averted his eyes from it.

"Yeah, we were," I said, continuing with the lie.

I tried to sound like I didn't just cry ten seconds ago, but there was still a lump in my throat that made me sound like I was in pain.

"Can I ask a random question?" Taylor asked. I was still slowly trying to forget the tears on my face. I hated myself for having tears in my body in the first place.

"Go ahead," I responded, clearing my throat.

"Do you remember that charm necklace that Mom had? The purple one." My eyes slowly widened.

"Yeah, it was like a children's toy, right?" I asked.

I realized I was barely making eye contact with him and just staring at his carpet floor.

Taylor started reaching behind his desk and brought out a small paper box. He plopped the box in my hands. I looked at him questionably.

"Open it." He suggested.

I opened it. I was speechless when I saw what was inside.

"D-did you make this?" I was stuttering over my words.

"No, actually." He said with breath-ey laughter. "When I was packing for college, I found this is some of Mom's old stuff. I was meaning to give it to you, but forgot about it."

It was the exact charm necklace Mom had. It was as clear as I remember it. It almost didn't look real.

When Mom was alive, she had this purple charm-looking thing. I strictly remember that she would wear it 24/7. She refused to take it off, even for showering or sleeping. If you find any photo of Mom past her thirties, this necklace is on her in every photo. For some reason, it was *very, very* special to her, for reasons unbeknownst to me.

"Are you sure you want to give this to me?" I asked, trying to be considerate.

I was never close to Taylor and sometimes I forget that he was also affected by Mom's death. He didn't express much emotion or change when I asked him about it. To this day, I'm not even sure how he feels about it.

"Yeah, I don't really have a use for it, and you seem like you need it more than me." He looked up at me and smiled.

"Okay thanks, it means a lot to me." I put it in my pocket immediately. I felt a quick rush of adrenaline and goosebumps the second it hit my pocket. I felt like a new person just because of one stupid necklace. I wouldn't dare wear it, though. It was too sacred.

Taylor had to leave for his lecture and after that, he had worked for a few hours. I asked him if I would stay in his dorm for a bit and read a little more of the book that I took from his shelf. He, without question, said yes. These casual favors are probably normal for regular siblings, but Taylor and I's relationship is so loosely knit that I was worried he'd say no.

I waited a few minutes until I knew for a fact he wasn't coming back. I checked his desk to make sure he didn't leave his keys or his textbooks. When the coast was clear, I reached into my bag and brought out three small security cameras. Our old house in Atlanta was surrounded by quite a bit of crime, so Dad bought seven small cheap security cams and we still had them, thankfully. I was worried they'd be so cheap and outdated that they wouldn't connect to my laptop, but they did.

I looked around the small dorm to see where I could place them. There were only three rooms in the house, the bedroom/living room, the bathroom, and the closet. I found a spot on the shelf that would hide the camera in plain sight, one behind his lamp and one in the closet, behind some dirty clothes.

My heart was racing for no reason like I was committing a crime (which I was). I told myself I was committing a crime to stop a crime. I wanted to see, for myself, if he changed. I had a strong conviction that I had to do this once I had the idea planted in my head.

I double-checked that all the cameras were on and connected them to my computer. I had this program where I could see all three angles at once. The quality of the cameras was so terrible, so it only detected every other frame. It was very laggy.

I closed my laptop and got out of there as fast as possible. I looked flushed when I walked out of the dorm, so people were looking at me weirdly when I was walking back to my car. It was written all over my face.

When I was driving home, I tried not to think about the camera. So, I wondered if Taylor ever thought of Mom like I did. Did he give me the charm necklace out of generosity, or because he resented her? That thought didn't sit well in my mind. It should be obvious what the answer to that is, but I wasn't sure what side of Taylor I was talking to anymore.

When I parked in the driveway, I took a second to take everything in. I didn't feel like myself. The way I sat in this car, my grip on the steering wheel, the music I played didn't sound the same, the way I parted my hair slightly to the left (your right) didn't feel correct.

I don't like to give these types of things a title, but I was having a minor identity crisis in my driveway. I decided to take out Mom's necklace out of my back pocket and stare at the details of it for a second. I looked at every detail. The charm was made out of plastic wires that were woven together. The cord of the necklace was made out of wool. The colors of the wire were black, white, and purple. There was a little star engraving near the bottom of it, signifying it was, in fact Mom's.

I smelled it, yes, I smelled it. It smelled like Mom. How does Mom smell? Not-so-strong perfume from the 1990s. The smell was exciting, exhilarating even. I couldn't believe it still smelled like her after all these years. It forced a smile on my face, probably the widest one I formed all year. A lot of guilt entered my body subsequently. Once again, having one of Mom's things in my possession felt like I was damaging it.

I spent the rest of the day helping Dad unpack everything from our move. It shouldn't take four days to unpack things, but to be fair, Dad is 80% of the manpower in the house, so he has to do most of the heavy lifting. The older he gets, the more worried I become that his back will just *give out*. We move pretty often, so that worry probably won't die down any time soon.

I think this is our sixth time moving in the past eight years? To be honest, I stopped counting after our third move. You know that smell of a new house when you move into it? It's like the smell of newly dried paint and years of dust.

Anyway, I'm used to that smell way too much. You don't get used to it either.

I wish I could say moving was a pleasant experience. Dad calls it 'traveling the world' but we've literally never left the state of Georgia. I don't complain though, since I realize how hard it is being a single Dad.

My younger brother isn't really old enough to fully decide if moving a lot is a good or bad thing. From what I observed, he tends to look on the bright side of things, which young kids tend to be good at. The first day we moved in, he was ecstatic at the fact that the past owners painted his room a dark blue.

Meanwhile, mine was painted a very light pink which wasn't noticeable at first, but after being in the room for more than three minutes, I felt like I was surrounded by very chewed bubblegum. I wasn't really happy nor sad that I got a new room frankly. I thought to myself, *this works I guess,* which was the way I feel about most things nowadays.

"Congrats, Lilith, we've officially moved in," Dad said to me after we finished folding the last box. We both dusted off our hands over the pile of collapsed boxes.

I feel like I've heard that phrase a thousand times.

"Yep. Thanks, Dad." I said blandly.

"Are you hungry? I can make you and Mason dinner if you want." Dad offered.

Dad probably saw how exhausted I was, emotionally and physically, and offered to make dinner. I'm usually the one that makes dinner, but I didn't have the energy that night.

"I'm just gonna call it a night." I rejected. Before I finished that sentence, I was already walking to my room.

To be honest, I really haven't been eating as much as I should be, at least for the last few weeks I haven't. I don't know what happened, but one day my appetite just seemed to dissipate. Just like one day, the idea of sitting down and eating something seemed so... *undesirable.* Whenever I get unbearably hungry, I just drink two glasses of water and try to sleep on it. Lately, that's been the source of my dinners and I've been losing a bit of weight because of it.

I looked at this kind of stuff online, and they said this is how some eating disorders start, but I convinced myself that I didn't have an eating disorder and this was just some sort of weird phase.

I spent the rest of the night writing *this*. I've always wanted to write a diary, like Mom, but never committed to it until now. So, if anyone else besides future me is reading this, first of all: shame on you, second of all: Welcome to 17-year-old Lilith's life.

I'm not saying I'm gonna die or anything, but I want to have something documented, not to be remembered, but to look back on when I'm older. Reading Mom's diary made me learn so much about her. When you write about yourself, you get to the *core* of yourself, maybe stuff you don't even know about yourself. The core of Mom was a lot to take in when I first read it. Some good things and a whole lot of bad things, but she was far from perfect, which was my mindset going into it.

The last written page in her diary was a message to Mason and me. Mason was, and still is very young, so he hasn't read it yet. I plan to show him when he gets into his mid-teens, so he can understand it. I bet if I showed him right now, he wouldn't fully grasp it.

I was tempted to write my diary in the missing pages of her journal that her diary was in. There are about fifty pages left in that journal I could write in. I'm willing to bet that Mom would have encouraged me to write in her journal if she was alive, but I couldn't bring myself to do it. I have trouble opening it to read sometimes, let alone putting my own writing into it. It's already been torn and beaten up throughout the years and I feel like putting my pencil strokes into it will damage it to its breaking point.

There was an extreme bittersweetness to reading those diary logs. On one hand, I get to know more about my mom and can fulfill myself with the fact that I can connect with her through her writing. But on the other hand, I always feel terrible before and after reading them. Traversing through every word was hard, without the constant urge to put it away in my bag. A notable spark hits me in the heart that makes it hard to keep going. It takes me a good ten minutes to open the diary itself without having some form of hesitation.

When I read this in a few years or decades, I want to see what seventeen-year-old Lilith had in her brain at the time. I just want to have something to write down. Mom wrote things down. That's why her writing was so mesmerizing to me as a kid, and even now. I know how terrible it sounds to somewhat idolize a fucked-up woman who almost brought down her family, but there were some good things about her. Things you would only know if you've read her diary.

Tyler Bansil

Lilith: Day Five

I was supposed to meet with an assistant principal today for a formal introduction to the school. I transferred to the school less than a week ago, but I was apparently supposed to talk to a staff member on the first day.

When I came into his office and talked with him, he was very surprised by how much I knew about the school's layout and its programs. Over time, I learned quickly that a lot of the schools in Georgia have the same layout, so I knew I wasn't going to get lost.

Transferring to a new school is weird. Everyone expects you to feel nervous or something in that nature. I just feel nothing, as depressing as that sounds. School, and the idea of getting an education before college, was almost a joke to me. I learned after my first year in middle school that the curriculum for every district is the same, so now I study everything in the summer. And I mean everything. The legal bounds were the only thing keeping me in school at this point.

A lot of my teachers did the usual transfer student thing where they make you introduce yourself to everyone in the class. I kind of half-assed it, so everyone probably thought I was depressed or something. In my math class, some assholey-looking guys called me sexy behind my back and said they would "totally have car sex" with me, which I told them to fuck off for.

It seemed like everyone in high school had something to prove to everyone. That either meant trying to fuck every girl they see or study themselves to death. I know it seems stereotypical, like the stuff you see in movies, but sometimes stereotypes are 1000% true. Whenever I'm walking from class to class, I swear I see either a dude in a varsity jacket pinning a freshman with glasses to a locker, or a kid with oily hair trying to stick his hand down a girl's shirt. This isn't anything new to me, but after seeing it half my life, I've gotten too desensitised about it.

I figured out quickly that I really didn't have to pay attention to most of my classes. I just sat in the back and pulled out one of Mom's journals and tried spacing out. I already knew what was being taught, so there was no point in paying attention to the lesson.

Of course, there are some power-hungry teachers who told me I couldn't do that. There was no point in arguing or telling them I supposedly knew everything. I did argue with my English teacher about it though. She was being a real bitch about it too, in English out of all classes. She was yelling at me, in the middle of class. A normal response would be to apologize, but I didn't have the patience to think of one. Instead, I just said that I already knew the English curriculum, in the least asshole-y way I could. She took offense to that and 'threatened' to give me the final. Naturally, I said I'd be fine with that, but she also took offense to that and sent me to the assistant principal.

I know this whole diary so far has been me just complaining and venting on paper, but I swear I never get angry that easily. It takes quite a bit for me to actually get angry. Thanks to my arrhythmia, getting angry becomes a regret, rather than an emotion. I even have to carry a bottle of pills in my backpack in case it flares up.

The first week of school and I was already being sent to the office. Fun. It ended up being the same assistant principal I met with in the morning. He was incredibly surprised that I already got in trouble just a few hours after being a student in this school. I explained what happened, and he sided with the teacher, naturally. He let me off with just a warning though, because it was my first week and that teacher was known to snap at students. Someone should've told me that sooner. Now I know not to even touch a book in her English class.

At lunch, I found a curb outside near the baseball field to sit down on. Nowadays I don't pack myself lunch, because I already spent the majority of my mornings preparing Mason's. I wasn't that hungry anyway, which is probably another factor to why I'm losing so much energy and weight. I'm starting to get minor headaches too, ugh.

After lunch was my last class of the day, which was history. This day was already off to a horrible fucking start, and I just wanted to stay in my room for the rest of the day. This teacher seemed pretty chill, so I carefully pulled out my book to read. I pulled out one of Mom's journals as well, to make it look like I was taking notes. Mom had a journal where she would just take random notes about literally anything. I write in it pretty often, even though sometimes I feel extremely guilty. Why do I bring them to school? I generally like to have all of them on me at all times, for spiritual reasons. It's also pretty beat up, like the other journals. The leathery cover had many holes, had different color splotches, and the spine was almost nonexistent.

After school, I'm responsible for picking up my younger brother, Mason, up from school. Dad has work from the usual 9-5, so if I wasn't able to drive, we'd be having a lot of problems. There was this one hectic period in my life where I wasn't old enough to get a license or a permit, so picking up Mason from school was always stressful. Sometimes I had to drive and hope to God the police didn't look in the window and see how young I was. Do you know how terrifying it is to drive when you are fourteen or fifteen years old and don't know a damn thing about driving? Meanwhile, begging to God that no one notices that someone that looks like a middle schooler is controlling the wheel. That was probably one of those stressful periods of my life.

Whenever I pick Mason up, he always has a slight frown on his face. I can tell he tries to hide it, but you're eight years old, it's hard to hide any emotion.

"Hey, buddy. How was school?" I asked Mason. He put his backpack in the trunk and jumped into the back seat.

"Okay, I guess." He said solemnly. I couldn't see behind me, but I can say for almost certain he was pouting.

Mason never really enjoyed school, as harsh as that sounds. That's one of the things we have in common as siblings. It might just be in our DNA or something. It doesn't help that we move all the time, so he can't grow any attachment to friends or teachers.

I was tempted to make more conversation with him about the school, but it was written all over his face that he would rather just be left alone in the back seat.

"Stay here. I'm gonna pick up something," I told Mason.

Mason nodded his head, and I made sure to lock the car and leave the windows only slightly open.

I stopped by a comic book store. I always passed by it when I was buying groceries and always thought I could stop here one day after school and buy one for Mason.

I picked up a random red comic book and ran to the cash register. The cashier could tell I was in a hurry, so he rang me up quickly. I stuttered over half my words since I wasn't used to talking to other people, so he was probably freaked out.

"Here, buddy." I dropped it in his lap.

"COMIC BOOK?" He screamed. I had the windows open, so some people probably heard.

"I thought you needed some cheering up." I smiled at him. He was too encased in the book to look at me, though.

"THANKS, LILITH!" He started flipping through the pages like a Christmas gift.

I normally don't hear Mason's childish-exciting-scream-tone very often, but it always brings a smile to my face when I do hear it.

"No problem Mason." I ruffled his thin brown hair, but he was too deep in his comic to notice anything.

I knew Mason wasn't exactly into comics and stuff relating to that, but I knew he liked anything that was designed to cheer him up.

It kind of dawned on me a few weeks ago that I acted more like a mom to Mason rather than an older sister. This probably makes sense to nobody besides me, but I've been thinking about it for the past few weeks. I make all of his meals, I take him to, and from school, I help him with homework and a million other things that a mother should be doing. That includes doing little things to cheer him up. It's not exactly a bad thing, but I wonder sometimes if Mason sees me as anything else than an older sister. It doesn't help that he didn't have a physical mother for most of his life.

When I was pulling up in my driveway, I noticed someone standing by our front door. I couldn't tell who it was since they were facing directly away from where my car was parked.

"Who is that?" Mason asked, a little worried. We're not used to having visitors unless it's mail.

"I don't know…" I said, with a scared undertone in my voice.

I quickly parked my car in the usual spot and turned off my car. The person kept knocking at the door, then checking their phone.

"Let me go check."

I got out of my car and Mason opened his door, too.

"Can I help you...?" I didn't get close to them, but close enough for them to hear me. But the second I could see the details of their person, the tight jeans, leather boots, the long reddish-brown hair. I knew who it was.

"Long time no see, Ms. Andrews."

"You're fuckin' crazy," I said, jokingly. A wide smile started appearing on my face that I couldn't control.

My close cousin Tess turned around and smiled at me. We haven't seen each other in some time now, so our smiles were wider than they'd usually be.

"What?" The both of us started laughing.

Tess always had this radiant, fun girl energy that I've gotten accustomed to. Her obvious southern background and accent added to her personality as well. I would never see myself tolerating her if it weren't for the fact that we were around each other so much as kids.

Mason jumped out of my car and ran into Tess' arms. Mason went nuts. Tess always adored Mason and Tess was the fun, upbeat sister that Mason never had. Their age difference is pretty apparent, but Mason was never intimidated by her age.

"Oh my god, he's grown so much!" Tess commented while fluffing Mason's hair.

"Tess, you saw him a few months ago," I said while laughing.

Tess is one of the few people in the world that can activate the 'fun girl' inside me. I don't see myself talking like this to anyone else. It sounds depressing, but I'm not used to laughing while talking. Those were usually separate things.

"Ye'ah, but kids grow so darn fast."

I brought Tess inside the house so I could cook lunch for her and Mason. I thought that Tess being around would put me in a mood to actually eat for once. But when I was in the middle of cooking potatoes, I couldn't bring myself to commit to eating. I stared at the boiling pot for like 30 seconds and that was long enough for me to almost gag. Something's fucking wrong with me.

"How's Mason been?" Tess and Mason sat down at our dinner table and Tess went on her phone while I cooked. Mason had headphones in, listening to whatever he listened to, so he couldn't hear anything.

"Same old Mason, I guess. Doesn't particularly like school." I said blandly. I had no reason to sound bland, but it was hard to sound excited when talking about Mason. Also, I was trying to hide the fact that I almost gagged at boiling food.

"Why doesn't he like school?" Tess asked. Her hands wrapped perfectly around the glass of water I gave her.

"It's hard to enjoy school when you move every year, Tess. We both know I learned that long ago." I said. Looking back on this conversation, I sounded more depressed than I would like to sound. But around Tess, I'm the most myself. That probably says a lot about who I am.

Tess had that look on her face that looked like she agreed with me, but didn't know what to say, or if she should even say anything. I kept looking at Mason to make sure he couldn't hear us.

"Darn, I admire that father of yours. Raising a family of three kids is hard, but sometimes I wonder where his head is at. Moving all the time ain't healthy for a household." Tess' southern accent became especially thick this time.

Family of three kids. I haven't heard that in a while. It didn't feel right to call us a family of three kids. Mason and I are fine, but thinking about the third kid left a bitter taste in my mouth. It's hard to wrap my mind around Taylor being considered family.

I kind of wanted to tell Tess about my visit to Taylor's dorm yesterday. The event is still fresh in my brain, so my emotions were still attached. Of course, there's no way I would forget about the security cameras. That is one of those events that will go with me to the grave. But Tess is the last person on earth I should talk to about Taylor. And I'm willing to bet she's the last person on earth that wants to hear about it.

"What brings you here, anyway?" I awkwardly asked, mostly to change the subject.

"I just wanted to check up ya. You don't respond to my texts." She jabbed at me. I literally never check my phone unless Dad calls me, so that's my excuse.

"You didn't have to drive for two hours to be here, haha. You could just call me or something." Atlanta is two hours away from Macon, where I live right now.

"Eh, I missed you anyway. It was about time I visited." Tess said with a wholesome tone.

Tess is the closest thing I have to a best friend, so these gestures mean a lot to me, even though I barely show it on the outside.

I served Tess and Mason their food. I was worried Tess would ask if I was going to eat, but she just started eating immediately when I plopped the plates on the table. I stared at the pot of potatoes one more time. I didn't gag that time, but I felt some sort of mental resent towards it.

When Mason was done, I told him to go to his room to do homework. Once again, feeling like a mom. I was worried that he could somehow hear our conversation through his headphones. We were sort of talking about him like he wasn't sitting right there.

"Yo Lith!" Tess called out.

Tess had a speech impediment as a teenager, so she had to call me Lith instead of Lilith all the time. After a long time of not seeing her, her saying that felt a little unfamiliar to my ear.

"What's up?" I turned off the water.

"Hand me that picture frame." She pointed at a blue glass picture frame next to the TV.

"This one?" I picked it up and held it up.

"Yeah, hand it to me for a sec." I handed her the frame.

She stared at it with a questioned face, tilting her head to the left and right like the picture was upside down.

"God, I don't remember the last time I saw the five of you together in one photo," Tess said out of awe.

I was trying to process the fact that I used to be a part of a family of five. Five whole people. For some reason, my mind couldn't wrap my head around that. Even right now, as I'm writing this, I still can't fathom it.

"I'm pretty sure this is like the one photo we all have together. Even when Mason wasn't born, we didn't have photos when there were four of us."

"How old were you in this?" Tess asked, still staring at the photo.

"What colored shirt am I wearing?" I asked in response. I didn't remember the photo that deeply, even though it's framed in the living room.

"Yellow with a star in the middle."

"I was probably nine or ten," I said with confidence.

"You can tell by the color?" Tess looked up at me in confusion.

"Mom always bought my clothes when she was alive, and she would always buy colors based on what age I was. First, it was pink, then red, and before she died, yellow." I walked back to the dishwasher.

"I'm surprised you remember those types of things. No offense, but as of late, I can't remember nothin' about your moms." Tess said as she put the frame back in the correct spot.

"None taken. It was a long time ago. To be honest, you probably remember a million times more than Mason." I said passive-aggressively.

This conversation wasn't making me uncomfortable exactly, but I didn't expect Tess to drive two hours here to talk about my dead mother. But to be fair, if I was her, I would have so many questions as well.

Something Tess didn't notice in that photo was that Mom didn't smile in that photo. In fact, if you look at any photo of Mom, she never smiles. She wasn't unhappy outwardly, but she would not smile. Dad and she always argued about it whenever we had to take photos, but that woman didn't smile.

"Lith, can I ask you some'n?" Tess asked with a sort of regretful tone in her voice, like she was forcing herself to say it.

"What's up?" I said for the second time. I wiped my hands as I turned around to face her.

"Do you ever blame your mom for anything? It's not uncommon for kids of dead parents to be a little bitter." Tess asked as she stared directly into her glass, not having the confidence to face me. When you talk to Tess long enough, you realize her southern accent becomes thicker if she says something serious.

I kept repeating the question in my head, not really having an obvious answer come to me. I've never thought about it that way. The weird part is, I bet all of Dad, Mason, and Taylor would have separate answers to that question if they were asked.

"You..." I looked down at a very specific speck of dirt on the floor. "You shouldn't blame dead people for things, that's my answer," I said to myself, rather than to someone I was talking to.

Mom was a terrible person, but I had trouble blaming her for things. It's hard to blame dead people for things. Dad is the best example of this. I know in the back of my head that a lot of the things in my life are the way they are because of Mom.

We changed the subject and Tess talked about her life in Atlanta before she had to go back to work. Even though I sat with her as she rambled on about things like school, her boyfriend, and whatever was going on with her, I struggled to listen. I was basically in my own head for the rest of the day, even going into the night. While I was reading Mom's journal late that night, I kept repeating Tess' question and my convoluted answer in my head, not even sure if what I said was how I truly felt.

While reading that night, I tried to picture Mom as a good person and a bad person and see if that would sway my opinion at all. Picturing Mom as a terrible person isn't hard, but picturing her as a good person was.

Some pages are written differently than others. It was like reading from the perspective of two different people. One was emotional and wrote like an insane person, the other wrote like an angel. Sadly, the insane part of her was the part I saw the most. The angelic part went into her writing, and now I'm reading it nine years after her death. I bet this all sounds poetic from an outside perspective, but it really isn't. She was a monster and her writing is trying to pull me away from that reality.

I remember at her funeral, I held back my tears so much. My whole face was scrunched up for the entirety of that day and then some, trying not to cry. I wanted to test myself and I passed. If I failed and cried, it proved that I wanted her to live. Crying would mean that I had physical proof that I wanted to stay with her on this earth. To this day, I keep that standard to myself.

No one had anything good to say about her at her funeral. It was basically a silent room of people wearing all black. The priest said the most generic funeral lines. "She lived her life the way she wanted to. She's doing better in heaven. She was a personality-filled person." We aren't even religious. I think Dad just wanted to hear someone of authority to say that his wife was in a better place.

Mason cried a lot, and rightfully so. Even if Mom was an axe murderer, he'd still bawl like crazy. That's just how two-year-old are. I tried to shut him up by covering his mouth, but Dad pulled me away from him. I don't regret what I tried to do, even though it wasn't the most ethical decision of mine.

Tess and Dad often ask me why I obsess over Mom's journals so much. There are only five journals worth of information to read, yet I've been trying to absorb information since her death seven years ago. When Mom was alive, she kept to herself a lot. She didn't have many friends and didn't make any effort to show me things about herself. When you're 10 years old, like I was, you don't realize that learning things about your own mother is crucial. I was basically deprived of knowing who Mom was. Mason is a more extreme case of this, being only 2 years old when she died.

These journals are all I have. Dad doesn't seem to show any interest in telling me things about Mom, so I try to absorb as much information as I can from reading them. Even if that means reading them on repeat until the day I die. To this day, I still don't know much about her. Yet I probably know more about her than Dad or her own parents. A sick reality, as I call it.

"Reading your mom's diary again, eh?"

Dad popped into my room and looked ready to go to bed. I looked up, and he smiled at me. I thought he would be asleep since he had work in the morning.

"Yeah, when I'm bored, I read them. Have you read these?" I asked. I heard Mason's snores through the walls.

"Not really. They seem too sacred to me, y'know?" I knew what he meant, but I didn't see that as an excuse.

"Do you miss her?" Dad asked.

I found it really confusing that a dad has to ask his own daughter if she misses her own dead mother. That should be a no-brainer for any other instance, but it really wasn't.

"More or less," I admitted. My brain didn't have a natural response to that. It wasn't a clear yes or a harsh no. "I think I just miss her for the sake of missing her, y'know?" Tess' southern accent was rubbing off on me a little. I cleared my throat.

That was a convoluted answer, but I didn't want to disagree bluntly. The answer was more complicated than a yes or a no. I bet Dad felt the same way, too.

Dad looked down and just sighed at the floor. "Do you miss your wife?" I asked, trying to get personal with him, which was a hard thing to do with him most of the time. It felt weird.

"Yeah, of course, if I didn't miss her, I don't deserve to be your father. She was an incredible woman, but you couldn't see that before it was too late." His words cut a little deep, for reasons unbeknownst to me.

I gripped the journal harder than usual as a sort of coping mechanism.

"I called Taylor today." Dad brought up. His voice sounded unsure, like his name carried a burden on him.

For some fucked up reason, whenever anyone said that name out loud, my heart dropped to my stomach. That was probably one of the reasons why I forgot that he's my older brother. Or maybe I choose to forget subconsciously.

"Yeah...?" I said with a lump in my throat.

"He said you visited him the other day. You didn't tell me that." He said like I was supposed to tell him.

"Oh yeah, I did," I said blandly. I wanted to say more in response to that, but I think the fewer words said in this conversation, the better. "I just wanted to see how he was."

"That's very considerate of you, Lilith. I didn't know you-"

"What did he say?" I blurted, interrupting him. I wanted this conversation to be over as soon as possible. I started to clench my fist out of some sort of spite.

"Oh yeah, uh, this might be a bit of a surprise, but he asked if he could move back in relatively soon." Dad struggled to say.

"..."

"Of course, he wanted to make sure you and Mason were okay with it. I haven't asked Mason yet. I wanted to hear your input on it first." Dad's voice went deeper.

I stared at my closed laptop across my room with all the security footage waiting to be watched. "Dad, I'm feeling kinda sleepy. Can we talk about this in the morning?" I said, hoping that he'd get the message.

I didn't want to look up, but when I did, Dad seemed very distraught and defeated. He was leaned up against my door frame, still as a board. I could tell he wanted to say a lot in response to that but knew he shouldn't. He just let out a slow exhale.

"Yeah, sure..." Dad's voice went deep and raspy. "I'll head in for the night then. Good night Lilith."

I slowly closed Mom's journal and put it by my bedside.

26

Mark: October 28

"Mark, I got you a baked potato." I heard a girl's faint voice to my right. I looked up from what I was doing and she was walking towards me.

"You know we're not allowed to eat in here, right? I'm pretty sure every classroom in the country has that rule." I responded.

Nicole dropped the potato wrapped in foil next to my bucket of paint.

"What? You said you were hungry and culinary class had just finished." Nicole said as she sat down next to me, eyeing down what I was working on.

I looked around the art room and the other people seemed to be snacking on stuff, too. The room was pretty confined, so it was easy to see what everyone was doing.

"I'll eat it later. I don't want to be kicked out."

"Relax, people come to the art room to do all sorts of stuff. There's literally a couple in here doin' some weird shit." Nicole pointed to a couple in the broom closet who was trying to hide the fact that they were making out, but I think everyone in the room knew what they were doing.

I was in the middle of making Nicole and I's Halloween costumes, so I had red paint all over my shirt. I didn't realize how hard it was to work with paint until now.

Nicole and I plan our costumes months in advance, usually in summer. We sit down at her computer and search the internet for costume duos. Last year we did Mr. and Mrs. Incredible and the year before we did Sharkboy and Lavagirl, one of our favorite movies.

A few days before Halloween, we either unbox the costumes that we ordered or we make them by hand. We're not exactly good at making costumes, or anything for that matter, but it's fun to do.

This year we chose Waldo from Where's Waldo. In the summer, we were deciding between that idea and being Bert and Ernie, but Nicole was not into the idea of being Bert, so we chose Waldo. It was a relatively easy costume to make ourselves, so last night I bought red paint, some white shirts, and two beanies. The pants needed for the costume were blue jeans, so we had that part covered.

"Did they add anything new to the festival this year?" I asked while painting stripes on my Waldo shirt. I looked at my watch since I was losing track of time. It was around five, so I knew the sun was going down or about to go down.

"My friend said the city upped the budget for the festival this year, so I'm expecting some new things. They add something new every year, so I'm excited." Nicole said, giddily.

"Dude, the Halloween festival is my favorite *thing* ever. I hope it's even better this year." I said, reminiscing on the time Nicole and I went last year.

I'm not one to over exaggerate something, but I wasn't kidding when it came to the Halloween festival. It completes the entire night for Nicole and me. The city rents out this big outdoor space and turns it into a Halloween theme park. There are haunted houses, live music, amazing food, games, and other things that make the $30 ticket worth it.

After we finished painting, we hung them in the courtyard along with the other artworks that were drying. It was getting surprisingly late, so Nicole drove me home. We normally hang out at her house after school, but I needed a way to get the splotches of paint off me.

"Jesus, dude, why is your phone ringing so much? Is someone texting you?" Nicole turned her head while she was driving. She also had some of the baked potatoes in her mouth.

"Sorry, I emailed some colleges earlier today and I think they're all responding at once." I didn't mean for that to sound depressing, but it just came out that way.

I took the phone out of my pocket and mindlessly scrolled through my email list.

"Why did you email colleges? We don't have to worry about that stuff until next year when we actually have to apply 'n shit." Nicole asked while making a U-turn. *Nicole, some people start worrying about college the minute they know what college is.*

"I just wanted to know about their law programs. I also want to see my options. Just to get an idea, y'know?" Nicole was trying to shove more potatoes in her mouth while we were at a red light.

At the beginning of this car ride, I was hungry enough to split the potato with Nicole, but receiving all these emails and the idea of reading them was sucking away my appetite.

"Isn't that stuff hella expensive? Law school is the opposite of cheap, from what I know at least."

"It is, but at least I'm thinking about stuff past high school. I don't think my parents can cough off enough money to pay for law school." I responded with a depressing exhale.

"Hey, if you get enough scholarship money, you could get into a really nice school for that. A lot can happen in one year, dude. You got this."

It's cheesy, but that's one of the reasons why I like having Nicole around. Not every friend of yours will support you as much as she does. Besides, we've been friends since kindergarten. I couldn't get rid of her even if I wanted to.

Nicole dropped me off, and I ran straight to the bathroom to wipe all the paint off my arms. It's been on there so long, the redness of the paint started to blend in with my skin. I had to pour a ton of soap on a towel and rub my arms with it until either the paint scraped off or my skin.

"Are you trying to get a rash or what's going on here?"

"Nah, I just spilled some paint on myself," I responded, washing paint off my fingers.

My dad came home from work and the bathroom is next to the front door. As soon as I heard him come home, he was already standing outside the bathroom.

"How was work Dad?" I asked.

My dad works as a police officer for Macon County Police, so it's always somewhat interesting to hear what my dad does. And of course, it gives me an insight into law.

"Kind of rough son, not going to lie." My dad looked really tired just by turning around and looking at him. His eyes seemed heavy, even though he probably wasn't sleepy.

"Did anything bad happen...?" I stopped my towel scraping to ask.

"Nothing immediate, but we got a sexual assault report today." My dad said depressingly. My dad leaned up against the bathroom door.

"Wow, that's not something we hear every day," I commented.

"I know. I was just as surprised as you are."

The town I live in, Macon, doesn't have that much crime. Of course, there are the usual number of petty crimes, but when it comes to *big* forms of crime. It's pretty rare. Hearing the words sexual and assault was pretty new.

"Luckily nothing extremely terrible happened, but it was attempted rape. It happened at a college party the other night." He said monotonously.

"That's unsettling..." I also commented.

At this point, I didn't know what else to say. The tone of my voice said more than my words themselves.

I didn't know what to say. The idea of that kind of stuff happening to kids similar to my age was a kind of scary. I'm going to college in less than two years, so that was even scarier to think about.

"I'm gonna look at the case more when I come into work tomorrow. I'm gonna head to bed. G'night." My dad's voice started to become fainter as he walked towards his room.

Mark: October 31

Yesterday I was hanging at Nicole's house doing some last-minute Halloween preparations, but I ended up staying the night. Even though it was a school night, neither Nicole nor I could get sleepy enough. After we finished the preparations, we planned to watch movies until one of us got sleepy, or both of us, and I'd go home. We watched two-and-a-half movies until Nicole said that I should just stay over for the night, which was a regular occurrence. I was too lazy to drive back home anyway, so I agreed. Our friendship has gotten close enough to where we are comfortable sharing the same bed. Nicole's bed was queen-size, so it could fit two people, unlike mine. When she sleeps over at my house, she has to take my bed and I always sleep on the floor.

Around 3 AM we 'tried' to sleep. I'd like to note that I had a good sleep schedule until that point. I *need* sleep to get through the day, let alone a school day, so I normally sleep at 10:30 by choice. If I sleep any later than that, a good third of my day is ruined. I was hoping the excitement from Halloween could cushion that, but I already knew when I woke up it'll be a bad time. Meanwhile, Nicole could sleep at any hour and have enough energy for the day. I guess all that partying and procrastinating on school work has its perks.

Once Nicole hit the bed, she fell asleep instantly, which wasn't surprising. I, on the other hand, was still trying to fall asleep. I wish I could lie and say that sleeping in a place other than my own bed was the reason for me not being able to sleep. I kept tossing and turning and changing sleeping positions. For my whole life, I've had one sleeping position, which was on my back, but somehow that didn't do the job. Also, sometimes sleeping next to Nicole is a nightmare. Some nights she'd snore loudly and when she finally stops, she starts sleep-talking, which I didn't think was possible. Tonight, was one of those nights where her periodic snoring and sleep-talking occurred and, combining that with my excitement for Halloween, made sleeping impossible.

Finally, at 4 AM, I fell asleep after laying on my side, away from Nicole, which felt off. When it became morning, Nicole had to wake me up, because my body slept through her alarm clock. The first thing I woke up to was Nicole shaking my torso.

"Wakey-wakey asshole," Nicole said. I heard her ongoing alarm clock in the background and extreme fatigue started hitting me.

"What time is it? I asked, with what little voice I could muster.

"Six in the morning."

"Why did you wake me up so early? School starts at 7:30." I complained.

"I thought I could make us breakfast."

"Can I just go back to bed? I'll be awake in thirty minutes. Besides, both of us don't eat breakfast."

"If there's any day that we need to start with a full stomach, today is that day. And thirty more minutes of sleep won't do anything, anyway." Nicole said like a drill sergeant.

Nicole pulled up on my side of the blanket and tugged on my legs. I lazily jumped out of bed and the both of us got ready. Nicole cooked us breakfast while I showered. The water woke me up a bit, but I was still very *out of it*. Getting two hours of sleep really does a number on me.

"Don't you need to shower?" I asked, drying my hair in the kitchen.

"I'm gonna be smelly tonight one way or another, doesn't matter to me," Nicole said while making pimento sandwiches.

I was pleasantly surprised to see how many people wore costumes at school. Usually, as you progress in school, the number of people that wear costumes decreases. Everyone did it in elementary school and now, only a percentage of people in high school bother to dress up. But this time, almost everyone in our building did it, which was a nice sight. A lot of the people went *all out* in their costumes, which made mine and Nicole's look pathetic. I still liked our costume though, mostly because I made it myself.

The bell rang for the next period and a bunch of commotion came from the courtyard. Nicole and I ran over to see what happened and two freshmen, who were both dressed up as Teletubbies, somehow got into a fight. The red one knocked on the purple one cold, and it was hard not to contain my laughter after I saw the red one swearing out the purple one who was unconscious on the floor. Something about two characters from a children's TV show getting into a form of violence tickled my funny bone a bit.

Two teachers had to pull away from the red one, presumably to the principal's office, and the purple one was taken to the nurse's office. At that point, a bunch of people were just stalling themselves to not go to class, so a teacher forced us to go even though we were late.

"Party? You mean festival, right?" Nicole said something about a party, but I was still laughing about the fight to hear what she said.

"Oh shit, right, I didn't tell you. My friend from college invited me to this Halloween party. Apparently, it's supposed to be legendary, since the girl hosting it has a big, mansion-like house."

"Nicole...really? Another party? You didn't get enough from your birthday? And we're supposed to go to the festival." I said, sounding frustrated.

Nicole had her birthday party last week, and it ended up being a whole mess. Long story short, she got drunk, and that never ends well for anybody.

"Listen, I won't drink, I promise. I'll be with you the whole time if need be, but I *really* want to go. If the party is a flop, we can ditch it for the festival. But I really want to go. Please?" Nicole pleaded.

I thought about it. My head still hurts from her party the other week. I didn't need another episode of 'Saving Nicole from her partying bullshit'. And I was really looking forward to the festival too.

"Fine, we'll go," I said with a bitter taste in my mouth. Nicole squealed in excitement.

In all fairness, even if I refused to go, going to the festival by myself or with my other friends wouldn't be the same.

It was around 4:30 when we arrived back at Nicole's place. As soon as we got inside her room, I plopped in the middle of her bed and passed out.

When I woke up, the room was significantly darker. I looked outside, and the sun was no longer there. I freaked out for a second and thought it was the next day. I stood up and looked at Nicole's clock. 9:32. *Phew*.

"Did you have a bad dream or something?" I turned around and Nicole was.

sitting on her desk, laughing to herself.

"I didn't think I'd be asleep that long. Why didn't you wake me up?" I asked. I looked at my arm and they had a bunch of nap-wrinkles.

"You look so peaceful when you sleep, I didn't wanna wake you haha." I turned on Nicole's lights and my eyes started to adjust. "And besides, I was gonna wake you up in a few minutes if you didn't do it yourself." I looked at Nicole for the first time and her face was covered in white and black makeup.

"WHOA!" I yelled. Her shirt and jeans also had plenty of holes in them. She looked like an abandoned spirit, which was the look she was going for, I guess.

"Looks good, huh?"

"I mean, yeah. It's a little much, no?"

"Boys drool over this kind of shit. Half girl and half dead." I was flabbergasted at the way she described herself.

"You're really trying to get a date tonight? Out of all nights? There are plenty of weirdos at these parties and you know that better than I do."

"I'm willing to take my chances. If I'm not drinking, I'm gonna hit on a guy. If I'm feeling really outlandish, I'll do both." I wasn't sure if she was using that word correctly, but I got her point.

Nicole and I got in her car and we started driving to God knows where. Even after sleeping on it, I still felt bummed that we weren't going to the festival. I wanted to be mad at Nicole for that, but it wasn't like me to be petty for more than five minutes. We drove by the festival and I felt like a kid who just drove by Disneyland. There was an incredibly big bonfire, which wasn't there the year before, so my mind ran wild, speculating about what was going on.

Nicole wasn't kidding when she said the party was at a mansion. Macon, and Georgia in general, didn't have many large estates. Maybe in the larger cities, but in small towns like Macon, not so much. There were an incredible number of cars. Nicole and I had to park five minutes away from the house itself. By the sheer number of people, I was expecting to be jumped at any moment walking in a secluded area. I saw some scarily realistic Halloween decorations outside the house, and there were plenty of them. Some people even acted as props to scare people entering the property. This wasn't just a party, it was an *event*. There were some college kids and maybe adults outside in the lawn area playing beer pong and throwing eggs at each other. So, far, I haven't seen anything I didn't expect.

"How did you even get invited? I don't see many high schoolers here." I asked. There was some background music, but it wasn't deafening.

"I knew some seniors last year when I was a sophomore. I stayed in touch with some and they hooked me up with an invite, but I honestly think anyone can just walk in and just blend in."

"We don't exactly look like college students, y'know?" I pointed it out.

"*Pfft*, you look older than you think, and my makeup makes me look mature-er. And everyone is wearing costumes. There could be a nine-year-old here and no one will know."

When we walked inside, it was as chaotic as I imagined. The light made it so I could barely see my surroundings. I realized quickly that college parties are like high school parties, but dialed up to an eleven.

There were a ton of people, and this was only the first floor. Even Nicole looked intimidated. There were multiple colors of light flashing from multiple directions. Of course, there was *deafeningly* loud music, but at this point, every party-goer should expect that. All I could think about was how Nicole. would handle this. I doubt she's been to something like this.

"I'm gonna follow you around for a while. I need to get comfortable in this place. I'm a little star-struck right now." She admitted it.

Nicole and I just walked around and looked at what was happening. People were watching sports in the theater area, dancing in the living room, and smoking outside. Almost everyone's costumes were so 'out-there. It made our costumes look lame, but then again, some people didn't bother to dress.

I was immediately attracted to the dining area since I hadn't eaten a candy apple. I dragged Nicole to the snacks area, and I took some chips and sat down. Admittedly, we looked a little lame, just two Waldos sitting down, looking lost. I saw Nicole eyeing down the fun-looking shot glasses. They had little shot glasses that had devil horns and spider legs attached to each glass. She was incredibly antsy, and I didn't know if that was a good or bad thing.

"I see you eyeing the drinks," I commented, like a warning.

"Mark, I need *something* to get me going. Anything. Two shots and I'll be set for the night."

I concluded that Nicole's uneasiness was a bad thing. People near us were doing crazy party things like throwing pies in each other's faces and doing shots, and Nicole kept looking at them from afar.

"I'm not gonna boss you and stuff, but you know your limitations, right? If you get intoxicated and wander off, I'm not sure I can save you. *Again.*"

I was starting to sound like a parent. I found it incredibly ironic how my father encourages me to go wild and drink, meanwhile I try to prevent my friends from drinking. If this is a foreshadowing for how strict I will be as a parent, that idea scares me.

"I just need two shots, dude. *Two* shots and I won't even be drunk, I'll just be *relaxed*." I silently questioned the legitimacy of that statement. I let her go at some alcohol and I watched her down two shots in five seconds. "Okay, it should start kicking in soon."

"I'm gonna look around the place, you can do whatever you want." I nonchalantly said.

I could tell Nicole was holding herself back because of me. I didn't want to be known as the friend who makes parties unfun, as much as I wanted to, for safety reasons.

I left the kitchen area to wander the place. This was the first time I've been inside a house of this size, so I wanted to see what rich people's homes consisted of. The first floor was what you'd expect a home to have. Everything was just a lot bigger. Next to the entertainment room, they had a small library, which I was jealous of. Not because of the library part, but because it would be a perfect place to study. There were a couple of girls silently reading in there and they gave me dirty looks when I opened the door, so I apologized and left.

When you walk upstairs to the second floor, the first thing you see is a game room. Four flat-screen TVs with video games on them, ping pong tables, pool tables, and laser tag? You can buy equipment for laser tags now? There were a decent number of people up here, and the people here were pretty calm. Downstairs had a few bad apples, but this just seemed like a lounge area of some sort. I was tempted to hang out up here, but I held off. For some reason, parties kill my motivation to be social, which is ironic, I know. So, I didn't want to have to deal with playing with some people I didn't know. Maybe I was an ambivert.

Not much else was upstairs. A few locked bedrooms, some were unlocked, so it made me question if some people were 'sleeping' in there. I felt odd just exploring a house for the sake of it being a big house.

Some girl took notice of me looking around and confronted me. I lied and told her I was looking for my friend, which probably sounded more suspicious than I just admitted to looking around. I guess Nicole was right about me looking older than a high schooler. When she approached me, I half-expected to be called for not being a college student.

There was one more floor to the house. All the lights were shut off and nobody was hanging out up here. I pulled out my phone flashlight and started looking around. I didn't think till now that there was a high chance that there was a security system, but I proceeded anyway. For a moment, I felt like I was exploring an abandoned mansion and I was searching for ghouls or something. There was nothing interesting, though. I think it was a storage area. There were a couple of boxes that I didn't bother looking into. Other than that, there was just a small bathroom.

The longer I stayed, the more creeped out I felt. You can't ignore the feeling of being watched, no matter what you try to do to shake it off. It being Halloween, and a party didn't help my insecurity either.

To the left of the room, there was a door labeled: *"Roof Access"*. Creepily enough, the door was slightly open. I heard some people talking too, which made me both more freaked out, but slightly relieved at the same time. My curiosity, once again, got the better of me and I committed to climbing the stairs to the roof. I opened a heavy door that led to the roof of the house.

I breathed in the fresh air, which was incredibly refreshing. There were no visible lights on the roof, so I had trouble seeing where I was going, even with a flashlight. The people that were 'talking' ended up being a couple making out. Once again, nothing surprising. The guy had a Willy Wonka costume on, and the girl had a very skimpy Tinker Bell costume. The sight of that almost made me laugh. Luckily, they didn't notice me and I explored the other side of the roof.

From what little I saw; it was just a flat-topped roof. I could tell how unvisited this part of the house was. The door at the beginning was very hard to open, and it was a danger in itself to be up here. The only thing up here was a small electrical room. I didn't have any business opening it, but I did anyway just to see if I could find a dead body in there or something. There was nothing, though.

I checked my phone, and it was only 11:30. I sighed at the fact that I would be stuck in the perimeters of this house for a while. I completely forgot Nicole and got worried for half a second. I tried washing the worry away and told myself that I would give Nicole the benefit of the doubt.

After exploring the perimeter, I looked back to see if Willy Wonka and Tinker Bell were still making out, and to my surprise, I saw that they were gone. They probably heard me walking around and ran off. The party music was almost mute from up here, so them hearing my footsteps wasn't out of the question.

I got the sudden realization that I had this whole roof to myself. For some reason, I found that fact very cool. Everyone had to share a floor with hundreds of other people and here I was, one hundred feet in the air, with no one on the same floor as me. I layed down on the cold concrete and marinated myself in the environment.

I expected there to be a view from up here, but it was pitch black out and there wasn't another house in sight. It was just me and the night sky. I caught myself staring deep into some stars without even realizing I was doing so. I wouldn't say it's a type of meditation, but just looking up into the infinite sky and bright stars made it really easy to lose yourself in the void of your thoughts. I started thinking about a lot of things, stars being one of them.

I feel like stars are too good for humans, like we don't deserve to have them or be in view of them. The concept of stars themselves seems too mystical for it to exist in our world. It's like one day a genie granted a man three wishes and one of them was to have these sparkles of light come out every night to watch over us from the sky.

It's strange how I find so much zen out of staring into something that's billions of miles away. There was something poetic about staring into a celestial figure such as a star on a night like Halloween. I became comfortable in the environment, which was something I couldn't say about a party till now. My eyes started becoming heavy, and I let myself doze off, barely aware of my circumstances.

Lilith: Day Ten

I kept playing with the necklace every night before bed. I still couldn't believe how real it looked after years of forgetting about its existence. The colors haven't faded at all, at least from how I remember them.

It was just some children's toy with a string attached in reality, but to me, and to Mom, it was *so* much more than that. This toy represents years of Mom's life. It says more than her journals ever could.

I really want to thank Taylor, in some way, for giving this to me. I'm in shock about how he found this is. I would've certainly thought that it got lost somewhere when we moved out of our original house in Atlanta. I might just buy him a gift or something and drop it off later today. Although the idea of that left a bitter taste in my mouth.

Today is October 31st. You know what that means, right? Today is Halloween. Exciting, right? *If there was a sarcastic font I could handwrite, I would definitely use it right now.*

I almost forgot about the holiday's existence if it weren't for Mason bringing it up to me. He is a kid, so naturally, he loves Halloween. That's just how kids are, everyone except for me, apparently.

When I was a kid, I never particularly *enjoyed* Halloween. I didn't hate it; it was just something I didn't give much thought. I never did trick or treating or the whole costume thing. Now that I'm older, I wish I forced myself to do those festivities just for one year. Just to get a feel for it.

I made Mason some lunch and chose to not make myself any. I've developed the habit of not eating/not making meals for myself so many times now that it's built into my instinctive day routine. My body is getting used to being hungry and I'm not sure if that's a good thing or not. The feeling of hunger is still there, but it's not as alluring anymore. When a normal person gets hungry, the idea of eating food pops into their mind. When my body gets hungry, food is the last thing on my mind.

"Hey, kids." Dad came through the front door, presumably from work. Mason and I quickly turned our heads towards him.

"Hi, Dad." Mason and I said in unison. I was washing dishes while Mason was just finishing his sandwich. "You have any plans today, kid? Either of you?" He said, mostly looking at Mason, giving him a bit of attention.

I wonder sometimes if Dad thinks I just have no social life. He doesn't ask nor say anything about my supposed 'friends'. That either means he doesn't worry about it or he has accepted the fact that I'm just hopeless when it comes to socializing.

"I'm gonna finish the comic book that Lilith bought me!" Mason said excitedly. I couldn't help but let out a quiet giggle to myself.

"That's great, kid." Dad ruffled Mason's hair until Mason pushed away his hand.

Isn't that just the most *dad* thing ever? I bet my dad could win the award for the most dad of all dads. He even does that thing where he randomly grunts and clears his throat loudly.

"What about you, Lilith?" Dad turned his attention to me.

"Uh, nothing really." I was a little spaced out, watching Mason and Dad. I forgot where I was for a second.

I realized that not eating much of anything was taking a toll on my health. I noticed I'm more irritable. My head hurt a bit, and it was affecting my mood quite a bit. The simple solution was just to eat, right? But I can't bring myself to do it. Last night I made a sandwich for myself and I ended up just staring at it for fifteen minutes until I just put it in the fridge. I told myself I can deal with the pain.

"I might visit Taylor again tonight and give him something as a thank you. I don't know though." I said quietly while wiping my hands with a towel.

"Wow, that's generous." He did the dad thing where he folded his arms as a reaction to *anything*. He wasn't even upset. That was just something he did. "What did he do? You two haven't seen each other in like what? Three, four years ago?" *It felt longer than four years.* I thought to myself.

"Something like that," I said, not even knowing the number myself. "He just gave me some books to read, that's all." I lied, awkwardly scratching the back of my head.

I know I didn't have to lie. It was just a stupid charm after all, but when it comes to telling Dad personal things, especially when it's things about Mom, I can't bring myself to spit out any sort of truth. There has to be some sort of twist or bending of the truth. Either that or a straight-up lie.

"Wow, I didn't know he read." He admitted it.

Me, neither Dad, me neither.

"I'm glad he's alright. I worry about that kid every day." Dad said whole-heartedly. "Even though he's not the greatest of people, he's still my son. I'd take a bullet for that kid if need be."

My natural reaction was to smile at what he said, but I simply refused to. I just let out a heavy exhale.

"Well, I'm not sure today is a good day. Taylor is gonna be out the whole day." Dad said while opening a Diet Coke. I heard the crackle and pop of the can from behind me.

"How do you know?"

Mason put his dishes in the sink and started walking quickly towards his room. I couldn't tell if we wanted to leave because of his comic or the fact that we were talking about Taylor. A person he isn't familiar with in the slightest, even though they are brothers.

"I called him yesterday to just check up on him. I do it every other day to make sure he's doing alright." *Wow, I didn't know that.* "He said he's going to a Halloween party with some friends. I guess he made some friends at college." He explained while shoving the half-empty can of soda in the fridge.

A sinking feeling spawned in my heart when Dad said Taylor was going to a party. It's hard to put into words, but I couldn't help but think something bad would happen when I pictured that scenario. I knew I needed to stop this somehow.

I tried my best to hide my expression. I wiped the bottom half of my face with a paper towel.

"Do you know where he's going?" I asked.

"No, he didn't say. All he said was the party will be at a 'sick mansion'." Dad put in quotes.

I processed that for a second. I haven't been in the town long, but are there any big estates in Macon? I thought. All the houses I've seen are regular homes and apartments.

Dad went to take a nap. Mason's door was closed, which meant he didn't want to be bothered. He never specifically told me that he wanted to be left alone whenever his door was closed, but I noticed over time that whenever I entered his room when it was closed, he seemed to snap at me a bit.

I was finishing up dishes when I heard a knock at the door.

"Hello? Andrews Residence? Anyone home?" Someone said through the door. The voice was muffled, but I could recognize that voice from anywhere.

"Jesus Tess, you scared the daylights out of me." I opened the door and Tess was standing there.

For some reason, when I saw Tess, the southern-ness inside of me came out. I used to sound way more southern when I was younger and was surrounded by very southern people. My accent sounds more *normal* now, if that makes any sense.

"You're home Lith? I thought you'd be in school. I was gonna wait till you got home."

"I just wanted to skip today, so I did. I also skipped a day last week, but that was for a... different reason."

I didn't want to say out loud that I visited Taylor. Taylor and Tess have a *history* that I rather not take time to write out. It is not a rich history, but it goes deep. That's the reason why whenever I see Taylor, I automatically think of Tess; and almost vice versa.

"Geez Lith, you be actin' like me now." She wasn't wrong, but not right either.

Tess and I went to my room, where she sat on my bed and I had to sit on the desk. Our positioning reminded me of when I was in 6th grade and she was in high school. At that time, the age difference was so obvious, so I was forced to see her as an adult-like figure and she probably saw me as a little kid.

`I would always go to her house after school and do homework on her bed and she would normally be on the phone with her boyfriend on her desk. This time the roles were reversed, minus the boyfriend part of course. In my mind, it shown how much things have changed.

"What brings you here this time?" I asked. I was trying to lighten up my mood for Tess, but I still felt like shit. I kept tapping my foot on our wooden floors as an anti-headache mechanism.

"I was at a friend's house last night. I saw a road sign that Macon was a few miles away, so I thought to visit-"

I was tired of keeping this inside my mouth. I needed to say this to anyone, anything. The fucking wall next to me would've been satisfactory. It was making me go insane. "Tess. Can I ask you a favor? And you have to promise to say yes." I looked her dead in the eye and she was taken by surprise.

"What is it...?" She said slower and with a heavier accent. Tess almost stuttered over her words.

"I'm thinking of spying on Taylor tonight. He's going to a party and I have a bad feeling about it." I said softly.

Tess didn't say anything for what felt like forever. My eyes almost refused to look up at her. I couldn't tell if she was looking at me in some sort of disbelief or at my door to leave. Either way, it felt like a million things were staring at me at once. The longer the silence was prolonged, the harder I tapped the floor.

"Lith, you promised to never even *say* his name in front of me again. And you want me to potentially *see* him again. Are you outta your fuckin' mind?"

Tess' accent always thickens up whenever she's mad or sad.

"Okay, I understand, but this is serious-"

"No, you *don't* understand!" She cut me off and immediately stood from my bed. "There are billions of people in the world and you thought to ask *me*?"

You're the only person I can ask.

I heard Mason's door open from outside my room. He took a peek in my room and I shooed him to leave. If Mason can hear us, that means Dad can hear us.

"Lilith, the worst part is," She used my real name. My eyes widened. I haven't looked up at Tess once, but she was looking down at me with all the anger her body had. "The worst part is that YOU WERE THERE! We were in the same place, same time, and our eyes saw the same thing!"

She's right. The memory is the most vivid thing I can recall. We were camping together in the woods. Our shoulders were even touching when it happened. Eyes parallel and everything.

"I know it was four years ago, and you were just in middle school, but you don't forget that shit, Lith!" My eyes finally looked up at her's. I swear she wanted to kill me. Her hands wanted to grab my neck and strangle it. I don't blame her in the slightest.

"I'm sorry..." I uttered. I wanted and should've said much more, but that's all the words I could muster.

"I'm out of here." She aggressively grabbed her jacket and started stomping towards the door.

"Wait! Tess, listen!" I commanded. I reached out my hands towards the door as if I could pull her back in.

Tess, who was already a foot out the door, looked back at me. When we made eye contact, I opened my mouth to say something, but nothing came out. My brain froze when it came to saying something.

After a second, she looked back down at the ground beneath her and realized I had nothing to say.

"I really thought you were the one person in my life that understood me, Lilith. I guess not..." Her voice was broken, about to cry or already started.

She quietly walked out of my room. A few seconds later, the front door opened and gently closed. The sound of the front door closing kept repeating in my head for a while.

Tess was kind of the last person on earth that I wanted to be mad at. As a kid, I was always mad at her for doing a variety of things, but when it was the other way around, it felt horrible.

The void in my stomach kept growing as I laid in my bed. I continued to play with the charm necklace, but I couldn't think of Mom while doing it, which made things both better and worse.

"Lilith?" I didn't hear Mason's tiny footsteps leading up to my room. His voice caught me by surprise.

"What's up, Mason?" I asked, in the happiest way I could muster.

"Are you okay Lilith?" I sat up to face him. He looked a little distraught, like Tess yelled at him instead of me.

"Of course! Why wouldn't I be?" I said, forcing a smile on my face. I hated how artificial I sounded.

"Is Tess mad at you? You two were yelling at each other." *I know Mason. I was there.*

"No, we just got into an argument. Sometimes I get into an argument with Dad, but we still love each other." I wanted to use Mom and Dad as an example, but we both know how that ended.

"Are you guys still cousins?" Mason did that kid thing where his voice got quieter when he felt guilty or sad. I guess adults do that too, but it's more apparent in kids. It kinda made me realize how much of an 'effect' this kind of stuff has on kids, especially Mason.

"Of course, dude."

I gave Mason the same hair-ruffle that Dad gave him less than an hour ago. I don't know what that means in terms of how similar that makes me to Dad. I'll just say Mason's hair is fun to mess with.

After Mason left my room, I tried calling Tess. I almost never use my phone for anything, so this was unfamiliar territory for me, even though it was just pressing a few buttons.

To no one's surprise, she didn't pick up. My first thought was that she was still driving to Atlanta, where she lived, but I've seen her texting people while on the freeway, so that theory was ruled out.

I contemplated sending her an apology text for a while. I laid down in my bed and just stared at the blank messages board for more time than I'm willing to admit. I kept writing half a sentence, then frustratingly erasing it. No combination of words in the world would've satisfied me, so I just put the phone down and took a nap.

The sound of Dad coming home from work woke me up. I didn't realize how thin these walls were until today.

I looked outside, and it was almost pitch-black outside. That was in part due to it being the dead middle of fall, but I don't usually fall asleep for that long. I looked at my watch: 11:10. *I was asleep for that fucking long?*

A wave of urgency slapped me across the face. That same feeling of a void inside my stomach started appearing once I gained consciousness. The thought that Taylor could already have done something bad was overpowering. I hopped out of bed and immediately started getting ready.

"You going somewhere?" My dad popped in. I didn't realize my door was open, even though I always keep it open for Mason.

I looked so suspicious, putting things in my bag with no lights on in my room.

I took a deep breath before I said something stupid. "I'm gonna go look for a gift for Taylor. I also need to get gas, so I have enough for the week." I was surprised by how convincing I sounded. My voice was calm and everything. It's amazing how fast the human brain could come up with a lie.

"Okay, have fun."

Dad seemed like he was ready to go to bed. If that was the case, I could be out of the house for a long time. I genuinely didn't know if I was going to be out for five hours or none at all. I took another deep breath before leaving the house. *Taylor, I'm coming.*

Mark: November 1

"**Y**ou know how easy it would be to push you off right now? That'd be a murder I'm almost sure I can get away with." I heard an unfamiliar voice behind me, and my eyes burst open. I shot up and yelled in surprise.

"Christ, you scared me." I plunged my hands into my face in reaction. I turned around to see a girl in a cat costume. Her all-black clothes seemed to blend in with the darkness of night. I had to rub my eyes a few times to see her clearly.

"My bad, I thought you were awake." She said, giggling to herself.

"Is the party over? I don't know how long I was asleep." I kept scratching the back of my head. Laying on concrete for a while does that to you. It was also unreasonably cold for what I was wearing. My costume only included a t-shirt and jeans; my arms were freezing cold. But for some reason, I was still very content with where I was.

"It's around one, you're fine." She responded.

The girl sat down next to me, which I was a little weirded out by. Both of our legs were dangling off the roof at different lengths. I checked my phone, and I got a text from Nicole twenty minutes ago asking where I was. I wanted to respond, but I didn't want to come off as rude to her.

"Let me guess, you're not much of a party person, eh, mate?" I don't know the last time I heard someone say 'eh' or 'mate'.

"Yeah, how'd you know?" I responded with one eyebrow raised.

"Because you took my idea. I was gonna hang out here until the party was over. I'm not much of a party gal myself."

I wasn't particularly weirded out by her. I actually appreciated her company, but her accent caught me off guard more than anything. I only hear variations of southern accents where I live, so her Australian accent was unfamiliar to my ear.

"I bet that can get frustrating." She said, finishing her thoughts.

She started lying down and staring at the sky like I was earlier. For some reason, that made me smile.

"What's your name, by the way? I didn't ask prior." She asked.

"Mark. What's yours?"

"Sky. The place we're both looking at right now." I looked over my shoulder and her head was parallel towards the Sky, eyes gazing like they were trying to understand rather than admire.

We kept talking on the roof for some time. I wasn't the best at talking to strangers, but after a bit, I got more and more comfortable talking to her. It was hard to pinpoint what made her cool, but she was just a chill girl. I could tell she was introverted, though. Introverts and extroverts almost have different dialects. I find them more down to earth and if they're willing to talk to you, they can be outstandingly chill.

"I'll leave you alone, mate. Try not to fall asleep, or else someone might try to make you sleep forever." She winked, which made me laugh out loud.

"Okay, I'll see you around," I said. I sounded like my dad whenever he would have a friendly talk with strangers. It was frightening how naturally I said that.

"We'll meet again... I can feel it." She said as her voice started to dissipate from my hearing.

I kept repeating her words in my head. Her unique voice made it easy to imagine her saying it as well. How does someone know, for sure, if they're going to see someone again? How does anyone know anything? What is knowing? My mind started going into an infinite loop. The ones that keep you entertained in class. In the corner of my eye, a star shined bright enough for me to break my train of thought.

I eventually went downstairs and looked for Nicole. The party was still going on, as I expected. The lights dimmed a bit from the last time I was down here, but at least a lot of the party craziness calmed down quite a bit.

I found Nicole, and she was drinking a beer by herself, nearly drenched in sweat.

"You seem like you had a good time," I commented.

Nicole's eyes looked at mine almost immediately, so she wasn't that drunk, which relieved me.

"You know it." Her voice was *out,* though.

"You ready to head out? I'm kind of sleepy, not gonna lie." I asked, hoping Nicole was tired as well.

"Yeah, why not? I've done more than what my body could handle." She admitted.

Nicole's voice was a little woozy, but she could still stand on her own two feet. Her body is small, so I was a little surprised that she wasn't completely drunk after two shots and whatever else she decided to drink.

Nicole needed to use the bathroom, which made me want to use the bathroom, too. There was an eight-person line for both the bathroom downstairs and the second-floor bathroom, so I hesitantly suggested using the third-floor bathroom. The bathroom no one is supposed to have access to, supposedly. Nicole was slightly drunk and her only objective was to empty her bladder, so she blindly agreed.

The room was still pitch black, so I had to guide Nicole to the bathroom with my phone light.

Nicole offered for me to use the bathroom first. My eyes had trouble adjusting to the bright lights of the bathroom. I splashed some water on my face to wake my eyes up.

When Nicole went to the bathroom, I heard a short, discrete sound across the hall. I looked up and flashed my light at the door, where I thought the sound was coming from. After like ten seconds of staring across the hall, I brushed it off and assumed it was from the roof or something. It sounded like a person hitting something. I tried ignoring it, still thinking it was someone on the roof. All my senses became heightened, and that's when I felt something was wrong.

After a few seconds, the quiet sounds turned into a loud banging, not on the door, but on something hard. At this point, I couldn't ignore it and I turned my phone flashlight on again.

"That felt good-!" Nicole slam opened the bathroom door and started blabbering. I jumped at her and put my hand over her mouth. *"Mrk wht th hell!"* Nicole yelled with her mouth covered.

"Quiet! There's something over there." I whispered.

Both of us turned silent, and the banging became loud and clear. Nicole let out a quiet *"Oh shit."* and I slowly let go of my hand that was over her mouth. I started getting closer to the door, taking quiet and slow steps. Nicole followed and held on to my arm. The tension in the room was so high, I couldn't hear a thing besides the banging and the eerily quiet air.

It was a long hallway, but Nicole and I were making progress. The banging stopped, and I paused my movement. I was about two feet in front of the door.

"Nicole, I'm gonna open the door, stay back." I guarded Nicole with my arm and slowly put my hand over the doorknob.

"Mark, they're probably just having sex in there. Don't open the door." Nicole whispered, aware of the tension. Her voice sounded worried. I don't think Nicole could even convince herself.

I gently pushed Nicole back with my arm and did a countdown in my head. As I counted down, I could hear my heart beat louder and louder. I heard Nicole squeal like a pig, which dropped my heart a bit.

I slammed open the door, revealing a broom closet. I heard two voices yell, a guy and a girl. I heard a slam and the sound of something resisting.

"HELP-" A girl yelled out loudly.

I flicked my flashlight up at ground level and I saw a guy pinning a girl down on the floor, who had her skirt torn. He had his hand over her mouth and her arm in another hand. Nicole yelled in the horror at what she saw.

"Hey! Get off her!" I yelled at him.

I felt my mouth begin to stutter even before I opened my mouth. The jump from terrified to horrified took over my entire body. My eyes blinked twice at the sight of everything.

The guy finally turned around and had a terrifying smile. It was wider than any smile I'd seen. It wasn't a costume either. It was a genuine baring of his teeth. His hair was so messy and he was sweating profusely.

He started to reach for something and I half-knew what was coming.

"Don't. Fucking. Move." I couldn't see much, but I saw a silhouette of a gun pointed right at my face. The shine of the silver gun reflected.

He started changing his aim between Nicole and me. Behind me, I heard Nicole on the brink of tears, in pure fear. I put my hands in the air like I was being arrested. I had the phone in my right hand with the flashlight, so I could see how he was looking at us. I could feel the cold sweat coming down my head and my breathing became heavy.

"If you move, I will shoot." The guy said, tightening his grip on his pistol.

The girl who was on the ground started all-out crying. Her face was red, and she had cuts all over her legs. The guy turned his head and put the gun barrel on top of her forehead and her crying got even more intense. He started laughing maniacally. I could hear the breaths between his laughs. It was the most horrifying thing I've ever seen by far.

"RUN! HE'LL KILL YOU!" the girl cried out. I heard Nicole swallow behind me, and it made me do the same.

My mind started racing at a billion miles an hour, quick to think of a way out of this. I heard Nicole's legs trembling, as well as some sniffling. When you're held at gunpoint, you can hear everything and nothing at the same time. You can see everything and nothing at the same time. You can feel everything and nothing at the same time.

Nicole was behind me, so while the guy's back was turned, I mouthed 'run' as dramatically as I could. I kept repeating the word with my lips while his back was turned. I kept switching my attention between the guy and Nicole's expression.

A few seconds later, I heard Nicole shift behind me, making a run for it. I heard her cry out, "HELP! HELP!" as she ran away. I could tell she was running fucking fast because her voice became quieter and quieter with every word.

"WHERE IS SHE GOING?" The guy yelled. The guy's voice when yelling was terrifying, and it stunned me for a moment. He turned back towards the door and shot at the door. The bullet was very close to my face. I could swear that as soon as the bullet left the barrel, life started going in slow motion. I felt, saw, and heard the bullet *woosh* across my face.

The girl, still pinned, suddenly punched the gun out of his hand. Before the gun hit the floor, I pounced on the guy, dropping my phone light. I was on top of him, half wrestling, half punching the floor. The room turned dark and I couldn't see anything besides arms and bodies flying. The guy couldn't help but laugh, which added to his terrifying aura.

I was still terrified of him, but I threw my punches with no fear. My adrenaline was so high that I didn't feel a single punch he was throwing. I just felt our bodies make contact.

"GET HIM OFF YOU!" the girl yelled. I violently shoved him off me and the girl cocked the gun and pointed it right at him. I got up and stood next to the girl. Her vibrant blonde hair was all messy, and it stood up on its own. The cuts on her legs started to show, even in the darkness.

When I was able to see and process reality, the guy, still on the floor, put his hands up. He was still fucking laughing and didn't look fazed at all by being at gunpoint. I could barely see him, but he was smiling with sweat running down his face, even more than before. It was like his body was reacting, but his expression wasn't. He was loving and hating every second of this.

"D-don't move! You're cornered!" I stuttered over my words, but I didn't *feel* the stutter.

The courage I had from earlier started dying down. I heard a bunch of footsteps coming up the stairs. I was slightly relieved to know people were coming to help. I looked at the girl, who was still pointing the gun at him. She continued to shake and went on the verge of crying again.

The lights flicked on and I heard gasps from ten different people, including Nicole. I looked back at the guy, who was still smiling and looking smug. "Nicole, call the police," I commanded. I looked behind me and there was a whole group of people huddled around us. The sight of multiple people, in costumes, backing us up was amazing.

"We already did. They're on their way," a girl said. The guy started laughing again, and some people started freaking out.

"What the fuck is this guy's deal?" Another girl disgustedly asked.

"He tried screwing with me." The girl with the gun responded, turning her back.

Amongst this chaos, I was incredibly impressed with how confident the girl was speaking, even after all that.

The second I turned my head away; I heard the sound of glass shattering behind me. Without even knowing what happened, I felt my heart drop a few inches. I turned my head a split second later, and the guy was gone. I looked down and there was a layer of broken glass on the floor.

Everyone gasped and ran over to look at the broken window. In the corner of my eye, I saw the movement of the guy running away. The second I saw it, something inside of me kicked into gear.

"MOVE!" I yelled.

My fight response started kicking in, and I bolted out of the closet, mindlessly shoving people out of my way. I ran out of the closet, down the stairs, and made a sharp right turn to the front door. My mind was extremely blank, and I just started *running*.

I saw the trees that he jumped into and blindly ran into the mini-forest. As soon as I was engulfed in the forest, I couldn't see a damn thing. The tall trees blocked all sources of light. It felt like I was running into a void.

I barely knew where I was running. I don't know if this is true, but I feel like my hearing, and my other senses, were dialed up because all I was doing was running towards the sound of footsteps. I felt like a wild animal trying to catch its prey.

"GET BACK HERE YOU SHIT!" I yelled.

My field of view widened and before I knew it, I was out of the trees. I looked to my right, and he was running towards a hiking trail and, without hesitation, I followed. I was getting on his tail. He turned a corner behind some bushes. I blindly turned as well.

This is the fastest I've ever felt in my life. The wind grazing against my face has never felt this powerful. My legs moved at a speed I was never able to achieve before. At that moment, I was faster than anyone on the planet. Well, second-fastest.

When I turned the corner, I couldn't see where the guy was. The corner was behind a giant boulder. I paused for a second to see where he could've gotten and I turned around to see him hovering above me.

The next thing I know, he jumps on me and shoves me. I tried to grab his shirt to take him down with me, but my reaction time was way too late.

I look down and there is literally no immediate ground below me. The feeling of myself falling started to come over. But before I fall completely, my eyes catch a glimpse of a girl to the right. Her eyes looked as hopeless as mine. I reached out my hand to her as if she could catch me. Complete darkness follows...

Lilith: Day Ten cont.

Dad said that Taylor was going to a party in a 'sick mansion'. After a quick Google search, there was only one house in Macon that was big enough to be considered a mansion. I was worried I was gonna have to drive around for hours trying to find the correct mansion.

Driving alone on Halloween night was a pretty surreal experience. I interpreted all the hellish decorations and lights as a sign of what was to come. For a second, I really wanted to turn back and go home. All the U-turn road signs were taunting me in a weird way. I almost committed to turning back. Then the vivid memory of what Taylor did to Tess that night four years ago shot up in my brain. It's one of those memories you can't forget, no matter how much you burn it away. I don't want that to happen to another person ever.

I had to drive into a pretty isolated place in town to reach the mansion. I was surrounded by tall trees wherever I went. There weren't many street lights either, which added another level of scariness to everything.

This definitely was the place. The second I saw the mansion, all the orange lights and loud music popped out at me. I've never done this sort of thing before. I've never gone to any sort of party that was social. I didn't see how any of this could be enjoyable, and I still stand by that opinion. When I walked inside, the whole place was how I expected it.

Hot, loud, and messy. Do you know what else has those traits? A vacuum. I'm not sure about the hot part, but anything that vaguely resembled a vacuum was a no-go for me. But apparently, I'm in the minority.

People who were dancing and doing 'party' things kept bumping into me. I don't consider myself short, but when everyone was jumping and wearing things that made themselves taller, I started to look like a child in comparison. Keep in mind, I wasn't wearing a costume either. I wasn't really intimidated, more like confused. If I wanted to find Taylor, it was gonna have to be nothing short of a miracle.

I went around asking people if they happened to see Taylor. I described what he looked like and had to pray that Taylor wasn't wearing a costume. 50% of the people here weren't wearing costumes, so theoretically, there was a 50% chance of him not wearing one.

Everyone I asked was either confused, drunk, or the music was too overbearing to hear me. My overall impressions of this party so far: Pretty fucking shit, and that's me being generous.

I sat down with a bottle of water and apparently that was an invitation for multiple guys to sit down next to me and hit on me. I told the first guy that I was under eighteen and that made him try even harder. After suppressing the feeling to throat chop that guy, I got up and went upstairs. I had no time for people like him.

If Taylor was going to be somewhere, it had to be upstairs. He wasn't a party person, he probably hated them as much as I did. But I was starting to lose hope that Taylor wasn't here. Maybe there happened to be another mansion in Macon, Georgia that didn't appear on Google Maps. Or maybe, the more logical theory, that he wasn't at a party at all.

I was making my way upstairs when I heard a *bang* from the floor above me. Everyone at the party gasped, and the house went silent. Somehow, my heart already knew what was coming, and skipped a few beats. A crowd of people started rushing upstairs. I hesitantly followed, being the last person in the line of people.

I closed my eyes, and when I opened them, Taylor was standing ten feet away from me. Everyone gasped and wondered what was going on. A boy in dark hair and a Waldo costume was standing near Taylor. The boy had blood on his face and there was blood on Taylor's hands. *I fucking knew it.* I either wanted to cry or run away. I did neither, though. I held my ground.

Next to the boy was a blonde girl with knife cuts all over her legs. The fact that Taylor did that to someone sickened me to my core.

In the crowd of people, Taylor couldn't see me, but I could see him bright and clear. I was shooting eye lasers at him. The Taylor that I talked to a couple of days ago wasn't the same Taylor that I was looking at. Where's that Taylor? The Taylor, who read philosophy books, wore a button-up to school, and color organized his textbooks. I wanted to believe that he had changed. I thought I was stupid for going to this party to spy on him.

Suddenly, Taylor jumped out of the window. The glass shattered loud enough to echo in my head. The boy in the Waldo costume started bolting towards the door. A second later, I followed, running towards the door as fast as the both of them. I knew immediately that they would try to kill each other and Taylor would probably win.

I followed both of them. When I got outside, I thought I had lost them for a second, but I heard a yell coming from inside a small forest next to the mansion. Without hesitation, I ran head-first towards the origin of that yell.

It was so fucking dark in that forest. As I got further inside, the outside light sources quickly dissipated into nothing. Next thing I know, I feel like I'm running into nothing. I kept bumping into random branches and rocks, but the pain didn't faze me.

Suddenly, I heard the sound of police sirens coming. *Fuck*. I kept running faster, dodging the trees. My brother might kill someone, that's the only thing on my mind.

I made my way out of the forest and near a cliffside. I shift my head to the left, and Taylor and the boy are standing dangerously close to the edge of the cliff.

"TAYLOR NO!" I yelled.

Taylor shoved the boy off an edge. The boy's eyes met mine as he fell down the ledge. I only saw them for less than a second, but life seemed to go into slow motion when our eyes met. He reached his arm out to me as if I could do something. I was the last thing he saw before hitting the ground. After that, I heard a big *slam*.

"....." Taylor and I stood in complete silence for a half-second.

"WHAT DID YOU DO?" I grabbed Taylor's shirt and started shaking him, getting on the edge of tears.

Taylor didn't say anything. All I heard was him trying to catch his breath. I don't even think he heard himself breathe. There were bloody cuts all over Taylor's face. Seeing his bloodshot, scarred face was terrifying. I truly didn't recognize this person.

He looked down below the cliff and stared down at his creation. I looked below the cliff and was relieved to see the cliff wasn't that steep.

"Speak to me God damn it!" I kicked him in the shin and he barely reacted to it. For a second, I thought I wasn't speaking to a human.

"What could I have done? He was catching up to me!" He said as calmly as he could, but it came out as a scream.

The sirens started getting louder.

"I DON'T KNOW? ANYTHING BUT SHOVE HIM OFF A CLIFF!" I cried out. Taylor's eyes started to tear up. It reminded me that he was a human being.

"*MOVE MOVE MOVE!*" The sound of police officers coming towards us flooded the forest. Taylor and I turned around towards the trees and both of our eyes widened.

"Taylor, you have to get out of here," I commanded, looking back at him with a great sense of urgency.

"Can you hold them off?" Taylor asked, looking me dead in the eye. He turned his shoulders around, ready to break away any second.

"... I'll do what I can," I said with a lump in my throat. At this point, anything could happen to either of us and I would be prepared for it. I tried to imagine the worst. I definitely heard the police getting closer and closer to us. All the flashing red lights and people from outside the forest yelling didn't make it easy on my heart. *Spark*. My heart started to tighten.

Behind me, I heard Taylor's footsteps get quieter as he bolted away from me and into the other part of the forest.

"Wait, Lilith."

Don't say my name like that, like we've known each other for our entire lives when I don't know a damn thing about you.

"Go, Taylor..." I said, with a clenched fist, trying to suppress the urge to punch in the face. I mindlessly kept tapping my foot on the ground. I felt like a ticking time bomb.

"Lilith, you can't tell Dad. Please." He pleaded. The fact that he wasn't running for his life was pissing me off.

"Taylor. Go." There was hair over my eye, making it impossible to see him. I preferred it that way.

Why did it matter if I told Dad or not? He's running away from the police, not Dad. In a life or death situation, Dad would take a bullet for Taylor. It literally didn't matter if Dad knows or not.

I started to feel lightheaded, sickly, all the bad adjectives. The combination of not eating and resisting the urge to kill Taylor was sending me into an out-of-body experience.

"Lilith, please. Promis-"

"TAYLOR FUCKING GO!" I yelled as loud as I could. My heart couldn't take me yelling at that volume. The things I was doing were already taking a toll on my heart. It tightened more with every word I yelled.

I turned around to face him, hair over my face and tears down my cheek. His hopeless face was the only thing I could see. And my mangled face was all he could see. It was both beautiful and disgraceful.

Taylor opened his mouth, trying to say something, but turned around and ran away. His footsteps disappeared into the forest. I didn't look back at him, but if I did, I might have chased him. I slowly released the tension from my fist.

"FREEZE!" A police officer came out of the forest.

I didn't freak out, knowing that he wasn't looking for me. That didn't stop me from putting my hands in the air.

"Where did he go?" An officer asked, with a wide-eyed expression.

"Look down here!" I yelled.

The officer looked below the cliff and tried to find a way to get down there. I heard more people coming from inside the forest, so I knew I had to start getting out of there. I ran out of the forest, probably faster than Taylor did. I wasn't breaking any sort of law by any means, but it definitely felt like I was. I made my way to the car and drove away as quickly as I could, running away from the mess I was leaving behind.

Running away from something that I knew was going to come back to bite me in the ass.

I didn't rest easy that night. My mindscape was a sandstorm and it wouldn't temper down. I kept asking myself why I saved Taylor. He was dead to rights if I didn't create a diversion for him. I was literally hitting myself over it. It bugged how instinctively I reacted as well. Us being family wasn't a good enough reason to save him. I don't know what he did, but if the police were called, it wasn't good. *Next time I see you, I'm ending this.* I told myself.

Mark: November 3

"You really don't remember anything, do you?"

"I remember a little, like people and little things, but not much else," I admitted, while putting my feet up on the dash. Nicole was driving me to school, since my doctor said I shouldn't be driving for a bit, among other things.

Nicole got done explaining what happened the other night. Apparently, I passed out after being tossed off a ledge. When I woke up, I thought it was just a faint dream that I had little to no memory of. It doesn't sound like me at all to chase down someone who could easily kill me, but Nicole told me it was a spur-of-the-moment type of thing.

"Does your dad know anything?" Nicole asked. My eyes shot open, imagining how my dad would react if he knew what happened that night.

"Nope," I responded, resting my head on my thumb. Nicole kept looking over at me, only being able to see her head-turns in my peripherals. I just kept looking forward, staring at my untied shoelaces. "He would be *furious* if he found out that I almost got myself killed."

"Really? I thought he'd be proud, being a police officer and such." The car came to a stop. Nicole parked in our usual parking spot and turned off the car. I looked at my watch to see how much time it took until class ended. There were only two minutes left, but for some reason, I didn't have any urgency to leave the car. Nicole seemed about the same. She reclined her seat a bit and leaned into it.

"You'd think that, but I don't think that's the case. He's stern about the most random things." I complained. I realized how teenager-ey I sounded, but my mind wasn't exactly in the greatest of places.

"Sorry, Mark," Nicole said, sounding incredibly distraught.

"For what?" I scoffed.

"Bringing you to that party. It wasn't even that good, anyway. We should've just gone to the festival." Nicole said, mirroring my position and overall mood. The car was now just an amalgamation of our terrible moods.

"It's fine," I said, slowly exhaling. "Just know that I'm not down for going to any parties anytime soon," I said exhaustingly.

"Me too dude..."

We waited like five minutes more after the bell rang, just sitting in silence. The only background noise was hearing other cars park near us. If someone saw us through the window, they'd probably think we were frozen in time or something.

For the next few hours, all I was trying to do was force my brain to recall some of the lost memories. When you're told something that you don't remember, especially something as important as a rape attempt, you try your best and conjure those memories back, no matter how intangible. My brain kept teasing with flashes of colors, rooms, and small details of people's faces, but no full picture was popping up.

Some people heard about what happened. Our town wasn't exactly big nor crime-heavy, so when something like this happens, it's a big deal. To my knowledge, it wasn't even in any newspapers or anything, so it had to be spread by word of mouth. Some of my casual friends and people who I've never talked to before started coming up to me during the passing period. They'd swarm me with questions and I'd have almost nothing to say besides an apologetic: "Sorry, I don't remember." I'm not exactly the type of person to turn down attention, but when it was in this form, it just made me want to isolate myself from everyone.

Before lunch, I went to the nurses' office to see if they had ice packs. Apparently, falling from that small cliff put a bruise on my forehead. I didn't think much of it until it started turning different colors. Now it was a darkish red with some purple mixed in there. Not the prettiest thing to see when you look in the mirror.

Nicole and I had lunch together, as usual. Every day, we sit at the bottom of our lockers, chatting about the most random stuff. Of course, we don't always have to talk to each other. One of the most underrated parts of friendship is not always having to talk about something to enjoy each other's company. It's cheesy, but great nonetheless.

Today wasn't exactly one of those days. We sat down and things immediately felt different. Neither of us really looked at each other. It wasn't exactly awkward, just *different.*

"I'm gonna get some water, be right back," I said as I tapped Nicole on the shoulder. Without looking up at me, she slowly nodded. Her eyes were fixated on a container of food that she hadn't even bothered to touch yet.

I walked outside to notice how dark the sky was. It was approaching winter, so the sky was darkened, even though it was the middle of the day. It's even supposed to rain sometime this week, too.

"Excuse me...?" A voice said behind me. I was filling my water bottle from a fountain.

"Sorry, give me a few seconds," I assured.

I closed my bottle and walked away without looking at them. I assumed they wanted to use the fountain, so I didn't bother to face them.

"Wait-" the girl said as I was about to turn a corner. I immediately stopped and turned back to face her. "Mark?" She uttered, looking unsure. I was confused at first because I didn't know who she was and she seemed sheepish for reasons unknown to me.

"Uh, hi? Do I know you?" I asked politely, scratching the back of my head. The way she looked at me made me think she knew who I was, but I didn't recognize her one bit.

"Oh yeah? I'm Sky. We met the other night. Does that ring a bell?" There was hope draining from her voice. It made me begin to feel bad.

I took a second to look at her in detail. She had dark brown hair with a tall-skinny frame. More apparently, she had a heavy Australian accent. It caught me off guard when I first heard her speak.

"Um, sorry I don't remember." I slowly admitted to her. I let my eyes drop down to the floor out of shame. "I lost my memory the other night at a party, so my memory is all over the place right now. Sorry."

"*Wow, so it is true...*" she whispered under her breath. My eyes widened at the fact that I could hear that. Normally I wouldn't, but it was deathly quiet out here where we were.

We stood in front of each other for some time. Sky pinched her chin to think to herself. I'm not the most awkward teenager ever, but the lack of meaningful conversation made me a little tense.

"Okay, can you do me a favor?" Sky asked, making direct eye contact with me. I nodded skeptically. I felt like this was one of those situations where I was in the wrong place at the wrong time. "My cousin wanted me to give you this note." Sky flipped her backpack around and pulled out a white notecard.

"If none of it makes sense, I'm super sorry, but it's really important to her that you get this." Sky's face went from unsure to stressed in world record time. The combination of everything was confusing the fuck out of me. But I had too much sympathy to say no to anything.

I reached out and grabbed the note from her hand. I was tempted to read it right in front of her, but Sky seemed like she wanted to leave as much as I did. Sky kept looking behind her as if she was yearning to get out.

"I'll read it sometime later. Thanks, I guess." You can tell I'm very good at handling awkwardness.

We both walked in our separate directions. I can only imagine how awkward it would've been if we had to walk the same way back.

I fished the note out of my pocket and read it while walking back to my locker. It was hard to read it through the shaky handwriting and crumples, but it was still manageable to read.

Hey, I'm not good at writing these things, so I'll explain everything as quickly as possible. If you're reading this, you had some sort of involvement at that Halloween party incident. I managed all the security footage they could from around the house. The problem is we know the lazy-ass police don't have time to go through hours of footage, and I can't bring myself to watch it. So, if it's not too much trouble... would you be able to watch it and try to find any clues? If you can, can you come to my house on Wednesday to pick up the footage? It's the same place as the party.

Thanks.

"Oh, you're back. What took you so long? Lunch is almost over." Nicole asked as I got back. When I looked up from a note, Nicole was putting stuff in her bag from her locker. I looked around and everyone seemed like they were ready to leave as well, cleaning up their lunch remains.

"Sorry, I was talking to someone." I honestly don't know that I spent that much time outside. "Can I ask a random question?" I was leaning up against the locker trying to act cool, but reading that note made me antsy.

"What's up?" Nicole responded, raising an eyebrow. Nobody ever asks if they can ask a question, so Nicole seemed sceptical off the bat.

"Did a brown-haired girl with an Australian accent pull you aside and give you a note of some sort?" I asked.

"Wow, that's super-specific- no, not to my knowledge," Nicole responded.

"That's surprising."

"How so?" Now Nicole was curious.

"Read this." I handed Nicole the crumpled note.

At first, I wasn't sure if I should give her the note, because it seemed private to me and that girl, but Nicole had as much involvement with the incident as I did.

"This handwriting is hideous," Nicole commented, squinting her eyes at the note.

"Just hurry up. Lunch is almost over." I said, staring at my watch. I felt like I was doing something illegal, even though it was some dumb paper. I kept looking around to make sure no one was in proximity to eavesdrop on us.

"Whoa..." Nicole handed me back the note, and I painfully nodded.

"I know, I was just as surprised as you." I put the note back in my pocket.

"Are you gonna go get the footage? She asked kind of big favor, y'know?" That comment rubbed me the wrong way.

"Yeah, I probably am. I was gonna ask if you wanted to come with me. You could be of equal help if we work together on this." The bell rang. I wasn't that keen on leaving, but Nicole started inching towards the door.

"Umm, I'm not sure if I want to do that, especially since we almost got ourselves killed that night." Nicole's voice went down a few notes.

"It's not that serious, y'know? We're probably just going to pick up some tapes and get out." I undermined.

"I can help if you *really* need it, but I prefer not to get involved. And you barely remember anything. How are you supposed to help?" Nicole slung her backpack over her shoulder, looking ready to leave at any moment.

"You're right..." I said before exhaling slowly. "I didn't even think of that." I had some other responses to her question, but all of them revolved around me sounding irritated at her lack of cooperation. I'd rather spare both of us the headache. "I'll let you know if I need help. Thanks anyway." I turned around to walk away in a sort of petty way. I know being petty is never good, but I needed some way to express my irritation.

Mark: November 5

In the days leading up to now, I tried finding the girl who wrote the note. I had a few questions because I had such a vague idea of what I was getting myself into. *Wouldn't it be ethical to give this all to the police?* That is what I thought. But going back to the note, it said they wouldn't because they're 'lazy'. That kind of hit me in a soft spot, being that my father is an officer and such, but I figured they had their reasons.

I didn't end up finding Sky on either Monday or yesterday. I asked some of my senior friends if they had seen her. All of them either said no or didn't even know who she was.

As I walked to my car, droplets of water started to fall on my neck. I looked up, and the rain started coming down very quickly; I had to run to my car. When I had a chance to catch my breath, all I could think about was if the rain was a sign of what was to come. You know in those drama movies, at the climax scene, where rain inconveniently starts to fall? That's what it felt like. Except for rain, those movies are poetic and dramatic, rain in real life is just sad and inconvenient.

As I drove myself there, a little of the memories started flowing back. Actually no, not the memories themselves, but the weight of those memories. The closer I got to her house, the heavier my heart started to feel. It felt like some anti-magnetism, where the closer I got, the more I wanted to resist.

I took a deep breath before knocking on the door. I emptied my brain of any thoughts, realizing that I was probably overthinking things.

There was no response for a good bit, maybe like thirty seconds or so. Hearing the rain droplets hit the ground acted as a form of time for me. A mental clock per se. I knocked a second time and someone from the other side called out to me.

"*Who is this?*" A voice called from the other side of the door. Even though it was muffled by the thick wooden door, I could tell they sounded very on-edge. It was a girl's voice. I figured she was Sky, judging by the accent.

"Uh, it's Mark. I was asked to come here to look at the footage?" I questionably confirmed.

The sound of three locks turning came from the other side, each one sounding heavier than the last. A short pause fills the air, then the door slams open, making me flinch.

"Whoa!" I said very audibly.

Sky and I made freaked eye contact for a few seconds, then she relaxed herself.

"Sorry. Random news stations have been appearing at our door all week. I should've known you were coming. Come in." She explained. I couldn't tell if I was overthinking it, but the rain made that statement a thousand times more dramatic.

I stepped inside and hung my wet jacket on a coat hanger. I avoided looking around the house to make sure I didn't trigger any memories. Somehow, there was still a level of familiarity to this place. That was probably me being slightly on-edge though.

"Forgive me for asking, but the girl from Halloween... Her name is Avery?" I asked, unsure of anything at this point.

Sky sat me down on a big dinner table with assorted candles in the center and a glass chandelier above us. I loosely recognized it from the party, except without the abundant amount of Halloween decorations.

"Yeah. I keep forgetting you lost your memory mate." I slowly nodded my head. Then she briefly looked at the bruise on my forehead. I waited for some sort of reaction, but she just slowly exhaled before averting her eyes. "Have you been told what happened?" She looked up at my eyes to ask.

"A brief summary, but not everything," I said, scoffing inadvertently. "It doesn't even sound like me, going to a party and such, so I'm a bit confused." I scoffed once again, but this time it was in this pathetic, irritating way; not exactly the impression I wanted to give off.

"Well, I hope you know you're a hero, even if you don't feel like one." She caringly rubbed my shoulder, as if to say that I should be proud of myself. I let myself smile. "I'm gonna get Avery from her room if that's okay." She said as she walked out of the dining room.

It took a minute for my brain to process those words fully. My brain wasn't focused. I realized I had been looking at a dent on the table for a good minute.

I slowly heard footsteps coming towards the dining room. In this big, spacious house, I could hear footsteps from a block away. In my head, I made them out to sound more dramatic than they actually were. I don't know why my brain does these things to me.

I watched as Sky helped Avery get to her seat. By the size of Avery's brace, I could already tell she wasn't able to walk properly. It wrapped around her entire leg. It was a sad scene. Avery had to lean on Sky for every step of the way.

Avery sat a few seats away from me, obviously wanting some distance. Even though she was somewhat away from me, I got a chance to look at her. My eyes felt awkward, but I felt the need to see what the damages were, as fucked up as that sounded.

There was an area of puffiness all around her eyes, one of them being a black eye. Her hands kept shaking as if there was an earthquake beneath her. Her bright blonde hair didn't seem as bright as it should be, probably due to being bedridden. There was so much about her that didn't seem right. It made me angry that a human would willingly do this to someone.

Sky looked over at me from behind Avery's seat, conveying to me that I should say something. Nevertheless, I still felt the need to break the ice.

"Hey," I said softly. I approached the situation like how you would approach a wounded animal.

"Hi." She said extremely quietly. If the room wasn't spacious enough, I wouldn't be able to hear her.

"How've you been?" I haven't heard anything from you since the night of the *incident.*" I had trouble letting that word leave her mouth. I looked over at Sky and she visibly cringed at me. I know it was a dumb question, but what else am I supposed to say?

"I've been fine," Avery responded, looking at the floor. Her hair cast a dark shadow over her eyes. It's pretty obvious that she was autopiloting her words. They were slow and short. She was mostly fixated on the loose thread on her sleeve. I supposed anything that would distract her was seen as a good thing.

Both I and Sky slowly exhaled, either in frustration or exhaustion. Personally, I was feeling a mix of both. I got the idea to ask more questions, but I figured I wasn't realistically gonna get anywhere. After a few seconds of not knowing what to say, I looked up at Sky and mouthed the words *'no good'*, to say that I had no more to say.

Sky gently tapped Avery on the shoulder. "I'm gonna show him the tapes now, okay?" Sky said in the softest voice she could muster. I started to notice that Sky's accent thickened up quite a bit when she was being serious. I wasn't sure if that applied to everyone with an accent, or just her.

"Go ahead," Avery uttered, barely moving her head to face Sky.

Sky walked to a nearby cupboard and fished out a folder from the top shelf. It was well hidden on that shelf like she didn't want someone to find it. She opened the folder to double-check all the contents were there and then nodded.

She placed the folder on the table in front of me and then told me to open it. I looked back over at Avery and her hands shook more vigorously than before. After staring for a few seconds, I slowly got this stiff feeling in my spine. It was hard to relax my shoulder. Nonetheless, I averted my eyes from her and opened the folder.

"Okay so, there are twelve cameras around the house. The other day I managed to get all of them on CDs."

I opened the folder to see a stack of disks on the inside. I slowly pulled them out and flipped through them. Each of them was labeled different things with a sharpie; things like *Upstairs 1, Backyard 2, Entertainment Room 1.*

"Would it be okay if you looked over these to see if you can find anything?" Sky asked. Before I could open my mouth, she said: "Don't worry, I made copies so I can look at them in my free time." That idea assured me slightly. Just the idea of having someone by my side was comforting, no matter how minute it might be.

"Sky?" Avery called out from across the table. Both of us immediately looked up at her. Surprisingly, I got to see the whites of her eyes after she moved a bit of her hair to the side of her face. They looked a tad bloodshot. The fact that it was noticeable from how far I was sitting probably meant they were incredibly bloodshot from up close. "Yeah?" Sky responded, sounding like she could break a sweat at any moment.

"I'm gonna head upstairs. Call me down when you make dinner, I can at least help with that." Avery said with a lump in her throat. To be honest, there was always some sort of lump in her throat, it seemed like, but at that time it was the most painfully obvious.

Avery stood up and made the slow journey to her room. I half-expected Sky to go over and help since Avery could barely walk, but Sky kind of just stood there, not really having any conviction to move. Her face was frozen for a long time, up until Avery's footsteps ceased and we both heard a door open and close. That sound echoed throughout the house for a bit.

My awkward teenage self-felt the need to break the silence, so I insensitively said something.

"It's okay, she's just probably not feeling well. I wouldn't want to be down here either if I were her." I said bluntly.

Sky slowly brought herself back to reality. As soon as I started talking, she did a little double-take and blinked a lot.

"Yeah, I know. I just don't know what to do, mate." Sky sat down and plunged her hands into her face.

I was trying to think of things to say in response to that. For some reason, my brain was either short-circuiting, or I was naturally bad at being reassuring.

"You know that was the first time she left her room?" Sky said as she looked at me dead in the eye. "It's been almost a week and Avery hasn't left her room other than to cook and use the bathroom."

"I mean she got the courage to come out and see me, someone who she barely knows, so I think that's progress, no?" I reassured.

"I mean, I guess, but I've been taking care of her since the party. It doesn't look good Mark, it really doesn't." When she said my name, I started to get increasingly worried. Her eyes grew wider and more hopeless.

"What about her parents? Haven't they been taking care of her too?" I asked.

"No mate." Sky slammed her palm flat on the table. "Avery's stupid *fucking* parents aren't even in America. They're in Germany or something on a business trip." Sky was in a position to hit the table again, but resisted the urge.

"What? Don't they know what happened? If they did, I bet they would fly back immediately, no?" My voice began to raise a bit. A slight echo bounced off the walls and into my ear.

"You obviously don't know how Avery's parents work." Sky scoffed pathetically. "The only way they would fly back is if she were dead, or the house burnt down. And even that last one I wouldn't bet money on." Sky's accent thickened again. I really couldn't believe what I was hearing. Are those people even considered 'parents' at that point?

"Wow, I'm sorry. I had no idea." I said, out of awe. "Who are you then? Her sister?" Judging by Sky's accent and Avery's… lack of accent, they probably weren't siblings, but at this point, no question was dumb.

"Nah, I'm her cousin. I actually live about an hour from here, but I figured I should stay with Avery for the time being so she feels safe." My heart lit up a bit after that sentence.

"Wait, why were you at our school then if you live that far?" I asked, remembering that Sky gave me the note at lunch.

"Oh, I snuck in, mate." She started laughing maniacally. "It's surprising how much you fit in when you just have a backpack on." I don't think I've ever heard something more true than that.

"Wow-wow. Well, I thank you on Avery's behalf. I don't know many people willing to do that sort of thing. That's very nice of you."

"Same for you, actually. I asked other people to come to get footage as well, but you're the only one who came."

Seriously? No one else came?

Sky admitted as she put the disks back in the folder. "But hey, all we need is us two. If we find out who this dude is, and get him arrested, then maybe Avery and I can sleep better at night." Sky handed me the folder and just smiled. Her sudden optimism was contagious. I felt a large beam of hope and determination strike my right in my heartstrings.

"Alright, I'll get on that." I grabbed the folder and stood up stronger than when I sat down.

Sky walked me to the front door to see me out. I looked towards Avery's door from downstairs and I could feel the life-draining energy coming out of it. If I didn't know any better, it would just be a regular-ass door, but knowing how long Avery was just suffering in that room, it gave off a bad aura.

"Thanks for stopping by. I wrote my number on the back of the folder in case you need to contact me." Sky informed me as she opened the front door for me. I flipped over the folder and her number was written in sharpie on the back.

"I'll look at these as soon as I can."

"Thanks, Mark."

Mark: November 8

It's been raining pretty hard the past couple of days. I know it's pretty normal in a lot of places, but not here. Rain is about as rare as holidays. In other words, they mostly happen towards the end of the year.

The rain only made watching the security tape a thousand times more depressing. I kept hearing constant pitter-patter on my roof while I was glued to my 1998 office chair and the only light in the room being the one from my computer screen. My older sister kept checking up on me to make sure I wasn't depressed or anything. I'm normally never in my room this much unless I'm sick, of course, so after the second day in a row of me being cooped in my room, she started to get a bit suspicious. I gave an obligatory excuse and just blamed the rain and my friends for not wanting to hang out.

After that, my dad started to get a little suspicious and asked some questions of his own. He found it odd that whenever he would come into my room, I would always be staring at a monitor, seemingly dead inside. When he asked what I was looking at, I kind of freaked out and 'sports' came out of my mouth. I don't know why I first thought to say sports, since I never really took an interest in any. My dad questioned me even more after that point, and I just told him I was planning to try out for the volleyball team this year to boost my high school resume, whatever the fuck that means.

After that, I was forced to watch volleyball with him for a whole hour while he explained stuff for that entire hour. At that point, I would rather have said I was watching porn rather than sports. At least he would've left me alone and not asked any questions.

That weekend, Nicole kept texting me to ask if I wanted to hang out at her place or get food. Normally, I would be yearning to get out of the house when it was raining, but I was very glued to the computer screen. The fact that Nicole wasn't very cooperative when I asked her to come with me to Avery's house still left a bad taste in my mouth. So, I said no to her text and didn't give a reason why. You can call me petty or an asshole, but at the time, nothing else seemed important. For one, I was trying to regain some of the lost memories that I lost from the party. The only sort of 'memory' I was able to recover was when I shut off one of the cameras. For some stupid reason, I went to the upstairs camera and shut it off. The worst part being, that probably the camera where all the shit was happening. Before I shut it off, I heard a guy yelling at Avery to go into a closet, but since it was nearly pitch-black, I couldn't see it. So, I blamed myself for that one.

Secondly, I was trying to find some sort of lead. Because for the past three days, I've been looking at swarms of people at twelve different bird's-eye angles. By day two, I've watched all twelve recordings two times over and haven't found much.

My determination was pretty low at this point. I kept reminding myself why I was doing this. The reason being, the person I'm trying to find is a criminal, but I was literally losing sanity by the hour. My routine for the past few days was: wake up, eat, watch, eat, watch, shower, watch, sleep, repeat. It was hard to believe that some people did this for a job. I couldn't see myself doing it for more than three days, so this morning I gave it a rest.

Some of my friends invited me to get burgers, and I agreed out of pure boredom. My sister was relieved to see me out of the house. Apparently, my dad told her about the whole volleyball thing and knew something was up. She told me about it as I was making lunch and my heart dropped. Thankfully, she didn't make much of a deal about it, since it wasn't her business to be snooping around in my life, but it's never good to be caught in a lie like that.

Lilith: Day Sixteen

Taylor hasn't picked up any of Dad's calls since that night. Of course, Dad didn't tell me this; I know this because I hear Taylor's voicemail through our walls, followed by a small grunt by Dad.

It's killing me inside to wake up every day and continue to stay silent. Every time I face Dad, or even Mason, I can't help but think of Taylor looking me dead in the eye and risking his life to make sure I didn't say anything. And now I'm here choosing to honor that request. Reason? It could be the way he looked at me, the hopelessness in his eyes, it could be the way he said my name, it could be the fucking temperature that night. I haven't pinpointed a reason if such a thing exists.

"Hey, Dad."

I walked into the kitchen, about to make Mason lunch. Dad stood next to the fridge like he spent the last five minutes pacing around the room.

"Hey, kid."

One little tidbit, in less than a year, I'm about to turn eighteen. I wonder if he will still call me 'kid' after that. At this point, he says it more than my name.

"You don't seem like you're doing too well." I looked at him with concerned eyes. Dad had his hand over his forehead and slightly bared his teeth.

"Your brother isn't picking up my calls. I called him like three times today and like five times yesterday." Dad aggressively pressed the off button on his phone and less aggressively put the phone on the counter.

"He might've broken it. He always dropped things as a kid, if you can recall that." I conjured up an excuse that didn't seem viable to me, to be honest.

I'm 99% sure Taylor has his phone working and he's just choosing to ignore Dad's calls. That's all the more reason to hate myself for helping him back out of the mess he's in. He could be doing more illegal shit for all I know.

"Just call back in a few days, he'll probably have it fixed or a new one," I suggested.

"Yeah, I'll give it a few days. If he doesn't respond, I'm gonna pay him a visit or something."

Please pick up the phone Taylor. I prayed to myself.

"Oh hey, I need to ask you something." I looked up from the fridge to give Dad a questioned look. "Are you free tonight?" Dad asked. I proceeded to accentuate my questioned look.

"Why...?" I asked as I took out a jug of milk.

I had no reason to be suspicious of Dad asking me if I had plans, but the teenager inside of me didn't want to give him the benefit of the doubt.

"I wanted to do our yearly camping trip tonight. My coworkers suggested this really neat spot by the mall." I don't think I've heard the word *neat* since middle school.

"Tonight?"

"Yeah, I have my day off tomorrow, so I thought we could do it tonight."

I wasn't exactly opposed to going camping tonight. To be frank, I've been kind of bored for the past couple of days, so I agreed.

Dad ate lunch and went to pick up Mason. I packed a clean pair of clothes (I wear the same thing every day anyway) and went to Mason's room to pack. Doing a task like that helped take my mind off everything.

I checked my phone, for once, to see if Tess texted me. I planned on calling her later tonight, assuming there was service wherever we were going, to apologize. I don't know what I was going to apologize for, but I felt sorry for *something*.

When I was done packing, I opened my laptop to check if I had any emails from my teachers (from missing an incredible amount of school and such). I briefly looked up my application tab and saw the program for the security cameras was open. I slapped myself in the face forgetting that I put cameras in Taylor's for that exact reason. There were many hours of unwatched footage that could explain what happened on Halloween. I knew I didn't have enough time to watch any of it before Dad came home, so I impulsively packed the laptop away in my bag.

Dad picked me up, and we started driving to the camping spot. Mason got extremely excited when he heard the news that we were going camping. It made me smile and made me temporarily forget about the things that happened. Seeing all three of us in a car together was rare. I pretty much drive myself all the time along with Mason. We felt like a broken picture frame of a family. Yes, the picture was still there, but the frame and everything else were shattered. *That was dark. I probably shouldn't have written that.*

We arrived at a place called Macon Hill. It's probably the highest elevation that I've been to in Georgia. There was an option to pay someone to drive us to the top, but Dad wanted the real camping experience, so he made us walk all the way up, tent and everything.

While aimlessly walking, all the feelings started flowing in again at once. It was overwhelming, to say the least. The combination of guilt from Tess and the anger and regret from Taylor all balled up into this storm of emotions. My legs were moving towards the top, but my physical body was pretty much on autopilot. I was encased in my thoughts that if someone yelled my name, it would be drowned out. The only sound I heard was my own head and the vague sound of my shoes scraping against the pavement.

"Hey, Mason?" I yelled out to him, trying to use him as some sort of distraction.

"Hi, Lilith!" I could *feel* the excitement in his voice. He was a few feet away, trying to throw pieces of rock and dirt off the hill.

"Hey bro," I said with the brightest smile I could muster. It felt a little wrong, not gonna lie. "How are things?" I couldn't force myself to talk in the little-kiddy voice that I normally use when I talk to Mason.

"I'm good!" Mason punted a pebble off the cliff we were standing by.

Watching him do things independently made me happy. The recurring, uncontrollable smile on my face started coming back. I don't like admitting it, but it was a proud mother moment. He was standing on his own two feet and it felt like he had just graduated college.

"Lilith!" He yelled, while still kicking rocks off the ledge.

"What's up, Mason?" The happiness boost allowed me to talk in a kiddy voice.

"How is Taylor? Dad told me you visited him at his collegg." College, he means. Mason was never able to say college correctly.

Something in my heart shifted down when he asked me about Taylor.

"He's good," I said blandly.

My heart wasn't in it to give more of a detailed description of what I thought of him. That wasn't just because I was talking to Mason. I would've responded blandly no matter who I was talking to.

I felt like such a piece of shit, allowing myself to lie to my own family about Taylor. As I said earlier, I have no idea why I'm even doing this for his benefit. He was manipulating me without doing anything to manipulate me. That makes no sense, but it was somewhat of a reason I gave myself.

A few hours later, Sky is pretty black and our tent and everything is set up. I'm not outdoors a lot, but I admit the breeze of the half fall/half winter is very nice. The air smells different here than in Atlanta. It wasn't a bad or good difference, it was just *different*. I was starting to like Macon quite a bit, not gonna lie. It's not good enough to call home yet. My heart still wants to call Atlanta home, and that hasn't changed ever. But Macon is a suitable substitute.

Dad and Mason were having some father-son time inside the tent, probably playing with his toy cars or something. I went outside to get a view from up here. There was a small cliff near where Mason was throwing rocks. I sat down to let my legs hang off the edge and it was easy to encase myself in the space. It was pitch black by this point, but the city lights and old Halloween decorations were enough to illuminate the ground below.

Even though the ground below was nice and beautiful, the sight above was charming me more than anything. Remember when I mentioned that Mom used to sit on our balcony and stare into the sky at night? Ever since she died, I started doing that as well. Nothing bad ever enters my mind whenever I stare into the night sky. It's impossible. Trust me, I've tried. I think Mom felt the same way, too. She would always smile and even laugh sometimes, like someone just told her a joke. seven-year-old Lilith would call her crazy whenever she did that. Now that I'm older, I see eye to eye with her on that. I don't like the idea of calling Mom and me similar, but I'm fine with the idea of how we see the stars.

92

Lilith: Day Seventeen

"How long have you been out here?" Dad asked. I didn't notice him sneaking up behind me. It was like the world was soundless for a few hours.

"What time is it?" I asked, trying to not sound startled.

"12:20. I put Mason to bed an hour ago." Dad sat down next to me, also having his legs dangling down the cliff. I wasn't uncomfortable, but I don't remember the last time that Dad was this close to me, physically.

"I think I've been out here for two hours. I think." I admitted, just realizing it myself.

"You've been staring at the stars for two hours? Wow, that reminds me of your mother."

For some reason, the idea of Mom's necklace popped into my head. Then I remembered it was in my pocket. I took it out and stared at it for a few seconds, got the idea to put it on, got too anxious, and put it back in my pocket. It sounded right to put something that Mom owned while looking at something Mom loved, but I can't bring myself to do it.

"That takes me back to my college days. When we were going out, I remember seeing her outside, staring at the sky for hours and hours. I didn't know why until we got married."

Dad rambled on for a while, talking about Mom. I wasn't very interested in Dad talking about Mom, to be honest. Dad *never* talks about Mom and that's something that bothered me slightly. Now that he was talking about her in a way that I would never expect, it didn't interest me at all.

I took out my laptop while Dad was making a fire for us. With nothing to do, I mindlessly watched the footage of Taylor on Halloween night.

It felt so fucking weird, watching my own brother on low-quality security cameras, that he doesn't even know that exists. He was just doing everyday things like doing homework, sleeping, occasionally using the bathroom, etc. And here I was analyzing every bit of it. For a few moments, I thought I was deranged. After all, this is very fucking illegal, regardless of him being my brother. But I reminded myself that I was doing this for a good reason.

"What is that?" Dad snuck up behind and peered over my shoulder. He sounded a little disgusted.

"Nothing." I quickly slammed the laptop shut. I didn't hear his footsteps behind me. *Shit.*

"No, wait. Open that up again." He demanded. I remained still like I was playing dead or something. I didn't move a muscle. "Lilith! What is that?" He grabbed the laptop from my hands. I yelled out a quick no, before giving up my muscles.

I didn't even turn around to face him, knowing what was coming next. The sound of my laptop opening followed by the sound of the footage came into both of our ears. I couldn't see Dad, but I experienced his disgust from where I was sitting. I was getting my justification ready in my head. The same thing a ten-year-old does when he breaks a vase and hears his parents coming home from work.

"Is this your brother?" Dad asked, seemingly pissed off already.

"No, it's Mickey Mouse," I said in a *tone.*

"Hey, hey, hey! Why are you filming your brother? Do you know how fucked up and *illegal* that is?" He pulled my shoulder so I could finally face him. His face was turning a bright red.

"You said you wanted him to move back in with us, right? I wanted to make sure he was normal! Is that so fucked up?" I said defensively.

My volume started amping up. Instead of looking away like a kid, I looked him dead in the eyes. Everything started rising in my head and arms. Clenching my fists didn't do anything. After a second, it was like I didn't have fists. It felt like I only had a head and heart. I started to feel a painful spark in my heart.

"LILITH! HE'S YOUR FUCKING BROTHER! HE'S OUR FAMILY! FAMILY DON'T DO THIS TO EACH OTHER!" He yelled. His face was fully red by this point. It took every fiber of my being to not just shout what happened a few nights ago at the top of my lungs.

"HE'S FAMILY HUH? DO YOU KNOW WHAT FAMILY DON'T DO? THEY DON'T *RAPE* THE ONLY PERSON THAT HAS EVER UNDERSTOOD ME RIGHT IN FRONT OF MY EYES!"

This feeling of non-suppression felt so different. The blood was flowing differently, the sky turned a different color, and the air I breathed was angry. I screamed so loud that it echoed throughout Macon. I probably looked and sounded like I was about to cry, but I was tired of holding in my anger. Years of anger just unleashed and I couldn't stop it. The feeling of no longer feeling like myself it wasn't just a *feeling* anymore. For once in my life, I embraced it. *Spark.*

"YOU WEREN'T THERE DAD! FOUR YEARS AGO! YOU DON'T KNOW WHAT IT FELT LIKE WHEN I WAS *GENUINELY* WORRIED I WAS GOING TO DIE THAT DAY! TESS DIDN'T DESERVE WHAT TAYLOR DID TO HER!"

My eyes started to bawl like crazy. I was forcing my words through the waterfall of tears. I didn't feel the tears. I was lightheaded and dizzy, but I didn't feel it. I couldn't feel anything but anger and resent towards everything in front of me. I don't think I've ever heard my voice like this before. I sounded desperate, in pain, and miserable. It was hard to believe my own voice.

"YOU THINK I DON'T KNOW THAT? YOU DON'T THINK I WAKE UP EVERY DAY AND REALIZE HOW FUCKED UP THIS FAMILY IS?" His usual raspy voice was gone, and he grew up. He graduated, got a job, had kids, retired into a scream. His words echoed throughout Georgia, and maybe South Carolina. His eyes went fiery. I could swear there was a literal fire in his eyes. I started to fear, instead of resent.

My legs gave up, and I collapsed on the floor. Signifying my storm of emotions was over with. No more spark.

"WHOA, Lilith!" The past ten seconds seemed like they had never happened. The sky went back to normal, my blood flowed normally, and the air was oxygen. My heart started to ache like crazy. I think it was hurting before, but I was too encased in my emotion to feel anything else.

"I'm okay. I'm okay." I said calmly, trying to stay conscious. The atmosphere around me went from 100 to 0 quickly. "Can you get my medicine and water? It's in the purple bag," I asked, and he immediately raced over to the tent.

I took a second to take in what I said and did. My brain tried its best to erase it out of my memory, but I remembered. A lot of regrets and confusion entered my body.

"Here's your medicine and water."

Dad kneeled down to my level, still collapsed on the floor. I was barely able to sit up to drink my water. Sometimes I forget I have arrhythmia since I don't usually do anything to trigger it, but it's a medical reminder of what happens when I let my emotions get the better of me. Whenever it triggers,

I feel like sparks are tightening my heart until it breaks. It's the strangest yet most painful thing ever.

"Don't do that next time, sweetheart," Dad said, trying to calm me down. "Sorry for yelling, I forget you can't take that stuff without hurting." He was bad at comforting. His words sounded artificial. They made me feel a mix of resentment and empathy.

"Sorry, Dad. I've had a rough week. Like one of those weeks that you remember for the rest of the month." I said wholeheartedly. I swallowed my medicine.

"Yeah, sorry about that kid," my dad said understandingly, or at least I think he understood. If someone yelled at me as violently as I did to him, I wouldn't be so forgiving. "Listen, if you need more time, to get to know him better and stuff, that's fine. But he deserves a second chance at being in this family. I don't care how long it takes, just please give him a chance. I don't want to lose another one of our family." Dad reassured me.

There was no way in hell that I'm giving Taylor another chance, especially after Halloween. If he appeared right in front of my face, I would kill him, even if that meant going to jail. I've never felt so much hatred towards someone.

"Whoa whoa, are you okay?" Dad asked as I got to my feet. The lightheadedness was still present, but it was the least of my problems.

"Yeah, this medicine is pretty instant. I don't take it that often for a good reason."

I looked back at the tent and there stood Mason, peeking his head out through the opening. I wanted to smile at first until I saw his face. He looked like he wanted to cry. Now I couldn't even look at him. I walked up to Dad again, who was by the little campfire we set up earlier.

"Is it okay if I leave for Atlanta for a few days?" I asked.

"Who are you gonna be living with?" Dad asked. He didn't seem concerned, which surprised me. I was expecting him to almost freak out and I would have to explain myself quickly. His attention was still directly at the embers. His eyes didn't move at all, which concerned me slightly.

"Tess. She doesn't mind since she lives in a dorm by herself." I explained.

"Don't stay too long, okay?" Dad added.

"I won't. Will you be okay with Mason?" I asked.

"Yeah, I need to spend more time with him, anyway." He said with a raspy, undertone

voice. He didn't look at me, but I smiled in his direction, hoping he could feel it somehow.

Events like these make me remember that I have a dad in my life. That sounds awful to admit, but more often than not, I think of him as just another person who lives in my house. I don't know if you noticed, but he's not good at being a dad, especially a single one. He has his moments though, he's a good person and I also forget that sometimes.

Lilith: Day Seventeen cont.

I had never driven at night before, let alone in the middle of the night. It was probably the *least* stressful thing I've done in a long time. There were still plenty of cars on the road with me, but I felt isolated and remote. I didn't need music either, just the sounds of the road and car were enough to keep me at peace.

More importantly, though, I felt free...? Is that the correct word? As soon as I got in my car, I felt a lot of weight lift off my shoulders. I felt like a different person, but it was a good feeling this time. There was a smile on my face the entire ride to Atlanta and I didn't even notice till after.

Entering Atlanta, there was a sign saying 'Welcome to Atlanta'. It was a reddish-brown sign that's probably been there since the existence of the city. I got injected with twenty pumps of nostalgia as soon as I crossed that sign. It was a combination of good and bad nostalgia, but it was the type of nostalgia that people yearn for. Like finding a toy you loved as a kid or visiting your old elementary school. I was home, not my house, but my home.

I had a hard time remembering where Tess' college and the dorm were. I've only been there a single-digit amount of times before today. I had to go through our text messages and find the address for her dorm. Getting out of my car and walking into her dorm, I tried preparing some sort of apology or *something* to say to her. I felt like If I didn't have something prepared, I would make it worse.

I didn't want to knock in case Tess was asleep or with her boyfriend. I remembered Tess kept a spare key under her welcome mat. There were multiple occasions where she's gotten drunk and left her keys at the bar, so this key was just in case.

When I got inside, I checked Tess' bedroom to see if she was asleep. It was around three in the morning, so I expected her to be home, but she wasn't. Tess was probably at a party or something. I don't get how people can go to parties and like them enough to go again. I think those parties should be treated like a once-in-a-lifetime event, like bungee jumping or paintball. Sure, people do them multiple times, but more often than not, you just do those things once and you're done.

I wasn't sleepy and there wasn't much to do, so I plopped myself in front of Tess' TV and turned on a random movie. I don't normally watch *anything* for that matter, so I'm not exactly good at watching things if that makes sense. I've always been a book person, and TV just isn't the same. I guess you could argue that TV shows and movies are just books but real life. It just isn't the same, though. For the next hour or so I spaced out in front of the moving screen. The sound just drowned itself out and everything seemed so silent. I don't think I moved a muscle in that hour, not even my brain muscles.

"Wow, this is a sight to see." I didn't hear Tess come in. I felt like I just woke up and forgot where I was for half a second. "I was about to text you when I came home, but I guess there's no need."

"Surprise..." I said in a purposefully depressing voice.

"What are you doing here?" Tess asked happily.

"You're home? I thought you were at a party." I asked, ignoring her question.

"It's four in the morning, Lith." Tess started to giggle. "Parties don't go on forever." My eyes widened as I brought my wristwatch up to my face. *4:18.* I almost screamed. I could swear to you I thought it was only eleven or twelve.

Tess plopped on the couch next to me, making our thighs touch. A little spark went off in my body that I didn't see coming.

"Do you want a drink? I have some wine and beer in the fridge." Tess said out of nowhere. I was slightly paying attention to the movie, but still being mostly zoned out.

"You didn't get drunk at your party?" I just realized Tess didn't seem drunk. I've seen her drunk before, and it's very ugly, to say the least.

"Nah, the drinks there were shit, so I didn't bother. I rather get drunk at home."

"I'll take a beer." The idea of food came into my brain and I was starving. The feeling of yearning for food was so pedestrian till now. "Do you have anything to eat?" I screamed across the room to Tess, who was in the kitchen. The soft light from the kitchen and TV seeped into my eyes.

"Are you sure you wanna eat this late?" Tess asked. I looked at my watch again: 4:21 in the morning.

"I haven't eaten any *food* since Wednesday," I admitted. I could remember the individual countless nights where I drank one, if not multiple, glasses of water to fill my stomach. I realized how sad it was.

"Jesus Christ, uh... do you want a BLT or some grits?"

"Did your mom make the grits?" I asked.

"Yeah, I have a big container of it in my fridge." Tess' mom makes a lot of southern food for Tess and drops it off every now and then. "So, a beer and grits?"

"Yeah, thanks."

Tess tossed me an ice-cold can of Miller Lite and a white bowl of grits. For some reason, the food looked so delectable, even though grits weren't exactly the most exciting food. I shoved a spoonful in my mouth, probably the most *food* I've eaten in one bite. Usually, I nibble at my food if I'm forced to eat. Eating more only made me hungrier. My body has been deprived of receiving doses of food, so the pre-built hunger was all catching up to me now.

I finished the bowl in less than a minute. I would've asked for more, but I didn't want to take any more of Tess' food. As for the beer, I had never tried alcohol before. It's not a standard I hold myself to, I just never jumped at the chance. But I felt freer in Atlanta. My shoulders felt lighter. I had a natural smile on my face. I wondered if this is what a *home* felt like. I took a massive gulp, and it tasted like shit, but I kept taking in more liquid.

Earlier, when I embraced that familiar feeling of not being myself, I held on, held on tight. The combination of those two made me feel alive and, more importantly, better. I felt like I was controlling my world for once, rather than the world making me its puppet and having to dance till the end of time. I felt free and *powerful* enough to do anything.

I took out Mom's necklace. It's been in my pocket this whole time, a little after I got it from Taylor. I got the confidence to put it in my pocket after a lot of thinking. I was planning to just have it hung by my bedside, but I had the idea to have it on me one way or another like Mom did. I still didn't know about wearing it though. I was still on the fence about that.

"What's that?" Tess asked, turning her head away from the TV.

"My mom's charm necklace. Remember the one she wore all the time?" I said in a monotone voice. I was too focused on playing with the charm part of the necklace.

"That the one?" She asked. I nodded. "Why don't you put it on? I don't think I ain't ever see you with jewelry." Tess commented.

"I don't know, I just don't think it's right for me to put it on," I responded, speaking from the heart.

"Bullshit, let me put it on you." Tess yanked the necklace out of my hands.

My first instinct was to resist, but Tess has been doing things like this ever since I knew her. It's built into her system. And I took this as a sign from God himself that I should put the necklace on.

I pushed back my hair a bit, and Tess unhooked the necklace. The string of the necklace was all black, besides the fake metal chain at the end that connected the two ends. Like I said before, it was nothing fancy, but that didn't matter.

Tess wrapped the string around my neck with the charm attached and managed to hook both of the ends. I've never worn a necklace before, or any jewelry for that matter. My ears are pierced, but I don't own any earrings.

"How does it look?" I asked nervously.

"Amazin'. I'm surprised you didn't wear it before." Tess while looking at my neck. For some reason, my body didn't react well with this necklace on me. It was like individual thorns were pricking me. It was gonna take some getting used to. I knew I wanted to wear it though, at least for the time being. Having something relating to Mom on my body sounded like something I should do.

"Seriously though, why did you come?" Tess chuckled. She kicked her legs out from the couch and did a lengthy stretch. "Did something happen? You don't normally do this." Tess' voice went all serious-like. My mind raced for responses that could either make a joke or dodge the question entirely, but nothing was coming.

"I just missed you, that's all. I have a car now, I can literally go anywhere in North America." I wasn't particularly guilty of anything, but it certainly felt that way.

"*Bullshit*," Tess said under her breath, loud enough for me to hear it.

"What?" I responded, almost offended.

"I literally saw you *the other day,* Lilith. Just tell me the actual reason."

She said my actual name. My ears weren't used to her saying it. Anyone on planet earth could say 'Lilith' and I wouldn't bat an eye, but when Tess says it, it was powerful enough to open a new dimension.

Her eyes looked at me like I betrayed her. The last thing I needed was for Tess to get mad at me after what happened lately.

"You really don't think I just miss seeing you, huh?" I snapped, fully offended this time.

"No Lith, I really don't."

A feeling of 'now or never' came over me. Like this was an action movie and my next action determined the fate of the world. My sense of self felt so... restricted, trying to make a decision. A spark went off.

I continued to look up at Tess. Every millisecond that passed by added layers of tension in the room. The longer I stared, the more uncomfortable she got. I saw it in her eyes. It felt like the world itself was reduced down to just Tess and me. It felt like the walls were closing in on us. But I wasn't panicking.

Before the walls closed completely, I let out a brief smile that lasted only a half-second. I stood up and pressed my lips against Tess'. I shut my eyes and Tess almost screamed. Neither one of us pulled away nor wanted to. There was no push or pull, there was just a double pull. I was on cloud nine and I knew for a fact Tess was the same. After that point, the world boiled down to me, Tess, and the couch.

Mark: November 15

After those few days of watching the footage, I eventually told Sky about how I found basically nothing. I was expecting her to be a bit disappointed, but she was actually pretty understanding. She said that she couldn't find much of anything either. Granted, she probably hadn't watched as much as I had, since she is taking care of Avery and such, but we both didn't find much.

Thankfully, her determination hadn't deteriorated in the slightest. She asked if she could come over to my house to watch the footage together, in an attempt to make it fun for both of us. I agreed, and she brought over her computer and her own disks.

"How is Avery doing?" I asked as I popped open the *Front Lawn* CD from its case. I looked outside, and it was still pretty gloomy. It wasn't pouring like last week, but it was gloomy enough to evict a depressing scene in my room. This time I turned on my room lights to prevent my room from looking abandoned.

"Better. We went out to get coffee the other day, actually." I ejected the *Living Room* disk and put it in the *Front Lawn* one. "Granted, I ordered for her and such, but going into a public area was an accomplishment, I guess." I started to notice how Sky's patience was being affected. If she were any normal person, they would've snapped by now. The other day, she was telling me about all the crying episodes and sleepless nights she's had to endure because of Avery. I don't blame Sky for sounding a little worn out.

"Have you thought about getting therapy for her? That could help her heal a bit more." I suggested. I opened up the video application on my computer and violently slammed the spacebar to play the tape.

"We both agreed that it wouldn't be a good idea, mate. Therapists help with like behavioral issues and bad habits, not coping with being a fuckin' rape victim." She said irritatedly. "It would just be a waste of time and money."

I noticed that Sky was very hesitant when it came to authority figures. I remembered in the note she wrote that she refused to contact the police about this. To be honest, I thought about telling my dad about this but chose to honor her wishes.

"I thought about coming over to visit, but didn't know if that would be a good idea" I said in silence. The memory of seeing Avery post-Halloween-party was almost jammed into my brain. That was the closest I've seen to a broken person. Seeing the state she was in made me sick to my stomach.

"If you tell me in advance, then it should be no problem." She confirmed.

After that, we both kind of shut up for a while. I assumed that would help me concentrate on the footage, but it was the opposite, actually. The silence was deafening. It was so quiet that I heard the front door open and close. I looked at my watch and it was about the time when I'd expect my sister to come home.

"Claire! Is that you?" I yelled through my closed door, hoping my sister could hear. I then realized she normally listens to music when she walks home, so I didn't bother re-yelling. It was probably her, anyway.

Meanwhile, Sky was kind of in her own world. Her eyes were glued to her laptop monitor, not missing a beat. She would blink rarely. It was scary how long she took between blinks. Calling her hyper-focused would be an understatement. Her unrelenting determination was contagious, so it inspired me to focus on my footage instead of everything else.

I put back on my headphones when suddenly someone opened my door. I looked up, assuming I'd see my sister. But my heart dropped when I saw my dad's head through the door.

"Who's car is parked outside-?" My dad came in asking. He turned his head and saw Sky's head peeking over her laptop. "Oh hello. Mark, who is this?" My dad asked.

I awkwardly reached my arm over to Sky's laptop to shut off the video. "I'm Sky, Mark's friend from school." Sky reached out her hand to shake my dad's. I was breaking a sweat trying to close everything on my computer. I took the stack of disks from my desk and slid them under my desk, making sure my dad couldn't see me in his peripherals.

"What are you two up to?" My dad asked after shaking Sky's hand.

Sky's mouth was about to open when I interjected with: "We're doing a school project!" I blurted, overtaking whatever Sky was about to say.

Really Mark? You couldn't come up with any better excuses?

Sky looked at me with a quickly raised eyebrow. I shot her a look that *hopefully* signaled to follow my lead.

"Yeah, we're doing a research project. Is it okay if Sky stays for a bit?" I asked in a calmer voice. My face was starting to warm up a lot. I was petrified that my face was turning a bright red.

"Yeah, that's fine. Just make sure your folks are fine with it." My dad said as he started exiting my room, closing the door on the way out.

Sky and I sat in silence for a few seconds as I made sure I heard my dad's footsteps becoming more faint. After what felt like an hour, I exhaled a breath that I didn't even know I was holding.

"*What the hell was that?*" Sky yell-whispered. I double-checked that the door was closed before I opened my mouth.

"Didn't I tell you? My dad's a police officer! If he knew what we were doing, our asses would be gone!"

"You didn't tell me that!"

"I didn't think I needed to!"

I slammed my spacebar again to play the footage. If life wasn't fucking with me enough already, it started to rain outside again. I plunged my hands into my face to let all the frustration out.

"Listen, mate..." Sky said with her arms folded. "Can we do this at Avery's place next time? I don't think it's safe to be here... No offense." She said monotonously.

"Yeah, that's fine by me," I said, slapping my thigh hard enough to make it turn a different color.

After Sky went home, I took all the CDs and put all of them under my bed. As lame of a hiding spot as it sounds, I couldn't think of any other place I could viably hide them. I just have to hope no one happens to clean under my bed or something.

Mark: November 17

I was in the library with Nicole at lunch. I had a history test next period, and I needed all the last-minute study time I could get. Sky had to meet up with a teacher at lunch, so I couldn't have lunch at the water fountains with her today.

"Guess what?" She said,

"What?" I said with grit in my voice.

"I lost my second virginity." She said, very perkily. The library was relatively quiet, so some people around us judgingly turned their heads.

"What do you mean, second?" I asked, while neck-deep in a history textbook. I was trying my best to absorb the information, but it became word mush once Nicole opened her mouth.

"The first one was like a free trial, a simple taste of the real thing. The second time is when you can say you've had sex proudly." She said smugly.

"This was the first date?" I asked, raising an eyebrow.

"I mean, I initiated things. We were just watching a movie and when the sex scene came on, I just took advantage of the situation. I was just really horny." Nicole explained way too much and too loudly for a public area.

I didn't give much of a response. I scoffed slightly begrudgingly and cuffed my hands around the sides of my face. To be honest, I didn't even know why I bothered asking questions.

Nicole kept talking about... whatever the fuck she was on about, and I purposefully tuned her out. If we're being honest here, I kept trying to read the textbook, but nothing was registering. I could read each individual word, but words suddenly had no meaning. I was in that weird in-between where there was either too much in my brain or empty space.

"Yo! Yo! Mark! Mark!" Nicole yelled. Eventually, she hit me on the back of the head, which sent me straight back to reality.

"W-What?" I yelled out. We once again made everyone in the library turn their heads, and the librarian had to shush me from across the room. "*What?*" I whispered this time, rubbing the back of my head.

"You've been acting weird lately, dude," Nicole said repulsively. She flicked her fingers at my book in some sort of disgust.

"What do you mean, I'm acting weird? I'm studying for a test and you're talking about your fuckin' sex life." I said in a snap.

"You've been ignoring my calls, avoiding me during school, and you looked like you haven't slept in weeks. What is up with you lately?" I looked at the window behind Nicole to see my own reflection. To put it bluntly, I looked like shit. My hair was all over the place and there were obvious bags under my eyes.

"I've been staying up pretty late, working on something," I said vaguely. I couldn't look Nicole in the eye, even though I damn well knew she was staring at mine. I just continued to look at my dead reflection.

"Working on what?" She burst out.

"I... I can't tell you." I said, letting my eyes drop down to the ground.

"We know everything about each other. What the fuck do you mean you can tell me?"

"Hey! You two! Last warning, tone it down!" The librarian yelled.

"I mean, I can't tell you! What is so hard to understand about that? I'm not fucking required to tell you everything!" I said in an outburst, letting my arms and hands fly everywhere.

"Alright, that's it! Both of you are out of here, now!" By this point, I felt like the entire student body was staring at us. I didn't realize how loud we were until every single direction I looked. There was at least a pair of eyes staring at us both. But I was too angry to care.

"Fuck you!" Nicole yelled, slapping me in the face. I instinctively put up my hand to get her back. My hand was held firm in the air, and Nicole flinched at the sight of it. A brief gasp was heard around us. Somehow, my morals were strong enough to resist the urge. I slowly put my hand down and everyone in the library let out a loud breath.

"Fuck you too, bitch." Nicole turned around but almost went back to punch me in the face. I almost welcomed it. I looked at her as if to say *"Try me"*, but she realized it wasn't worth the trouble. She just bared her teeth at me.

I aggressively grabbed all my shit and walked towards the front exit while Nicole walked towards the back. I bit on my tongue to neutralize the anger. Every time I get angry, I'm reminded of what anger feels like. It's one of the more uncommon emotions to experience, at least for me. I've never sworn at Nicole, and neither has she at me. In a matter of seconds, we broke that act without thinking a second time.

Before lunch even ended, I marched to my locker and grabbed all my stuff, and left school. My other friends caught word of what happened and spammed my phone with messages and calls. I let all of those ring out fully until they stopped on their own. I got in my car and sped out of the school. No one tried stopping and even if someone did, I would've ignored them.

I didn't know where I was driving. I just kept going forward until something compelled me to make a right or left turn. All my frustration was seeping out the open windows. I cut off random cars on the road and beat every yellow light I came across. You can tell I'm not good at handling my frustrations well. If I let myself become more careless, I would've been gone, one way or another.

Hours of me riding around town go by, seeing my gas tank deplete to almost empty, and I eventually get home around two in the morning. By then, I felt like I'd completed a road trip all around Georgia. I told myself I would drive until I was too tired to feel angry. Seeing the magnificent stars also helped me calm down a lot.

I felt totally drained when I finally parked my car in the driveway of my house and turned off the car. I leaned back in my seat for a few minutes and thought about falling asleep right then and there.

When I got in the house, all the lights were off and the house was silent. I called out to my dad to see if he was awake. By this time, he would either be watching TV or getting ready to sleep, so it was weird seeing the house this lifeless. I got no response, so I assumed he went to bed or something.

I finally checked my phone while heading up to my room. I've been neglecting it the whole time I was driving. There wasn't much besides a few missed calls from friends, my sister texting me asking me where I was, and nothing from Nicole, as expected. There were also A LOT of missed calls from my dad. That made me worried that he was emailed by the school about what happened. He normally doesn't take that kind of stuff lightly, so I began to dread the conversation we're gonna have in the morning.

When I got to my room, I saw that the door was wide open and a dim light came out of it. I raised an eyebrow, knowing that I closed my door the last time I was in the house. And I knew for a fact that I didn't leave my lamp on. I suddenly got this feeling of ominous doom, like there was a robber in my room or something.

When I walked inside, I saw my computer monitor shining in the complete darkness. I thought I was in the clear, assuming I accidentally left my computer on from the other night... until I looked at who was standing behind the monitor.

"Dad?" I knocked on my open door. "What are you doing?" I said with a lump in my throat. Suddenly that feeling of doom began to ramp up.

My dad didn't bother turning his head or eyes to acknowledge my existence. His eyes were glued to my monitor, having a permanent frown on his face. There was a sound coming from my speakers, but it was so faint that even in the dead-silent house it was hard to hear.

"Dad?" I called once again, letting my worries marinate.

He didn't move a muscle. I swear I was looking at someone frozen in time. The fucked-up suspense was killing me. I walked up to my monitor to see what he was looking at. My brain knew what to suspect, but I chose to stay oblivious.

On the desk were all twelve CDs spread out on my desk. "H-h-how did you find these?" I struggled to utter it. On the monitor was Avery's security footage playing on fullscreen.

But how? I hid them under my bed. How the fuck did he find them? I thought to myself.

My dad finally slowly turned his head to me, breaking his eternal stare with my computer monitor. His expression didn't change at all, but he was looking dead into my eyes this time, which made things a thousand times more scary.

"I know w-what this looks like! I-" I exclaimed. I put both of my hands in the air as some sort of defensive mechanism.

"Looks like what? Huh? That my son is a fucking criminal? Is that what it looks like?" My dad slammed his hand on my desk, chipping some of the wood off, and threw some of the disks at my chest.

"Please! Let me explain! I swear-" My voice started devolving into pathetic screaming.

"Oh, fuck off! What is this? Your fucking 'volleyball' practice, huh? Yeah, good one Mark." My dad shoved my monitor off the desk. The screen instantly turned black while some of the wires broke off. The loose electricity lit up the room a bit before it hit the ground.

"No!" I screamed. In a heartbeat, tears started to well up on the sides of my eyes. I clenched my fist to fight the tears. I even squeezed my eyes shut so no water could break loose.

"What's happening?" My sister ran in and quickly turned on the lights. With it on, I could see my computer in shambles in the middle of my room. It made me squeeze even harder.

"Yeah, why don't you explain, huh, Mark? Your sister would *love* to know why you've been cooped up in your room for this whole week." My dad taunted. I squeezed so hard that I started to not feel my fingers or eye sockets.

"Fuck you," I uttered, with what little strength I had.

"Come again?" My dad stepped back to do a double-take.

"Fuck you!" I burst into tears, shoving my dad back a few more steps. "FuckyouFuckyouFuckyou!" I laid hands on my dad to push him again, but before I could exert any force, he sucker-punched me across the face.

"Stop!" My sister squealed.

I was sent to the floor immediately. The punch made my head bang against my dresser, and that's all I could feel. I began to hold my head in my hands and writhe in pain on the floor.

In the corner of my eye, I could see my dad go for another punch, probably using more force than the last. Suddenly, I felt something pulling me away from him.

"Dad! Stop! Leave him alone!" My sister begged. She quickly helped me to my feet.

"Get the fuck out of here, Claire! This is none of your business!" My dad screamed. He laid his hands out like he was about to kill me. I stood behind Claire in fear.

My dad charged at Claire and me. We both dodged to the left and he slipped on the broken monitor. As soon as he hit the floor, he violently screamed in pain. Claire and I looked down and there was a piece of black glass from the monitor stabbing through his foot. He screamed so loudly that it echoed throughout the house.

"Mark, get out of here. Run." Claire said through her teeth. We were both still trying to process everything, and it wasn't coming to me as quickly.

"What? Run where?" Claire kneeled to assist our dad.

"Away from here! Get out before this gets even uglier!" Claire forewarned. I looked down at her and she was holding down our dad. He was trying his best to get to his feet, even with a piece of glass in his foot. A crazed look in his eyes stared me down as I thought about where to go.

In a panic, I grabbed my phone and ran out of my room and house. Without even realizing it from the inside, it was pouring outside. I heard my dad's voice become fainter as I ran farther and farther away from the house.

I don't know where I was running, but I was running as far as I could. I felt primal running in the pouring rain in the dead of night. There was no care in the world besides what was in front of me and how long my legs could carry me for. Every car that drove past me made me want to run faster.

A car on the side of the road started to mirror my speed. My primitive instincts somehow saw this as a threat and I pushed my body to run faster.

"Mark? Is that you?" A familiar voice yelled out of her car. The heavy rain almost made it inaudible. I turned my head and saw Nicole's head peeking out of her car window.

"Nicole? What are you doing here?" I yelled, using what little lung capacity I had left. I had to do a double-take to make sure I wasn't seeing things.

"What're you doing here? It's fucking raining! Get in the car!" Nicole demanded. She quickly pulled over and slammed the passenger seat open.

Without thinking about it, I jumped into her car, drenched in rain water. Before I could close the door, she pushed on the gas like we had just committed a heist.

Lilith: Day Seventeen cont. again

"**W**ake up," Tess said in a half-awake voice. As I opened my eyes, I silently panicked, trying to remember where I was and how I got here. Once my senses became whole, Tess and I locked eyes. I was laying flat on her chest to the point where our legs and feet were exactly parallel. We were both naked on the couch, smiling at each other for a prolonged amount of time. The only clothing, I had was my underwear dangling off my leg. That thought didn't bother me. "Morning, Lith," Tess said in a comforting motherly voice. All I could do was giggle. There was nothing funnier in the world at the time.

"Morning, Tess," I said, overwhelmed with laughter still.

"You feelin' alright?" Our smiles got wider as we spoke. It became harder and easier to keep eye contact.

"Yeah, I'm fine. How about you?" I asked.

In actuality, I was more than fine. I wasn't engulfed in my emotions like yesterday. I was just *happy*. Waking up with some fire inside of you makes you feel nothing can go wrong.

"I'm a little hungover, not gonna lie," Tess admitted.

"How much wine did you drink?" I said, playfully.

Tess started petting my hair, which added even more happiness to the pile. I was still on top of her, my head perpendicular to her chest. I pressed my ear up against her heart and I could hear her individual heartbeats. They sounded as beautiful as heartbeats could. At that moment, I wish I could've somehow gotten closer to them.

She grabbed the bottle from next to us. It was ¾ empty. We both just laughed.

"How much beer did you drink?" I held up my already small beer can. It was only half empty. I barely remember drinking, if I even drank it at all.

"You weren't drunk at all?" Tess asked.

"No, no, I wasn't." We exchanged one wider smile until we both got up. I looked at my watch, 1:17 PM. The latest I've woken up in years.

I pushed my hair back a bit and my finger grazed the string of the necklace. I almost forgot I had it on. I was so worried about putting it on before, but now I couldn't help but smile. I clutched the charm that the necklace was attached to. It was perfectly laid in front of my heart, just like how Mom had it. It felt so... *right*.

"Yeah, at two, so I have to get ready soon." Tess started making us breakfast, even though it was the afternoon. I was still exhausted, but I didn't want to go back to bed. The thought of being home in Atlanta was more than enough to keep me awake.

I went to the bathroom to see how much of a mess I was. As soon as I walked in, I noticed a hickey on the right side of my neck. I barely recognize myself in the mirror. My first thought wasn't: *Oh no, a hickey!* It was: *That's nice.* I asked Tess if I could use her toothbrush and she said it was fine since we already exchanged multiple bodily fluids last night.

Tess was still butt-naked, making us breakfast, which was dangerous, among other things. But I think she was just trying to amuse me, which she accomplished. I couldn't help but smile or laugh whenever I looked back at her.

We sat down across from each other to eat. I didn't even think about the idea of *not eating*. I sat down and ate like I've been doing it that way for my whole life.

Now that I thought about it, I didn't have the usual minor headache or irritability I usually had. I knew that was due to my lack of eating, but I didn't realize that one night of eating could make the difference.

"Are you still going to work? Hungover like that?" I asked.

"I have to. I have already scheduled my shifts for this week."

We were talking like we actually lived together. There was a certain warmth to our conversations now. I wanted to stay here forever. The longer I was here, the more I hated Macon in comparison.

Tess started flaunting her naked body around the kitchen as she cleaned our dishes. I hate to admit this, but I was getting really turned on. I didn't even know I could get turned on till seconds after it happened to me. It's the weirdest thing in the world. You don't get used to it either. It was like a loud heartbeat. My leg started to shake like I was bored in class.

"Where do you plan on going today? If you even plan on leaving," Tess asked.

"I'm gonna try to relax for the most part. I might go out a little, but I want to take a break from it all. Is that okay?"

"Yeah, of course," Tess said blandly.

There was a moment of silence between us. This time, it was awkward. Our eyes locked at the most random time, and I knew we were thinking the same thing.

Tess pins me against the wall behind where I was sitting. Still naked, let me remind you. She started lifting my shirt up and reaching between my bra. My legs started to become weak, and we both collapsed to the floor. This time, she was on the top and I was on the bottom. I was severely overwhelmed by her sudden movements and moaning. I started moaning too, but against my will. A familiar spark appeared in my heart. The spark that your body doesn't forget the feeling of. Like stubbing your toe or getting punched.

My heart started to hurt. It hurt like hell yesterday too, even though I took my medicine. I chose to ignore it at that time, but this time my body won't let me ignore it. A little of my rational side of me started coming back. It didn't feel good.

"Hey-hey-hey-hey." I interrupted, trying not to sound like I was suffering, but my face probably gave it away. I used my hand to push her away softly and my other hand over my heart. It started aching like crazy. She immediately stopped. "Listen, last night was great. But you have a boyfriend. This is wrong and you know it... for multiple reasons." I said, I knew that the last part hurt her and myself. It was meant to be mean.

Our eyes were locked, but it became increasingly harder to say those words without wanting to pull my eyes away. I had trouble resisting my own desires. But I know it's wrong, very wrong. So, wrong that I don't want to say the other obvious reasons.

"Yeah... you're right." She said. Tess made a very obvious frown. I couldn't tell if she was mad at herself or me. I automatically blamed myself. Tess got up and went to her room to put clothes on. The spark feeling went away.

Tyler Bansil

Lilith: Day Eighteen

I told myself that I'd spend the entirety of yesterday staying and resting, but I ended up going out at night. I didn't do anything stupid like I expected myself to do. I just got myself a sandwich from a sandwich shop I used to go to all the time after school.

When I used to live in Atlanta, it was within biking distance and also on the way home, so I used my allowance to buy either a small sandwich or water. To be honest, I just went there to have an excuse to have a conversation with the Italian woman that took the orders. It was something I looked forward to every week. She was this short, old Italian woman that spoke a more-than-decent amount of English. I haven't seen her since I was nine, so about eight years ago or so.

When I walked in, a bunch of good nostalgia hit me in the face. The shop hasn't changed one bit. There was still the missing dog poster that was there when I was six. The wooden walls were still as dark and damaged as I remembered it. A bunch of people waved hello to me when I walked in as well. I don't think any of them actually knew me, but they waved anyway. It was like a little Italian community in this small shop. It felt homier than Macon is, that's for sure.

"HA! I knew you'd come back!"

I was still admiring the interior of the place when I heard that familiar voice. I looked back down and saw the Italian woman at the cash register. My heart expanded at the sight of her. I was almost star-struck, like I was meeting a celebrity. "You look no different, do ya?" Her English has improved a lot. The accent, not really, but her words made more sense to me. Her voice got raspier though, but that's expected with age. Other than that, she didn't look a day older than I remember.

"Nonna!" I ran up behind the cash register and just hugged her. That was probably out of line, but she didn't mind.

"How could you leave me here for nine years? You left me with Bolo. How could you-a do that?" Nonna said jokingly. I was slightly worried that Nonna would forget me, but that problem quickly washed away.

Bolo was her husband who helped cook in the kitchen. He was this old, but slightly younger than Nonna, man that didn't say much. The few words he did say, though, I remember them word for word. I wasn't nearly as close to him as I was with Nonna, but it still felt like I'd known him forever.

"I'm sorry Nonna. I'm visiting, so I thought I should see you." My voice got very excited, like I was nine years old again. By the way, Nonna means grandmother in Italian. That wasn't her real name.

"Don't be-a sorry. You needed to grow up. I stopped growing up fifty years ago." She said, laughing at her joke.

It felt like one of those movies where the student sees his master after a ridiculous number of years and he's still in the same spot as when he left.

"Ahh, what you want to eat? I feed you, I feed you. You were always very hungry as a kid." That last part both saddened and joyed me. The fact that young Lilith ate more than current me and the fact that she even remembered my mannerisms.

"Do you remember my usual, Nonna?" I asked, trying to fish for more nostalgia happiness.

"Ahh, my memory is no good anymore, Lilith. I'm-a sorry Lilith." I was a little sad about that.

She didn't remember, but it was to be expected. She was approaching 80 years old, so memory was a luxury at this point.

"It's okay. I'll take a ham and cheese with mustard."

I know that sandwich is a little childish and dull, but I would order that same sandwich all the time when I was a kid. I know it would taste better than any sandwich on the menu. At least to me, it would.

"Bolo! *Italian words that I don't know to write out, but it was probably my order*" Nonna yelled. Bolo just nodded as silently as a person could.

I took a step outside real quick to wait for my sandwich. It took me a moment to take everything in. The lights, the cars, the buildings. I've been looking at lights, cars, and buildings for my entire life, but it didn't feel as satisfying as it did until now. This time, it hit my heart at the correct angle. I let my eyes bathe in the city until something broke my train of thought, which happened to be a pigeon flying by.

I don't know how long I was out, but most of everyone who was eating there was all gone. Bolo and another employee were cleaning, and Nonna was at the cash register as usual. In my mind, I never wanted her to leave that spot. The restaurant was nothing without Nonna, and Nonna wasn't herself without the restaurant.

"Sorry Nonna, I was distracted by something outside," I said.

"I saw you-a stare at nothing for ten minutes." She pointed to a window that showed where I was standing and started laughing. "Don't worry, your mom used to do the same thing." Nonna laughed again. I tried to fake laugh with her, but it was a horrible fake laugh.

Usually, I would feel a mix of happiness and sadness in sentences like that, but this time it was just sadness. It didn't help that her death anniversary was tomorrow. I became aware of the charm in my pocket. It seems like I only *feel* it when someone talks about Mom, which is fitting.

I sometimes forget that Mom and Nonna used to be great friends. Mom was one of Nonna's first friends when she came to America. At that time, Nonna spoke barely any English, but they were still good friends. That story in itself was beautiful. It's one of the few things that I admired about Mom. Trust me, there were very few things, to begin with.

"You know her-uh, death day is tomorrow, right?" I said, trying to not make it sound depressing.

Nonna was one of the few people that didn't know about Mom's issues. I'm pretty sure the only thing that Nonna knew about Mom was that she had three kids, a husband, and a job. At her funeral, phrases like abuse, mentally unstable, tried-to-kill-her-husband and other terrible words were the topics of the funeral. Of course, Nonna doesn't know what those words mean, so she doesn't know anything about the *actual* her. Everyone at the funeral learned about the actual her one way or another.

"Ahh yes, I know Lilith. I visit her every year." Nonna said, endearingly. That usual mixed emotion hit me pretty hard. I still managed a smile, though.

"We're closing up soon. Hurry up with your customer." The employee said.

"Ahhh one moment." She yelled back.

I looked at my watch: 11:18 PM. It was eighteen minutes past closing time. Nonna always went past closing to talk with the customers she liked. I'm glad I was one of them.

"Okay, I'll-a tell you something. Nonna said discreetly. "If I see you tomorrow. I have a surprise for you." I smiled a bit.

"Okay, I'll see you tomorrow then, Nonna," I said happily. I took my half-eaten sandwich and left. The sound of the little bell that rang when someone entered or exited the shop injected more good nostalgia inside of me.

I stood outside my car for a little longer, looking at the roads and buildings again. *God, why couldn't I live here?* I thought to myself repeatedly. I diverted my eyes upwards, and the stars were there to greet me. Even the stars looked better in Atlanta. Of course, all-stars are great, but my eyes literally gravitated towards them. Maybe it's because I was happier, but they were brighter, better, and grander.

"Thanks for bringing me home," I said to the stars. The sound probably disappeared in my own breath, but I'd like to think something or *someone* heard it.

Lilith: Day Nineteen

Tess and I haven't said much to each other since our little scene in the kitchen two days ago. It felt much longer than two days, though. I felt like I've gathered enough experience to last a month. Anyway, we ate dinner together like once. I tried to make our conversations not awkward, and I think I did a good job, but in the back of our heads, there was tension. There was obvious pain in our voices. I heard it more in mine than Tess'. It stuck out like a sore thumb.

Tess didn't have any other bedrooms in her dorm, so last night we tried sleeping in the same bed. We slept in the same bed many times before, as kids, of course. And I thought things had calmed down by then, but then she asked if we could just kiss. It was so sudden too. I was reading one of Mom's journals with a lamp on, then she just blurted the question. It sounded like she rehearsed the lines, too. She said she'd been thinking about me all day and one kiss would satisfy her. I didn't even consider her request and coldly declined. If I gave it any amount of thought, the threshold to say no would've exponentially decreased. *God, why was it so hard to reject her?* If you told me a week ago that I'd be resisting the temptation to kiss someone, let alone Tess, I would've slapped you. I started to wonder if resisting was worth it. My excuse was that it was *wrong* and that it shouldn't have happened in the first place. Both of those arguments are very valid, but there's also the argument of *who cares?* No one else is involved, and it's not hurting anyone. Who cares if it's wrong? Life is short. But these were all mindsets that drove crazy people to do crazy things. Then I thought about Mom and then I became level-headed.

"Are you visiting your mom today?" Tess asked in the morning.

It seemed like she knew it was Mom's death anniversary. I was just about to go out the front door. She was doing some yoga in the living room in front of the TV.

"Yeah. I'm also meeting Nonna there." I don't even remember if Tess remembers or knows Nonna.

"The woman at the sandwich place? The one you used to go to a lot as a kid." I nodded. We blankly stared at each other for a few seconds, not knowing what to say. My brain seemed to shut off whenever I was talking to her. "Are y'all related or something?"

"No, just friends," I said blandly. I tried to end the conversation on a relatively high note, but that's all I could muster.

I stepped outside and I noticed it was raining. It wasn't a good type of rain either. A good type of rain is the light pitter-patters, the ones you think about when it's a rainy day. Today there was a depressing type of rain. The really heavy rain that makes the sky turn dark. Everyone on the street is all wearing black raincoats and looking down or else they'll get water in their eyes. It really doesn't benefit anyone. How fitting for the day of Mom's death. How fitting indeed.

I tried to numb myself to any emotion while driving to the cemetery. I knew the destination of the cemetery by heart, but I still used the GPS to distract myself from any emotions or thoughts. It didn't help that I read some of Mom's journals the night before, either. I didn't know what to think of them anymore, which scared me. They didn't make me feel any emotion like they used to. The words just turned into mush on the page. At that point, my brain goes into autopilot, jumping from word to word. So, I guess I wasn't really reading, more like looking.

Surprisingly, even though I've gone here every year, entering the cemetery itself makes my emotions go into overdrive. As soon as I park my car and stop the engine, my body tries to prepare itself. I try not to look at my surroundings because everyone knows how depressing a cemetery is.

When you think about the idea of funerals and the events surrounding them, it's a little shitty. First of all, it's expensive, which is an issue in itself. Next, I don't see how burying someone's dead body is paying it any sort of respect. I don't wish that on my worst enemy. Cremating someone is a little weird, but it seems more sensible than burying someone.

"Oh, it's you again." The funeral clerk said a little condescendingly, even though it probably wasn't meant to be condescending. I've probably seen this guy three to four times, combining my yearly visits to this same cemetery.

"You still work here? I thought you would've gone to college by now." I responded bluntly. I remember this guy telling me he was a senior in high school, but I don't remember when I was told this.

"For the field, I *want* to work in, I don't need to go to college. Seems like a waste of time." He said, sounding very opinionated.

"What field do you want to work in?" I asked, for the sake of conversation. Personally, this was just another mind distraction for me, so I didn't mind dragging out a conversation with him.

"That's none of your business, is it?" He was as rude as I remember. I just tolerate him, because his rudeness is the least of problems when I come here, so it ends up being one of the more pleasant experiences.

"Terry! Be nice to the guests!" An old woman from another part of the room, who was old enough to be my grandma, yelled at him. By the way she said it, it seemed like this wasn't the first time he spoke this way to the guests.

"Ugh, fine." He said, like any other miserable teenage boy. Technically, he was an adult, but his mindset from his teenage years hasn't moved at all. "Enjoy your visit, ma'am. Please make sure you don't trample the other guest's flowers." He said nicely. His voice was more wholesome than I thought, which is how he probably presented himself when he was interviewed for this job.

"Thanks, Terry."

I walked past him and the field of grass greeted me with its environment. It's always more surreal than my memories lead me to believe, even though I'm pretty familiar with the area. The rain made the area more depressing than I remembered it, that's for sure. It was just a flat field of probably fake grass as far as the eye could see. All the gravestones were organized ten feet apart from each other, like a row of soldiers. The flowers from the loved ones were dampened by the aggressive water droplets. It literally felt like I was surrounded by dead things. It wasn't just the caskets that made this place as dead as it felt.

In this whole field, there was only one woman here, from what I could view. I heard the faint sound of crying from a distance. It made me wonder if I would still visit here when I was her age. As long as I'm in Georgia, I'll feel obligated to come here at least yearly. Hopefully, when I reach that woman's age, that I'll be located somewhere else.

When I reached Mom's grave, the emotions started flooding in. Every time I come here, I force myself not to cry. It doesn't get easier with time, either. I haven't cried once, but it just bottles up more every year. Like continuously adding one drop to an already full glass of water and waiting for a bunch of it to spill out.

I kept reading the words on my Mom's grave repeatedly. *Theresa Sara Jacobs. 1969-2010.* The remaining petals of the flowers I left last year were still there. This was the one funeral tradition that I actually sympathize with. Flowers are a living thing and they give life to those who died. Replacing them every year makes sure the souls don't die. I don't know. I'm making this up as I write. All I know is that I appreciate the tradition. It was the one thing that gave this place a little color and vibrance.

A woman slowly creeps up right next to me. I didn't fully notice it at first, but Nonna came up next to me and stared at the gravestone with me. Nonna probably knew that I was deep in thought, so she didn't give me her usual one-line openers that she usually throws me. It was considerate of her, but I could've definitely used that to cheer me up a little.

I spent a long time staring at the gravestone. The rain even eased up a little. What was going on in my head? The same thing that appears in my head every time I come here. The memories, the flashbacks, the hospital visits, the drama, the sleepless nights, specific journal lines, the horribleness. I was having a little PTSD episode while staring at a piece of metal. If it were up to me, I would've screamed and cried, but my mind won't let it happen. It locked me in a train-of-thought chamber and wouldn't let me out until my brain decided that I had enough torture. You might question why I come back every year then if I described the experience as torture. Sometimes, it doesn't feel like a choice whether I come back or not. Emotional attachment is a deadly weapon. It's hard to let go of something when you have an emotional attachment. Children are pretty much designed to have an emotional attachment to their parents. No matter how bad or good they might be. It was a necessary evil that I only have bad things to say about.

"I'll wait for you inside. I still have your surprise." Nonna said softly.

It just popped in my head that I was probably torturing her with how long I made her stand there in the cold, harsh rain. She put her own set of flowers in and slowly walked back inside.

My little PTSD episode was over by that point. How did I feel? Blank. A mix of happiness and sadness. Weightless. The sound of rain and my footsteps drowned out even though I wasn't stuck in thought. Before going back, I wanted to talk to Mom. I kneeled on the wet grass and spoke my heart out. I was basically having a conversation between myself and a piece of metal. But to me, it was the most meaningful conversation of the year. I didn't receive words back. It was a one-sided conversation, but I felt heard. I held Mom's necklace firmly in my hand. That was all the conversation I needed. The words I said are personal to myself and Mom. I don't want to write those things out, sadly. The words exchanged between daughter and dead mother shouldn't be repeated to others. The few words I say to Mom should be personal.

"Are you okay?" Nonna asked, concerningly. Her voice went deep and sorry-like. I could tell she was a little saddened, too. It took me a while to realize that.

"I'm fine," I said unconvincingly. "It's a part of growing up like you said, Nonna." I smiled at Nonna, she smiled back. The warmth of her smile pierced through my heart and made it feel more whole.

"I'm-a proud of you Lilith."

Nonna was the best version of a relative you can get. We're not related, but it certainly felt like it. Future Lilith, if you're reading this. I don't care where you are in the world.

Visit Nonna. She probably misses you as much as you miss her.

"Are you okay?" I asked Nonna. The memory of Nonna crying at Mom's funeral jumped in my head for a split second. The first time I've seen her experience any strong emotion. In my mind, she was this invincible woman who didn't let anything affect her. So, that distinct memory stuck to me.

"I'm fine. Don't-a worry about me." Nonna said endearingly. "Say, where is your little brother? Is he with you?"

It just dawned on me that I haven't thought about Mason since arriving in Atlanta. That was weird to think about thoroughly. Usually, Mason is one of the top things on my mind. Even when they are contained in the same four walls, I'm always thinking about him. Things like: What will I make him for dinner? How is he doing in school? Should I check on him? And like a thousand other things. I started to feel awful as a person, but mostly as an older sister.

"No, he's with my dad back at home. I came to Atlanta by myself."

"Aww, is your father not coming?"

"Probably not Nonna," I said, not fully knowing the answer myself. Some years Dad

chooses to come or not come. That idea never fully bothered me until now. A husband skipping the trip to visit his dead wife. It didn't make sense at all. The more I thought about it, the less sense it made to me. It also started to anger me as well, but I felt bad at the idea of me getting mad at Dad again.

"Are you ready for your surprise?" Nonna asked. She probably heard the sadness in my voice and wanted to flip the script.

"Sure." I tried to say excitedly but failed miserably at it.

"Can you meet me at the shop?" Nonna asked. I agreed happily.

I was looking for any excuse to leave this place and Nonna's shop seemed like heaven. It's good that I only visit here once a year. If I forced myself to come here any more frequently, I would begin to hate Atlanta. The number of mixed feelings I have for this place is indescribable, but I truly love it at the end of the day.

Nonna's shop was normally closed on Sundays, so the shop was pretty empty and lifeless. I was used to seeing the groups of people as soon as I stepped in, but the chairs were stacked on the tables. At least Bolo greeted me. He asked me how it was back home in Macon. Instead of answering at first, I just looked at him blankly. Even though I've heard his voice before, it always confuses me. Whenever that man opened his mouth, it raised more questions than answers. He had the voice of a thirty-year-old when he was approaching his mid-80s.

I told him that I wish I lived here instead of Macon. I didn't try sugar-coating anything for the sake of mellow conversation. He joked that I could work here and live with them. If I didn't have any morals, I would say yes in a heartbeat, but I jokingly declined. Just imagining that it sounded like heaven. I could even see Tess every day if I wanted to, just like when I was a kid.

"Lilith, come in the back, please! I have your surprise!" I heard Nonna yell from the back room of the restaurant.

I opened the double steel doors to the back room. I've been in the back room many times as an elementary schooler. I used to think it was the coolest thing in the world, being in the behind-the-scenes area of an *actual* restaurant. Even 9 years later, it's still the coolest thing. At the end of the day, it was just a room with a bunch of raw meats, vegetables, and crates, but it felt way more than that.

"Should I be worried, Nonna?" I asked jokingly. Nonna had a huge smile on her face.

She held a small crate where the bread would normally be stored. I honestly had no idea what it was. My first thought was a dog, but the crate was too small to hold one. And I don't think Nonna was strong enough to carry one. She could barely bend down anymore. Yet she was strong enough to run a sandwich shop.

"No, you're gonna love this." She said with excitement, which made me a little giddy. "Open it." She handed me the crate with a black towel covering the top of it. It was very light. I thought there was nothing inside of it at first.

After lifting the towel, I couldn't tell what it was at first. After lifting it out of the crate, it was a dress. A very dark blue dress with yellow stars decorated all over it. I looked at Nonna who seemed to be expecting a reaction. The thing was, you could get me *anything* in the world and my reaction would be the same.

"A dress?" I blurted. I was afraid I sounded ungrateful.

"This used to be your mother's. I made it to her first prom. Back when I had good enough hands to make dresses by hand. She grew out of it and I saw it in my closet the other day and thought about you. You can-a wear it for the festival next month!" Nonna said in a heavy Italian accent. It took me a minute to process and understand her words. "Try it on! I want to see how beautiful you look in it." Nonna shoved me into the bathroom to change. Meanwhile, I still had plenty of questions. Mostly about this *festival* she was referring to.

I was a little hesitant about wearing the dress. It was a very nice dress, don't get me wrong. But I felt like wearing the dress wouldn't do it justice. First off, I don't really *do* dresses in general. The last time I wore one was at Mom's funeral, and it was an all-black dress too, so it wasn't exactly meant for elegance. Second of all, it wasn't just any dress, it was Mom's dress. It could literally be the ugliest dress in the world and it would feel sacred to me. The same level of sacredness as Mom's journals. I put on the dress without thinking about it too much. I felt exposed since this was more skin than I was used to showing, but that was the least of my problems.

"Holy *Italian word(s) I don't know how to write, but it sounded vulgar*." When I got out of the bathroom, Nonna saw me and took a few steps back. She put both of her hands over her mouth and repeatedly looked me up and down. I felt self-conscious. "You look just like your mother! *More Italian words*."

"I don't think dresses are for me, Nonna," I said uncomfortably. The blaring thought of being in a dress, let alone Mom's dress, made me tense. "Are you sure you want me to have this? I don't think I'll have a chance to wear it for something, anyway."

"What about the festival? Are you going this year?" Nonna asked. I was still very confused about this festival.

"I don't know what festival you're talking about Nonna," I said shyly.

"The star festival? You don't know what I'm talking about?" I shook my head. When she said the word, star, a light went off in my head. "Let me show you something. Stay here." Nonna went into another room and came back with a stack of photos in her hand. She seemed excited to show these to me.

Nonna and I went into the main area of the restaurant to look at them. She sat us down and gave me half the stack of photos. They seem to be from an old digital camera, and she just printed them. She even wrote the dates on them too. 1991, 1992, 2002, etc.

"Did your mom ever tell you how we met?" Nonna asked.

"No, I assumed she had just met you through the restaurant," I said.

"We met at the *star festival*," Nonna said with a lot of emphasis. Her smile got wider when she said those words. "I remember it like it was yesterday." I looked at Nonna a little confused.

Mom never mentioned anything about a festival. It makes complete sense why Mom would attend a festival revolving around stars, though. That woman ate, drank, and breathed stars. One of the few things I'm jealous of.

"In 1999. I first arrived in America from Italy. I was very excited to be in America, so I attended a lot of things. Sports games, movies, and festivals. I met your mom at one of them and we've gone every year since." I started flipping through the stack of photos and tuning out Nonna. I became entranced by these photos. The photos were of Mom, Nonna, and occasionally Bolo. Nonna definitely looked younger in these photos. Mom looked young as a teenager, even though she was around twenty at the time.

I saw quickly that Nonna and Mom were closer than I thought. The amount of happiness resonating in these photos were astounding. It dumbfounded me how happy Mom looked in these photos. It was like I was looking at a new woman. Photos at the star festival, beaches, sporting events, the mall, you name it. I've never seen Mom this genuinely happy in my life. Every photo of Mom in existence doesn't have her smiling. But somehow, these do.

"Lilith? Lilith?" Nonna tapped me on the shoulder, breaking my spacing out. She probably noticed that I wasn't listening and just drowning her words out.

"Yeah, yeah sorry. I was spacing out." I said in honesty.

"Are you okay?" Nonna started rubbing my back as I kept staring at the photos blankly. My eyes felt like they had never blinked before.

"Yeah, I just... miss my family. That's all."

It sounded like I was about to tear up, which I was. I was freestyling my words, but at that moment, I realized how much I missed Mason and Dad. I haven't thought about them all weekend and now it was coming back to bite me in the ass.

"I-a understand. You should head home now before the rain gets bad." I looked outside, it was raining pretty badly. I looked at my watch: 4:45. I looked at the photos again, Mom smiling with Nonna at the beach.

"Nonna, can I ask you one more favor before I leave?"

"Anything, Lilith. Life is short, don't be afraid to ask me anything." Nonna said excitingly, brightening my mood.

"Is it okay if I borrow these photos? I'd really like them and I'm sure Dad would want to see them too. Next time I'm here, I can return them to you." I said with some guilt in my voice. These photos probably meant a lot to Nonna. For a few split seconds, I wanted to take my question back.

"You know what? Keep it." Nonna said confidently.

"What? No-no-no, I don't want to take them from you. I-
"

"I insist. Keep them. If I keep them, then when I die. Bolo will throw them away." Nonna joked. "I rather have you have them and keep them safe." I looked at the photos again.

"Are you *sure* Nonna?"

"Yes, and you can show them to Mason as well!" My smile got wider. I felt like I was about to tear up out of happiness. I didn't care that I was in a dress or that it was as cold as Antarctica in the restaurant. I felt warmth from Nonna.

"Thanks, Nonna. I love you." I gave Nonna a big hug. It was probably tighter than what she can take, but she hugged even tighter back at me.

"I love you too Lilith." I stored the stack of photos in my bag.

I said my farewells to Nonna and Bolo and left for the last time. Before I got in my car, I looked at the shop one more time and shed a tear. I wish I could blame it on the rain, but it was genuine tears. There's gonna be a time where Nonna won't be alive in my life anymore. I try not to think about it, but she's almost out the door of life. Nonna will probably die before Bolo and I was going to have to accept that fact. But in the meantime, I wish for her to live as long as possible. Future Lilith, for the love of God, please drop everything you are doing and visit Nonna.

Mark: November 18

“What the fuck were you doing out there? What were you running from?” Nicole panically asked.

“Home!” I said, barely able to catch my breath. Each breath felt like boulders crashing between my lungs. “I was running from home!” I said while wiping off the drippage from my face. The seat below me became drenched in rainwater.

“Why? What happened?”

“My dad found out. He almost killed Claire and me. I had to run away!” I explained. The memories were recent enough to where reminiscing about them almost gave me a panic attack. *I think I had a panic attack*. I thought. Everything was so fast but so slow at the same time. *Did that just really happen?*

“Found out what?” Nicole yelled, confused out of her mind.

“I-I’ll explain later! Can you hurry to your house? I think my dad’s after me! Go!” I desperately uttered.

“Argh Mark! Are you stupid? My house is the first place your dad’s gonna look. We need to go somewhere else.”

I paused for a second, trying to think about what little rationality I had. An idea popped in my head to stay at a hotel, but there isn’t a hotel anywhere near here. We’d have to drive all the way to Atlanta, which didn’t seem plausible.

"I know where to go!" I screamed. "Do you remember where Avery's house is?"

"Who?"

"T-the Halloween party we went to? Do you remember where that was?"

"Uhh, vaguely? Wait, why the fuck do you wanna go there?" Nicole asked, trying to control the wheel to the best of her abilities. It's not every day where she drives at more than seventy miles an hour.

"Just trust me! We can stay there for the night. Almost certain!" I confidently proposed.

Without another question asked, Nicole, made an aggressive U-turn back to be on the track to Avery's house. I tried using my phone to call Sky, but it was severely waterlogged. When I pulled it out of my pocket, it wouldn't even turn on. I almost threw it out the window in frustration.

"We're here!" Nicole quickly parked in front of Avery's driveway. Seeing the house in the dead of night scared me a bit, but I had no time to be scared. I rushed towards the front door, not slowing down for the rain.

"Sky! Avery! Anyone home!" I cried out through the thick wooden door. I said a little prayer in my head, begging that either Sky or Avery would be awake.

Nicole ran up quickly behind me, probably equally scared and confused at what I was doing.

"Please!" I begged, doing one big bang on the door.

"Who's there?" A voice could be heard yelling through the door. I loosely recognized it.

"Sky! Is that you?" A sliver of hope could be heard in my voice.

"Mark?" Sky undid all the locks on her side and the door opened in a flash. As soon as I saw Sky, the sliver of hope turned into a beam. I've never been so happy to see anyone in my entire life.

"What're you doing here? Are you okay? It's pourin' out the there!" Sky asked with wide eyes, sounding and looking like how Nicole reacted earlier.

"My dad found out about the tapes! I had to run away!" I quickly explained.

"Oh, *those* tapes! Oh, fuck!" Nicole yelled, finally connecting the dots.

"Explain later! Get inside before y'all get a cold." Sky hurried us inside and closed the door behind us.

Nicole and I were dripping all over the living room. I constantly had to wipe my face and hair to be able to see anything. Sky quickly ran into another room and gave us towels. I was thankful that her house was heated because if I stood in the rain any longer, I felt like I would've frozen to death.

"Sky, is everything okay? Who was at the door?" Avery haggardly came down the stairs in her pajamas. In a sort of messed-up way, I was happy to see her in a better position than I was at that moment.

"It's just Mark and his friend. They got in'na bit of trouble." Sky answered. She was frantically closing all the blinds to make sure no one could see that we were here. Even though I wasn't doing anything illegal (probably), I still felt that weight on my shoulders.

I looked over at Nicole, who was using the towel to warm her arms up. She was looking around the house, just trying to make some sort of sense out of this. I couldn't imagine what was going through her head. I reminded myself that we had a huge argument not long ago, which, looking back on, was mostly my fault. And now she was sucked into this mess I created. I started to feel unreasonably sorry for myself.

"Hey." I gently tapped Nicole's shoulder with the front of my wrist. We were sitting on a couch with a towel beneath us. "Thanks for saving me back there," I said softly, struggling to make eye contact. "If you weren't there, I would still probably be running or dead." I scoffed.

"It's the least I can do to you after what happened at school." Nicole also scoffed. She started to mirror my demeanour. She didn't even try to make eye contact with me.

"What were you doing out there, anyway?" I brought it up.

"After school, I just started driving to take my mind off things. I almost made it to Atlanta, but I turned around when the rain started to get worse." She explained.

I paused and just stared at Nicole. For a few seconds, I couldn't believe what I was hearing and was convinced she was joking. After letting it fully register, I just started bursting out laughing.

"Mark? What's funny?" Nicole asked, on the verge of laughing.

I had to force myself to stop laughing because I found it that funny. My lungs were still weak from my excessive running. "Yeah, I'm okay, I'm okay." I said, calming down.

"Mark, Nicole, do you two need to stay here tonight? I don't think it's wise to go back home, being late and such." Sky offered.

"Oh uh shoot. I didn't really think about that part." I said, thinking out loud. "Yeah, I'm not sure I can go back, at least for a while," I admitted. Saying it out loud made the situation start to fully set in. The idea of me not being able to go back to my own home scared me more than I thought it would.

"I think I should go back home," Nicole said, with little to no hesitation.

"Nicole, don't! My dad is probably looking for the both of us." I warned.

"Yeah, that's exactly why I'm going back. Think about how suspicious it would look if I went missing the same night you did. If he comes to my house, I can just lie." Nicole's thoughtfulness took me back a bit. Along with saving me, she was doing a lot to cover my back. I almost teared up from it all.

Instead of saying anything, I just ran up to hug Nicole, hug tightly. I think we both needed it after what happened today. My heart felt a little lighter after that.

Mark: November 22

I was petrified of going back to school that next day. Other than being dead-tired, I had to try my best and lay low. I had no idea if my dad filed a missing person's report or something. It didn't help that Nicole and mine little argument in the library caught some words. Nicole and Sky advised not to really talk to anyone, including teachers. I considered just not coming to school until I knew it was safe, but that would probably raise more eyebrows.

It was hard getting used to living in Avery's place, at least for the first few days. Sleeping in a bed that wasn't my own makes me a bit restless. The only sort of comfort that I could lean on was the fact that this house was in the middle of the woods, semi-isolated from everyone.

Nicole told me earlier today that my sister got in contact with her. I forgot to tell Nicole that Claire was the one that shielded me from my dad, so she got a little jumpy when Claire approached her. Apparently, she's tried contacting me for the past few days, but didn't realize my phone got waterlogged. I've been using Sky's phone whenever I needed it.

Later that night, Claire came over with a suitcase full of my stuff. We greeted each other with a slight smile before I let her in.

"Whoa, this is a nice place. I didn't know houses like this existed around here." Claire commented. Her eyes wandered the living room like a little kid.

"As long as Dad can't find me, I'll take anything." I scoffed.

Claire placed the suitcase on the dining table. She started fishing out some clothes and other necessities I would usually need. Funny enough, I completely forgot about the concept of brushing and flossing until she pulled them out.

"Does Dad know you're here? He would usually be home around this time." I asked, looking at my watch.

"Who cares? I haven't talked to that old man since you left." Claire said begrudgingly.

"Is he that mad at you?"

"No, I'm mad at *him*. He had no right to attack you like that. You didn't even do anything bad." Claire took a pair of my jeans and tossed them down violently.

"How do you know that?" I asked, confused as to why she was so quick to take my side.

"Mark, you know you're my little brother, right?" Claire paused in real-time and turned her head toward me. "Even when you hide things from me, I know that you won't do anything stupid."

I didn't realize Claire, and I had that level of trust until that moment. I couldn't help but smile at her level of confidence in me. "I'm not sure if you need these still, but I managed to recover some of the disks for you." Claire handed me a plastic bag with some of the disks. Some of them were shattered, but it really didn't matter that much at that point.

I stared at the bag for a few seconds. It hit me that so many people were doing a lot to just keep me up on my feet. Claire protected me from our dad. Nicole visited every day to make sure I'm doing alright, and Sky and Avery were generous enough to make sure I had somewhere to stay. I wanted to repay them somehow.

"Mark, one more thing," Claire said, immediately changing the tone of her voice.

"What's up?"

"I found a flyer for your little star festival. I thought you might want to go to that, so I grabbed it when I saw it at the mall." Claire handed me a purple paper ad about Atlanta's star festival. I awkwardly squinted at it for a few seconds, not knowing what to think of it.

"I'm not sure if I wanna go," I said dispiritingly. I put down the paper next to the jeans that Claire slammed earlier.

"What? Why? You've gone like every year since middle school." Claire pointed out.

"I don't know. I just feel like everything else is more important right now." While talking, I was taking out more clothes, but my eyes were fixated on one spot. I felt like all my systems were running on autopilot.

"Like what?" Claire asked, unable to comprehend anything I was implying.

"Figuring out who hurt Avery. I didn't forget about that, y'know?"

"Yeah, I can imagine," Claire said with an understandable irritation.

"I won't feel comfortable coming home until I've proven Dad wrong. I owe it to a lot of people; I'll say that much." I said with boulders over my words.

"Alright, I won't get in your way." Claire smiled with both emotions and started walking to the door. "Sky," Claire called out.

Sky was in another part of the living room, reading a novel. "What's up?" Sky looked up from her book.

"Make sure my brother doesn't kill himself alright? I need him alive for Christmas." Claire said lightheartedly.

Sky and Claire exchanged a hearty laugh, which made me join in. "Alright, take care mate." Sky and I waved to Claire.

Mark: November 25

After that night, my sister dropped off all the disks. I took a good look at them and thought about how useless they were. Sky and I knew these disks like the back of hands. There's no way we missed anything. I needed to take some sort of action, so Sky suggested something smart.

Sky remembered that in the footage, you could barely hear the sound of the guy's voice before he went after Avery, so she did her best to make that audio as clear as possible and downloaded it to an audio device. I even gave Nicole a copy, and we went around the school asking if anyone knew anybody who sounded like him.

I went into this extremely optimistic, thinking at least *someone* would recognize it, but we got a whole lot of nothing. A person can only hear "No." and "What the fuck are you talking about?" so many times until they go crazy. Nicole and I did this so much that people started labeling us 'Police-wannabes' when we walked around campus together. I mean, they weren't wrong exactly, but it still hurt.

"No dice, huh?" I met up with Nicole as she walked to our locker. She looked pretty dead inside, so I assumed things weren't going well on her end, either. The rain was still pretty consistent, so that only added to the dead-ness.

"Nope. I think we've literally asked every person in the school. *Nobody* knows this guy. It's ridiculous." Nicole violently opened our locker, and a notecard fell out. The two of us stared at it as it slowly fell to the ground. "What's that?" Nicole asked as she looked back to her locker to shuffle through her books.

I picked up the card off the floor and noticed the handwriting on it. Not only was it bad handwriting, but I think the ink smeared a bit as it fell to the floor. I had to squint at certain words to even understand.

"Is it a love letter?" Nicole joked.

"No. I think those stopped after middle school." I jabbed back.

"What does it say?"

I was hesitant to give it to Nicole, but since she's involved with the case now, there was no use avoiding her. I handed her the note.

Hello! It has come to my attention that you want to figure out who raped Avery. I'm very close with Avery and might know who you're looking for. If you're interested, meet me at this address TONIGHT.

He put some address at the bottom of the note, in slightly better handwriting.

After reading it, Nicole looked at me as if she were queasy. Something didn't sit right with her and neither did I.

"We should talk to Sky about this," I suggested. Without saying a word, Nicole grabbed her keys and pointed out the door.

"Where did y'all find this?" Sky said, still trying to comprehend the note. Nicole and I rushed to the house and were trying to catch our breaths after running in the rain for a bit.

"In our locker." Nicole and I's arms were folded. "We couldn't see who put it there, but it's probably someone at our school."

"I've never even heard of this address. Are you sure it's even real?" Sky questioned.

"It's real. I looked it up while in the car. It's near the edge of the town." I informed.

"*I'm very close with Avery.* What the fuck does that mean?" Sky threw her hands up in the air.

"Maybe a friend or something? I don't know, maybe we can ask her. Is she home?" I asked.

"No, she's at a lunch with her parents. But even then, I would rather *not* bring this up to her. I promised that I wouldn't involve her unless we really needed to." Nicole and I looked up the stairs towards Avery's room and instantly understood. Sky dragged her hand down her face as she gave me back the note.

"What should we do then? I don't think this is the type of thing we can just ignore." Nicole said with gravity. We all looked at each other with some level of hesitancy.

"I'm willing to go. But what about you guys?" I said with artificial confidence.

"Mark, this could easily be a bait, you know that right? Think about it." Nicole forewarned. Her eyes were shooting lasers at me, trying to break what little confidence I had.

"I'm willing to take that chance. Thinking about it won't change that." I stared deep into Nicole's eyes, hoping to spread confidence. All it did was make her more apprehensive, though.

"I think Mark's right." Sky blurted.

"What?" Nicole and I said in unison, immediately looking at Sky.

"Sky, you know how dangerous this could be, right?" Nicole put her hand on Sky's shoulder.

"Yeah, but I feel like this is our one chance to get somewhere. Even if it is a bait, I would rather say that I tried than didn't." Sky asserted, inspiring even Nicole. It was powerful enough for Nicole to put her hand down.

Sky and I exchanged a confident smile. That fake confidence was turning real now that Sky was on board.

"We need to get ready then, Sky. The sun is coming down fast. I don't know if this guy has a fuckin' time limit or something." I started running to get the things and supplies we potentially needed. I stuffed the plastic bag of disks deep into my backpack, just in case we needed it.

"Alright, give me a few minutes. I need to make sure we have everything in case this goes south." Sky started running to her room to gather supplies.

"Wait, what am I gonna do? Are you two going by yourselves?" Nicole yelled.

"You stay here Nicole!" Sky requested. "Someone needs to watch the house to make sure Avery is safe when she gets home."

"I can do that! You two keep me updated."

This felt like a fucking mission. My heart was racing before anything was even happening. I took it as a sign of progress. *We're finally getting somewhere!* I thought to myself. I was over the moon.

Sky and I were out the door before the sun fully set.

Mark: November 25 cont.

Sky and I got in her car, and she started racing towards the place. Sky's car was old enough to where it didn't have a built-in GPS, so I had to use her phone to guide her as we went.

I kept looking over at Sky while driving and the nervousness was starting to show. It's hard to blame her since she was the one driving, but it was becoming contagious. The void in my heart was starting to grow.

"Mark?" Sky called to me, seemingly insecure.

"Yeah? Everything alright?" I was looking at the digital map on Sky's phone.

We were both trying to hide the fact that we were nervous, but I bet we heard it in each other's voices.

"Are you sure it's here? Look where we are. There aren't any houses in this area." I looked up, and we were at the beginning of a forest. It was far enough from the civilized part of town that we weren't even driving on the road anymore, just a trail big enough to fit a car on.

"It's supposed to be here..." I said with a deep undertone. "The address is the only somewhat neatly written part of the note." I looked at the note for what felt like the one-millionth time and it matched with the address that I put into the GPS. "Do you want to turn back?" I suggested. The farther I looked down the trail, the darker and more mysterious everything seemed. It was like an endless path of trees and nothingness.

I think Sky noticed it too. Her pupils started to dilate as she got further down the road.

"I'll keep going. If I see something bad, I'll go back." Sky pushed forward with forced confidence.

The deeper we traveled into the forest, the larger the void became. The feeling of incoming doom could be ignored anymore. I kept opening my mouth to say something, but I was trying to tell myself that I was overreacting. *It's just like any other forest at night.* I told myself. The dot that represented our car on the GPS was approaching the address at a speed I wasn't ready for.

"We're here," I said, breaking the dead silence. When Sky parked the car, I exhaled a breath I didn't even feel like I was holding.

Sky slowly turned off the engine and took her keys out of the ignition. The sound of keys clashing against each other filled my ears.

"Ready?" Sky asked with a lump in her throat. Her eyes looked at me with emotions ranging from: "*Let's get this over with.*" to "*I don't wanna die tonight.*"

"As ready as I'll ever be," I said, struggling to swallow my fear.

We both hopped out of the car and soaked ourselves in the forest atmosphere. Sky came prepared and grabbed an umbrella from the back seat and held it over both of us.

We started walking towards where the GPS was taking us. It said the location was less than a tenth of a mile away, so we were just looking around for something that resembled a house. All we saw were trees and rocks, though, the furthest thing from a house. The whole idea of this being a trap was becoming more and more real by the second.

You have arrived at your destination. Goodbye. My phone told us. The goodbye sent chills down my spine.

"We're here?" I questioned. "There's nothing here." I shined my flashlight in front of us and saw no sort of building.

"Look there!" Sky pointed to my immediate right, and I shined my flashlight on what looked like an abandoned construction site with stone walls. The darkness of the stone blended in with everything else.

"This is the place?" I asked, pointing at it.

"There's no doubt about it," Sky responded, taking a step towards it. I quickly followed. We were leaving trails of sound by the gravel we were stepping on. I swear you could hear everything going on in this forest. Every gust of wind, branch falling, squirrel running could be heard one way or another.

When we got into the building, Sky and I loosely split up to examine the place with our flashlights. From what I saw, there were no lights whatsoever. It was truly abandoned. The floor was littered with leaves, rocks, and crushed-up beer cans. The only good thing about this place was the fact it sheltered us from the rain.

"Find anything?" I called out to Sky. My mind was blanking from the sheer nothingness.

"I found a random pocket knife. It's pretty dull though." Sky put the knife in her back pocket and continued to look around.

"I don't think there's anyone here Sky if I'm being honest." I started to feel dumb that I was worried in the first place. I was actually disappointed, hoping to at least find *something*.

"Who knows, mate? Maybe we're early. Just keep looking around. Did you check the back of the room?" Sky shined her flashlight behind me. I checked my watch and it was approaching 8 PM. While not that late, it was late enough to be considered 'tonight' as per the note said.

Without saying anything, I went over to check. I shined the light towards the corner and I saw a construction-ey-looking wooden plank nailed to the wall. It seemed like there was nothing behind the plank, which made me raise an eyebrow.

The plank looked thin enough to breakthrough. Out of desperation to find something, I kicked it open, shattering the wood. Sky screamed in shock.

"Whoa, there's another room in here," I said. "Sky, come check this out."

I walked inside and realized there was a complete other sector to this building. The walls were wooden instead of stone, and there were multiple levels.

"Sky, did you hear me? Come look at this." I called out. I was so far in the other room that I couldn't see Sky or her flashlight anymore. "Sky?" I called out again.

I slowly stepped back into the original room and suddenly I heard something behind me move.

"Mark! Look out!"

I turned around and a shadowy, tall figure stood above me. Next thing I know, something strikes me in the head. It was so fast I didn't even have time to flinch.

Mark: November 25 cont. again

"Wake up! Both of you! Wake the fuck up!" I woke up to the sound of a man yelling. My mind couldn't fully catch up with what was happening. The place I was in was so dark. I could tell it was the stone room, but the room was even darker than before. It was so dark that I couldn't tell if the thing I was looking at was two feet away from me or two miles away.

I could barely feel my arms when I tried to move them. There was a rope tying my hands behind my back and another one tying my body and legs to the chair I was sitting in. My arms went numb from the blood flow being cut off. I couldn't *move* anything. I tried resisting with my torso, but I felt perpetually stuck. I tried yelling, but my mouth was taped shut. I ended up making a bunch of muffled mouth noises.

"Where's the fucking flashlight?" The man screamed.

Next thing I knew, he was shining a light in my face. As soon as my eyes started adjusting, I saw Sky tied up in a chair as well. My eyes widened past its sockets. I could barely recognize her with the rope and tape on her body. She was trying her best to resist and yell, but we were both stuck. It was useless. *What was happening? Am I gonna die?* Being able to see things only made my heart beat faster.

"Well, well, *well*. We finally caught the rats. How does it feel to be tied up and on the other side of things, you bastards?"

The man got in both our faces and spat on them. I tried to shake free out of anger, but I was bound to the chair. The sound of my chair tilting back and forth echoed throughout the room. Meanwhile, Sky was still shaking and doing whatever she could to break free. She was approaching exhaustion. Her limbs became loose and her face only grew more red.

I tried forcing words through the tape, angry words. I was saying probably every curse word in the English language. I stared deep into the man's eyes, hoping to send hatred his way. There were not enough words in the world to express my restlessness. Our eyes locked for a second, but he turned away.

"Should I remove the tape?" He asked himself, looking directly at Sky, who was about to explode. "You two obviously have something to say. Might as well." We were like caged dogs, waiting to lay our paws on them and willing to die for it.

He ripped off Sky's tape and then mine. Both of us started barking up a storm and he fired back with more yelling, mostly shouting at us to shut up. Each word shouted made an astounding echo that bounced from wall to wall, each yell being louder than the other.

"It's you! I should've fuckin' known it was you this whole time!" Sky screamed, knowing who this guy was. Her voice changed, evolved even. The beast within was out. I wouldn't be surprised if she turned into a werewolf right then and there and broke the rope.

"Let us go! You don't know who you're messing with!" I shouted even louder, testing the limits of my vocal cords.

"I don't even know who you people are." The man looked smug, the same smugness that the rapist had. It was a mirrored image. "You fucks are *done for. I'm calling the cops.*" He reapplied the tape to our mouths.

The man spat in Sky's face. She *did not* like that. Her anger alone almost cut the rope. I was astounded by how close she was to breaking free, closer than I was.

Suddenly, the three of us were shut up by the sound of footsteps from outside the building. We all heard the sound of leaves and sticks cracking. The room became dead silent.

"What is it now?" The man complained.

Without hesitation, the man went to the corner where there was a small crate. Next to it was the bat he beat me with. He reached into a box in the front of the room and grabbed a pistol. The man looked like a pro with the way he held the gun. The sight of it all made me sick.

The man left the building. Without the flashlight, Sky and I couldn't see anything. We had to rely on hearing. I heard his footsteps go from audible to not as he got farther away from the building. Sky and I looked at each other, not knowing what to do. Sky motioned to her hands, which were tied up behind her chair, same as mine. She tried to maneuver them to point at something, but she was struggling to coordinate her fingers.

After trying to process what she was doing with her fingers, I tilted my head as far back as I could and noticed the knife from before sticking out of her jeans pocket. I knew that resisting backward would tilt the chair back and I could lean the chair against the wall.

I channeled all my will and previous anger to resist enough to tilt the chair enough to try and reach for Sky's knife. She was trying her best to shake the knife out of her pocket, but it was barely any use. My hands still felt numb, but what little blood I had circulating to my fingers I used to reach for the knife. It was a matter of mere centimeters in order to grab it. If my fingers were any shorter, then I don't think I would've made it.

I knew I had to act fast. My heart was racing like never before. I opened the pocketknife with the tip of my thumb and sliced the rope. The blade was very dull, so I had to press hard, making my fingers look like contortionists while doing so. I freed my arms and cut off the rope holding my body and legs. I quickly got up and cut Sky's rope, dipping my head up to make sure the man didn't come back without us noticing. I was ready for a fight either way.

The blood in my arms started coming back and my brain was in escape mode. I swiftly made my way to the box and grabbed the last gun left in the box. I checked to make sure it was loaded, and it was. Three bullets to be exact. I felt like I was in a game of Call Of Duty.

"We should make a run for it?" Sky whispered, with a lump in her voice.

Before I could answer her, I heard footsteps again. They were getting closer and closer and reality started to take a step back, each step they took having more drama than the last. We both kneeled by the entrance, me on the left and Sky on the right. I looked at Sky and she motioned that we would run for it. I shook my head no, knowing that we would get shot or run into the police.

"What the fuck was that?" I could hear his voice through the stone wall. It was quiet and muffled, but I heard approximately how close he was to the entrance.

A clock started ticking in my head. *Tick, tock, tick, tock.*

A beam of light shined through the entrance. "Hey! Where'd they go?" He yelled. His voice was as clear as glass.

"Now Sky!" I sprung up and ran behind the man, tackling him and putting him in a headlock, applying the gun tightly on his head. *Cling clop.* His gun hit the floor and bounced away. Sky pounced on him and made sure to clamp down on his limbs. The man tried to resist, but it was obvious I had him pinned, even when he had two free arms. He started kicking my legs, and they left marks with every kick.

"The police will be here any secon-!" He said cockily. I made my headlock even tighter to shut him up.

"Yeah, for you! We're not the ones who raped his ex!" Sky said in response. I tried my best to keep the gun on Damien's head, but he kept shifting around.

"Sky, you k-know this guy?" My face was grimacing at how hard I was trying to keep him down. My words were running over each other.

"Yeah! His name is Damien, Avery's creepy as fuck ex-boyfriend. I should've known it was you!" Sky punched him in the crotch, which made him scream.

"No. You got it all wrong! He raped Avery! I saw it on the tapes!" Damien's face was turning red from all the pressure we were putting on him.

"What the fuck are you talking about? How do you know about the tapes?" Sky interrogated. Her eyes went bloodshot, and it was taking a lot of self-control for her to not kill him on the spot.

"Come out of the building with your hands up! Drop all weapons now!" We heard a yell from outside. It was the police. All of our expressions dropped.

We all paused for a second, trying to let our brains process what was happening. "Follow me! I know where to hide!" Damien shot up from my loosened headlock and started running. The rest of us got up immediately and followed him. Damien grabbed his gun and ran head-first into the other room.

The light from the other room started to fade as we followed Damien. In a few seconds, it was pitch black. I only ran where I heard Damien's footsteps.

"You have a lot of explaining to do later!" Damien yelled.

"You too, asshole!" I yelled back.

As I was running, I had no choice but to run right through some wooden walls. I burst right through them. Normally it would hurt like hell, but my adrenaline was pumping to the max. I looked behind me and Sky was a close second behind. I started to hear gunshots shot from inside the building. The police were on our tail. The fact that one of them could've been my dad scared me to my core. Damien turned around and randomly shot into the darkness while running.

"Damien, don't shoot back!" Sky yelled. "We can't have any casualties!" Damien stopped shooting and continued running. This building was a literal maze. I was starting to lose track of where we were going.

"In here!" Damien stopped and pointed to a box we could hide behind. I could barely see what was happening, but as soon as Damien leaped somewhere, Sky and I followed suit. I then thought about how likely our survival chance was. By how reckless we were, breaking walls and firing bullets into the darkness, this seemed not far from a suicide mission.

We ended up prone, positioning behind the box while trying to catch our breath. The combination of unrelenting fear and running for our lives made all of our breaths very audible. My heart was still running on a treadmill at max speed, trying to get blood to the rest of my body.

"*Shh, they're coming!*" Sky yell-whispered. The room was still dark as hell. The police could be in the very room right now and we wouldn't be able to see.

All of us remained still as statues. The second we heard footsteps, we all stopped breathing. The silence became unbearably loud.

"I think they ran out of the building." The police officer said. We couldn't see them, but we knew they were in the same room as us. Sky started freaking out internally. I could tell by whites of her eyes.

"I swore I heard footsteps upstairs." Another one said, I looked to the left at Damien and his face went from a fire-red to a tissue-paper-white.

"We shouldn't try. I heard one of them had a gun. They could be waiting for us to walk up there." Another officer said. My heart sank when my brain processed whose voice that was. I almost screamed, but I bit on my arm in an extreme attempt to shut myself up. It stung, feeling my fang pierce through a little of skin. If this was somehow a bad dream please someone wake me up.

"Alright then. We're clear! They got out!" He yelled to the other officers. They walked away and a minute later, we heard the faint sound of a police car driving away.

"Are we clear?" Sky whispered.

"Yeah, for sure," I said. I started to taste blood.

We all sighed in relief. The tension in my body all released at once and it felt like I just got a massage. I spit out my own blood like some sort of savage.

"We need to get out of here. Use your phone as a flashlight and stay on high alert." Damien ordered. We all nodded and tried to find a way out of here. I aimed my gun at random things as we left the building.

Now that I got a chance to see the interior with light, it really was an abandoned building. All the walls were stripped, and only the thin walls of cheap wood remained. That explains how I was able to run through it so easily.

We made it back to the stone-walled room.

"Okay, we all have a lot of explaining to do, but we'll let you go first." Sky said with an attitude. The anger she had when we were tied up didn't exactly go away. "How do you know about the tapes...?"

We all stood close together, facing one another. All of us looked trashed since we rolled around in dirt and dust from the inside of the building. A bunch of our clothes were ripped too, including my favorite pair of jeans.

"Before I answer, you two need to put down your weapons." Damien eyed my gun and Sky's knife. We looked like blood-hungry creatures with how tightly we grabbed our weapons.

"No, I'm not falling for that shit! Spill the beans or I'm calling the police back here. I know who you are Damien! Even if you didn't rape Avery, I can have you arrested for all the other shit you pulled." Sky shot eye lasers at Damien. It made me extremely curious what past these two shared.

"Alright, alright. Calm down." Damien raised his hands in defense. "When I dated Avery, she told me about the computer in the house that had access to all the security footage. So, when I heard what happened to her... I thought about breaking into her house? And maybe downloading all the footage from that computer into a drive?"

Sky and I's jaws dropped to the floor. "And you did that, why?" I asked. Sky gripped her knife even harder. It was taking a lot of anger control to not kill this guy.

"Hoping to get back with her? Does that sound so bad?"

I started to feel stupid that we got outsmarted by the likes of this guy. He was nothing more than a miserable ex-boyfriend. Something about his innocent yet not-innocent looking face made me want to punch it.

"So, you didn't rape Avery?" I asked to confirm.

"I would never. I love that girl with my entire heart." Sky and I let out a sigh of relief. I couldn't tell which I was more reassured by. The fact that we didn't get arrested or the fact that we didn't get shot or stabbed by this guy.

"Why the fuck did you think it was Mark then? All he's done since the party was trying to help Avery."

"Oh yeah... I remember seeing on the tapes that Mark disabled the camera on the third floor before everything happened." Damien explained, with irritation in his voice.

"You were the one that disabled that camera?" Sky burst. She hit me on the shoulder.

"Yeah, that probably set off a few red flags. That's my bad." I admitted it. I don't remember the reason why I disabled that camera, but knowing myself, it's because I hate being watched.

We all had a good laugh after we realized how dumb we all were. There was something funny about the fact that no one will ever know what happened here, being in the middle of the forest and such. The three of us will probably be taking this night to the grave.

Tyler Bansil

Lilith: Day Forty-Two

Hi? I'm back. I know this was basically just a page turn for you, but it was a month since I've written in this diary for me. I know I haven't written in this diary for a long time, but I decided to take a break for almost the entirety of November. Why? You might ask. I don't know if this is evident, but pouring your honest-to-God emotions onto paper multiple times a week is a little draining. After I got back from Atlanta, I had little clarity with myself, so I felt no need to write anything.

That clarity lasted about a week and then life started happening and I couldn't hold onto it for long. I felt it around when I had to go back to school and when my hunger started to disappear again. I went back to just drinking water for most of my meals. After coming back from Atlanta, life just didn't move as nicely as I liked it to.

A nice thing to see was my family again. I honestly missed them more than I thought I would. I never thought that I'd feel any sentimental emotion towards Dad, but after our little fiasco on our camping trip, I saw him in a new light. I'm willing to believe he saw me in a different light as well. We talked to each other more at home, smiled at each other more, and spent more time together. We actually started to feel like somewhat of a family, instead of just two people that just happened to live together.

Mason was just the same old Mason, which was honestly a great source of my happiness for a while. It still is, but I never realized how much taking care of him gave me somewhat of a purpose in life. He asked a billion and a half questions about my trip to Atlanta. It didn't occur to me until now that he missed Atlanta, too. I used to think he was just indifferent to everything.

Tess and I have been calling and texting each other more since I got back. She would send me photos and videos of herself talking about how shitty her schooling is and how she's so ready to go out into the world. I thought we were finally graduating from our brief love episode, but one night she sent me a nude photo and it was clear that she still had feelings for me. Was she probably drunk? Yes. But drunk people tend to be the most honest people on earth.

I would be lying to myself if I said my feelings for Tess completely stopped when I came back from Atlanta. No matter how I thought about it, there would be a small part of myself that felt some sort of attachment to her. I tried my best to shake the thought of it, but it wouldn't let go. I fell in love with the idea of Tess surprising me by driving down to Macon for a day and we could spend the day together. I had something/someone to look forward to, which was both amazing and terrible. It made me think about how shitty the concept of love was in general. I'm not experienced nor knowledgeable in that subject, but I knew it was miserable.

Nonna sent me a letter, and it came in the mail last week. She somehow found out my address by asking my relatives in Macon who came to her shop. Being at the age Nonna was, she didn't own a cell phone or a laptop, so she had to use letters. Here's what it read:

Dear Lilith, I am writing this letter to you. Thank you very much for visiting my shop. Please tell your father and little brother that I miss them very much. The STAR FESTIVAL is on December 5. I would love to see you there.

-Nonna

It was short and all over the place, but none of that mattered. Knowing Nonna, this probably took her an hour to write, because she didn't know English or how to write it. Bolo probably guided her through the entire thing. Every word in the letter gave me so much joy. I still have the letter she mailed to me on Christmas the year after I moved away from Atlanta. That one had borderline gibberish, but I still kept it. It's currently in my closet and this one was gonna go along with it.

I told Dad about Nonna and Bolo. He was happy that I had people that still remembered me in Atlanta. When I mentioned that I visited Mom, he seemed proud of me. He was honest with me for once and admitted that he couldn't bring himself to visit Mom. He truly contemplated it for a few days, weeks even, but it was hard for him. No matter what perspective I took, I couldn't blame him. Now that I had more of an idea of what Dad thought about Mom, it was undeniable that he had a hard time dealing with anything Mom-related. *'YOU DON'T THINK I WAKE UP EVERY DAY AND REALIZE HOW FUCKED UP THIS FAMILY IS?'* The memory of him saying that was unforgettable. It was hard *not* to think of that memory whenever I looked at him. It was fucked up to say, but there was some truth.

I didn't know at first if I actually wanted to go to the festival Nonna was talking about. It was a bigger question mark for me than I'd like to admit. Even when she gave me the dress, the letter and the talk we had before I left, I didn't know if I wanted to go. Then I looked at photos Nonna gave me. Nothing about the festival seemed all that excitable. Of course, that doesn't matter to me. The thing that attracted me was the smile on Mom's face. It was unlike any smile I've ever seen. The type of smile that takes more than half a second to realize what it means. The smile part didn't really matter, it was what was behind the smile that made it special. That was the core of Mom right there. I knew right then that I had to go if I wanted to know the core of Mom even more.

"Where are you going?" As I was packing, Dad came into my room unexpectedly. It was approaching midnight. I expected him to be asleep.

"Why are you awake?" I asked instead of answering.

"I was going to get some water, and I saw your lights were on," Dad mentioned.

"I'm thinking about going back to Atlanta for a day or two. I still don't know if I want to go yet." I admitted it.

"You should. Mom would be proud if you went." He said softly, somehow already knowing the reason for my leave. That made me smile.

Mark: December 4

“Yo mate.” Sky came into the guest room where I was sleeping. Actually no, that's a lie. I've been awake for the past few hours. Even though it was incredibly early, I couldn't go back to bed no matter how many times I closed my eyes. It felt like something was tickling the top of my brain.

“What's up?” I asked monotonously. I was laid flat on my back, head parallel with the ceiling.

“Your sister came over and wanted me to give this to you.” Sky sat by my bedside and hovered a piece of yellow paper over my head. I slowly sat up and rubbed my eyes. I didn't realize that the sun was already up.

I grabbed the paper from Sky's hands. My muzzy brain took a while to process what the paper read.

“What does it say?” Sky was staring at my expression as I read through it.

“Uh, you live in Atlanta, right? If my memory serves me correctly.” I asked, scratching my head.

Sky paused and slowly nodded. I think I accidentally invoked some kind of homesickness in her. Her expression dropped pretty quickly when I mentioned Atlanta. I keep forgetting that she's been away for quite a while.

“Have you heard about the star festival? It happens every year there. Surely you've heard of it.”

"I haven't, actually. Tell me about it." Sky adjusted her position on my bed.

"Well, it's exactly what it sounds like. The people running it choose the best night in the year where the stars will shine the brightest. And we all sit around and stare into them, I guess. It's actually tonight." I said passionately. The room around me seemed to be a little brighter when I reminisced about the past years I've gone.

"Whoa...are you planning on going?" Sky advocated in the most energetic voice she could muster. Granted, it wasn't much, but I felt the effort.

"I'm not sure. I might skip this year." I said bleakly.

I know I told my sister I would think about going, but I haven't got around to really thinking about it. Honestly, it hasn't even crossed my mind. I guess that's why she went out of her way to deliver me this.

"What? Why? You seem like you would love that."

"Aren't we meeting up with Nicole and Damien today? Isn't that much more important right now?" I reminded myself.

"Well yeah, but you can take a break, y'know? You've been doing a lot for the investigation. You deserve at least a night or two off."

I looked back at the yellow star festival ad. Funnily enough, the purple one that Claire gave me the other week was sitting on the dresser. Not, funnily enough, I haven't looked at it until now.

"Are you sure it's okay?" I kept switching my eyes from the paper to Sky, not knowing what to even think anymore.

"Of course, mate! I insist!" Sky's accent thickened a tad. "The three of us can handle ourselves. I'm sure they'll understand too." Sky shot me a much-needed smile, invoking some good spirits inside of me. Somehow, she told me exactly what I wanted to hear.

Tyler Bansil

"Alright, I'll go. Thanks, Sky."

Lilith: Day Forty-Three

When Mason saw me leaving in the morning, he wouldn't stop crying. I tried leaving early enough in the morning before he had a chance to wake up, but he somehow woke up at 8 AM on a weekend. Something in his consciousness told him that I was leaving and woke him up. I wasn't able to leave the house until I assured him that I'd be back tomorrow morning at the latest.

"Hey, bud. I'll promise you something. Listen to me, okay?" I said in my big sister's voice.

"O-okay." Mason struggled to say. Tears were still running down his face and he didn't know what to do with his arms, so he crossed them.

"Next time I go on a trip, I'll take you with me, got it?" I said affirmingly. Mason's face lit up.

"Wait, hold on a second" Dad interjected. He was standing behind Mason, and I shot him a cold stare. He immediately stopped talking.

"YAY!" Mason celebrated. He uncrossed his arms and hugged me.

The same 'Welcome to Atlanta' greeted me again. Only a little nostalgia was pumped into me this time. My shoulders felt light again. The recurring smile that I can never seem to control was back. It was like I was transported to another world and in this world, my worries in Macon didn't matter.

Of course, my worries in Atlanta were much grander than in Macon. My Macon problems seemed petty in comparison, which it was.

I called Tess the night before and told her that I'd be in town for a day or two. She seemed ecstatic that I was coming, which wasn't surprising. It seemed like I was the only thing she looked forward to now. Admittedly, that was the case for me. One of the main pull factors that got me to was that I'd get to see Tess again. For the entirety of last month, I'd been secretly hoping that she'd visit me like she did when I first moved to Macon. I've been trying to block that part of my brain out, but it always comes back to haunt me. One day I'd try to suppress the memory and the next day Dad would be watching a random romance movie on TV and the memory shot up straight into my brain. *God, I hate writing about this.*

I took a *deep* breath before I entered Tess' dorm. While driving here, I repeatedly told myself that I wouldn't engage in any romance with her, no matter what. I was supposed to come here for the star festival and spend time with Nonna, not distract myself with Tess.

"Ahh, look who came back," Tess announced to the room as soon as I walked in. She was relaxing on her couch watching TV.

"Aren't you supposed to be in class?" I asked, almost complainingly.

"I don't have classes today. Since finals are coming up and such, my professors want us to study alone. Of course, I'm using that time wisely." Tess said sarcastically.

I knew Tess was lying off the bat. When Tess is lying, her voice doesn't have the same confidence as her other statements do. I bet she would be in class right now if I didn't tell her I was coming.

"What are you doing here again? Something about a festival?" Tess asked, trying to change the subject. I put down my stuff in the kitchen as she asked.

"Yeah uh, Nonna invited me to a festival. It's only for a day, so I'll be out of your hair tonight." There was tension in the room, a lot of it. I tried to speak without inconsistencies in my voice, but it would slightly crack every other sentence. I haven't even looked Tess in the eyes yet since arriving here. I've been trying to avoid her eyes and seeing *her* in general. I knew as soon as our eyes locked, it was game over.

"It's not like you to attend a festival, or attend anything for that matter." Tess jabbed at me.

"I know, but apparently my mom went here a lot when we used to live in Atlanta, so I'm just curious. Plus Nonna is dying soon, so I want to come here as much as possible." Saying that last part hurt me, but I was trying my best to convince myself that I didn't come here just to see Tess.

I wanted to take a nap before it got dark. I knew I was gonna have to drive back in the middle of the night, so I needed some extra energy. I took Tess' bed and purposefully avoided her couch. It was hard to fall asleep at first, so I read Mom's diary to help me fall asleep. Mom never talked about any sort of star festival. I looked through all her journals to see if I somehow missed something after years of rereading her journals. It seems like she kept it a secret, even from herself.

The sun was beginning to set when I woke up. I kept staring at the dress until it was time to leave. For some reason, I didn't want to wear it. There was one photo of Mom in this same dress that I couldn't get out of my mind. It was a case of being too close for comfort. I've always wanted to get to the core of Mom, but this was too far. Going to an event that Mom always went to, in Mom's clothes, in Mom's hometown, with Mom's friend. It was all too much. The realities were too close to one another. My heart started to race. In the back of my mind, I knew this would help me know my mother more, so I wore it. I felt like I was wearing someone else's skin, personality, and character. Whoever was wearing this dress wasn't the person writing this diary.

"Since when did you own dresses?" I was changing into Tess' room when she barged in. I was sitting on her bed while I looked at myself in the mirror with the dress. She caught me at a vulnerable time.

"I was given this dress to wear at the event, so it would be rude not to wear it." Hearing myself talk to her brought me back to reality a bit, but I was still shaken up.

"It might rain tonight, you might want to bring a jacket just in case," Tess said. I nodded. My heart was still pounding.

She sat down next to me and we were both in the presence of the mirror. Our thighs were touching, which set off a little *spark* in my heart. This situation felt too familiar.

"Are you okay? You look a little off." Tess asked without hesitation. Our eyes locked for the first time I arrived here. Something inside me knew that was going to happen, but wasn't mentally prepared for it.

"I'm not sure if I like the dress, well, at least when *I* wear it. I feel like I'm ruining it." There was a whole plethora of things on my mind, but my brain decided to say this one. I pushed a bit of hair behind my ear.

"Well, I think," Tess tackled me onto the bed. She hovered over me like how I hovered over her last time. Her eyes were fiery, and mine were full of fear, conflict, desperation. "You look gorgeous in it." *Spark.*

We both raised our heads simultaneously to make our mouths connect, also known as kissing. My body did subtle things to not give into my desires like my arm would shake or literal sweat began to form. But there was nothing my body could do once Tess started going. I lost all control, or I gained full control. I don't know which. Something was making my body do these things, and it was overpowering. My sense of self was lost. But it made me happy.

There was something about Tess that made me lose control. She seemed to catch me at my most vulnerable moments. Ever since that first night, I've never come close to that intense, toe-curling feeling that she gave me.

The sun had fully set by the time we were done. My shoulders felt weightless again. My mind was left blank and Tess and I layed on her bed next to each other. None of us spoke a word. My dress was wrinkled, but that didn't seem to faze me.

"Tess, I'm late. I have to go. I'll see you aro-" I said, trying to contain my emotions. I sat up and put back my dress on.

"Wait!" Tess interrupted.

I looked back and our eyes locked again. Her eyes were the ones with desperation this time. "Lilith," she said my name and not *Lith*. That surprised me a lot. "I want you to *really* think about being my girlfriend." She looked me dead in the eyes and I kept staring as I processed her question. My ears were not ready to hear that.

"Tess, you know that can't work-"

I started to notice a pattern where I was unable to look people in their eyes when saying something I didn't want to say. I know this is probably extremely normal human behavior, but it bugged me when I was unable to face the people I love in the most vital moments.

"Lith, I broke up with my boyfriend! I told him why I wanted to break up and he

called me a fucking freak! He told a bunch of our friends and they also called me disgusting." Her eyes were suffering. I've never heard a voice so desperate until now.

Her words echoed through my brain for a second. My mind couldn't fully process anything at that moment.

"What your brother did to me that night a few years ago, could never be undone. I know I told you that I've moved on from it, but let's face it, not even fucking Wonder Woman herself could confidently say that she is immune to those types of things."

When she mentioned Taylor, I gulped in fear.

"But you're helping me undo that. Whenever we're together, all of that seems to go away, even if it's just for a few seconds. I didn't think that was possible. Not even drinking does that for me." She laughed at her own joke depressingly. "Just think about it, please." She pleaded quietly. Another pause ensued, trying to take in all of that.

"I'm sorry Tess. I can't fix what I have done." I said, once again, unable to look her in the eyes.

I did what I do best and grabbed my stuff and bolted out of Tess' apartment. Tess screamed, cried, and maybe even tried to chase me, but once I got in my car, it was an afterthought. *An afterthought, right? The way she looked at me, the way she cried for me, and the way I cried for her. Just an afterthought, right?*

I tried my best not to think about *anything* on the car ride over. I wanted to let my brain autopilot, but I would risk crashing my car. I hate the fact that when I'm doing something mundane like driving, my brain *has* to run laps. It shouldn't even be a question of whether or not I should be Tess' girlfriend. Even writing the phrase: *Tess' girlfriend* makes my stomach turn. As I'm writing this now, the thoughts are just flowing in and I can't stop it. I hoped that writing it down would rid me of these burdens, but they only enable them. I'm gonna stop now.

I arrived at the place where the festival would be. I had to drive fifteen minutes away from the main city to arrive in this forest-like area on a little mountain. The forest acted as a barrier to the disruptive sounds of the city, so it was pretty perfect for a festival like this. It wasn't anything grand like I expected. It was just a large circular camping area surrounded by trees. The circumference of trees had tons of purple and yellow star decorations.

There weren't many people here. Maybe like a couple of dozen if not less. It seemed like a small number of people knew about this sort of thing. That was fine with me because it would be sort of unpleasant if there were a ridiculous number of people here. But it was very mellow. When I looked around, there were just a bunch of individuals laying down on big tarps looking and pointing at certain stars in the sky. It brought a much-needed smile to my face.

"She showed up. I thought she forgot about us." Nonna said, making herself and Bolo laugh. The both of them snuck up behind me while I was admiring the sight of the people.

"Hey, Nonna." I went and hugged both Nonna and Bolo together.

I wanted to sound more excited but didn't force myself this time. But I was genuinely excited to see them. Nonna had on a dress of her own. It wasn't as flashy as mine was, but it showed off her elegance in her own way. Bolo was in his work outfit, which was just a white t-shirt and jeans.

"We're all set up Lilith. You can sit with us if you feel like it." Bolo said, in better English than Nonna. The both of them left to sit down on their tarp.

I leaned against my car as I looked up towards the sky like everyone else did. The people who set up this event picked a brilliant night to do this. The stars were just as vibrant and marvelous as I remembered them being. The background sound of people talking just added to the experience. I was reliving my childhood again, looking at the same stars that Mom looked at every night. The same stars that Nonna and Mom would stare at every year. The same stars that Mom dedicated an entire journal to.

I went in my bag and opened that journal. I opened to a random page and read this:

The stars have seen everything in life. They've seen life, death, happiness, sadness, war, peace, love, heartbreak. Most importantly, though, they're watching you.

I kept reading that line to myself over and over until the words no longer looked like words. I imagined Mom's voice reading that line to me. It made her seem human for those few minutes. *There was no way a monster would come up with something so beautiful and wise. Right?*

Suddenly it started to rain, raining hard. My ears started to pick up the sound of heavy rain and people yelling as they ran to their cars. Somehow, I didn't feel any of the rain, nor did I notice it.

"Runnnnn!" The world went soundless again. I might as well be on a deserted island.

I pulled a photo of Mom out of my bag. Even though the photo was still soaking wet, I was able to see it clearly. The photo of Mom and Nonna at this same star festival. Once again, same location, same Nonna and Bolo, same smile, same hair, same dress.

I never noticed it before, but Mom and I did look so much alike. I smiled in different ways to see if I was just seeing things, but no matter what I did, we looked alike. I literally couldn't believe what I was seeing. I felt like someone shot a bullet through my heart. *Spark*

My whole chest tensed up, trying to maintain the pain. It was so strong. All I wanted to do was scream. It was like God designed me to be as similar to Mom as possible. Hate for nobody but myself came over me. I punched myself in the face, looking myself dead in the car mirror. I started to leave red marks on my cheeks. *Good. More.* I thought. My heart was palpitating like crazy, but I kept punching myself in the face over and over and over and over and over and over.

Mark: December 5

The rain started pouring down at an alarming level. People got in their cars and fled the festival. The yellow and purple lights started to fall off the trees and break. The scene was breaking before my eyes, like a zombie movie.

I was about to drive off too when I saw a girl in a black dress standing in the middle of the rain. She didn't seem to want to move a muscle like she was frozen in time. What the fuck was she doing? I recognized the look in her eyes. I've seen those sets of eyes somewhere.

"Run!" I yelled from the window of my car.

She started punching herself repeatedly. The rain took up my field of vision, but I saw frames of her punching herself. This girl was going to kill herself, from either staying in the rain or from punches. I ran out of my car, leaving my car door open. The rain only got more and more intense as I stepped each foot forward and I barely saw where I was going.

"Stop!"

I grabbed her arms. She was freezing cold, only being in a dress. When I grabbed her arms, I thought I was grabbing icicles. Our eyes finally met. But her eyes didn't have life. It was like something consumed her consciousness and ran away with it. She passed out in my arms. She felt literally weightless in my arms like she hadn't eaten anything in a year. I thought she died for a second, but I felt the beat of her heart against my arm.

My first instinct was to carry her to my car. I could drive her to a hospital in town. Then the rain suddenly got more intense than before. Little water bullets smacked the top of our heads. There was no way I was going to be able to drive down a mountain in these conditions.

Needing to think fast, I ran straight into the forest with the girl in my arms. I took her soaked bag as well and I ran away from the rain. This area was camping grounds, so I hoped to find some sort of shelter. Anything to keep us out of the rain.

Out of the corner of my eye, I found a little cabin in the middle of the woods. But when I tried to get in, the door was locked. I let out an irritated sigh before setting Lilith down. Her body seemed so weightless that I had to check twice to make sure she wasn't dead. I walked around the cabin to see if I could find anything. The darkness from the woods and rainwater hitting my eyes made it really hard to see anything.

Eventually, I found a small window in the back and had no choice but to elbow it to break it open. The sound of the glass shattering blended in with the rain, but I was happy to see that it actually broke. My elbow was bruised from the recoil.

I did a small prayer in my head before entering to make sure it wasn't rat-infested or something. When I entered, it was just dark and plain looking. It looked like people have been here this season and it was just a random cabin. There were chip bags and random water bottles on the tables, but that was the least of my problems.

I laid Lilith's body down on one of the beds and felt her forehead. She was getting a burning fever, but the rest of her body was still cold to the bone. I took off my raincoat and wrapped her body in it. I was cold, but I could manage it.

My body started to calm itself down and untense itself. My senses were clear, and the rain made it obvious that we were going to be stuck here for a while. The water bullets harshly hit the roof of the cabin and each one seemed to penetrate harder and harder into my ear.

My eyes started staring into hers for a few minutes. They were closed shut, but they gave me so much to think about. My mind channel kept replaying the memory of her beating herself senseless. It kept hitting rewind over and over until the memory seemed like a fever dream. Except it was not a dream, this was real life. A real girl, beating her real face, with her real hands in the real rain. It only happened a minute ago, but I couldn't make any sense out of it. Like I said, I knew this girl from *somewhere*. Those eyes, even when closed shut, I somehow knew.

To pass the time, and to warm myself up, I made a fire using some of the logs that were left outside the cabin. I used the lighter I had in my backpack to light the logs. I owe Sky my life for putting it in my bag before I left.

My body calmed itself more, and I was finally able to view the stars in a calm state. After all, that was the reason why I came here, but there was an obvious change of plans.

The stars in Atlanta were always so much better than the ones in Macon. That's probably why they call the event here and nowhere else. Even in the pouring rain, the stars stood out like they didn't care if it was raining or not.

I started to imagine colors. The sky was purple. The starry sky acted as a blank canvas and I was painting it with whatever I wanted. I imagined a guitar, a pony, a shoe, a hat, literally whatever I wanted. I could picture everything right then and there, like a movie. My eyes grew wider, and I felt weightless. The chair I was sitting on didn't exist, the clothes I was wearing didn't touch my body, the ground my feet were touching wasn't there. It was a date between the sky and me. *This* is what I came here to experience. *This* is why I come here every year, whether or not it rained.

How We See The Stars

185

Tyler Bansil

Lilith: My last entry

Am I dead? The first thing I thought to myself. This wasn't one of those times where you would pass out and forget everything that happened. I remembered everything pretty clearly and accepted it. With that knowledge in mind, someone or something had to have saved me. I woke up in a small cabin area with a coat around my shoulders. It was a man's coat.

My heart was still trying to recover itself from the palpitations it took earlier. On the other hand, my face felt bruised. The whole entire right side of my face was a reddish purple. When I put my hand up against it, the skin was tender. My whole body felt some sort of pain, but I didn't seem to mind it all that much.

The first thing I thought of was Nonna. I wondered if she got back home safely or if she was worried sick about me. When I was trapped in my own world, I couldn't see her run to her car, or hear her call out to me.

Next thing I thought about was Tess. My phone got killed by water damage in the rain, so she's probably been calling me a lot. My mind kept replaying what she said to me before I left. *He called me a fucking freak.* Guess what, Tess? We're both freaks. The number of reasons I had for being a freak was limitless. She felt out of place for once in her life and it was tearing her apart. The way her eyes pierced into mine made that obvious. If we became a couple, it was over for her.

I was the reason that she was going insane. She pounced on me like she never stopped thinking about me. I would be lying to myself if I said that she hadn't been on my mind every day as well.

Tess wanted her pain from Taylor to go away so badly that she trusted me to fix it. I did one dumb thing, and it gave her hope. Looking back on it, it's a regret, a big one. I can't fix you, Tess. Even if we became a couple and had sex every day, lived together, slept together, watched movies together, and drank Miller Lite and ate grits, I can't fix it. The truth is, I am only hurting you, and I'm sorry. I'm sorry you have to be hurt by someone else in my family.

I looked outside through a window and there was a silhouette of somebody with a fireplace, looking up at the sky. That was probably the person who saved me from the rain, so I felt the need to approach them.

I opened the door slowly and closed it. The sound of the pounding rain on the cabin probably drowned out the sound. There was the guy. The second I saw his reflection from the window, I knew who it was. I both wanted to smile and cry when I realized who it was. We didn't know each other's names, and that was the most beautiful part.

"Are you okay?" He asked softly.

I snuck up behind him and he took notice. I leaned up against the cabin wall behind him, only being able to see him from behind. The rain was deafening, but I heard him loud and clear.

"Yeah, I'm fine."

We stood in silence for a while, staring into nothing.

"I'm sorry you had to see me like that. I don't know what came over me." I said, letting my eyes gravitate towards the ground.

My eyes weren't brave enough to meet his. But when I finally looked up, he was smiling. I wasn't expecting him to smile, but that's the reaction I got. He seemed to be content with us just being here, even though our current situation wasn't the most ideal.

"I'm just happy you're okay." His voice went deep, like the way Dad does it.

He poked the fire with a stick, which activated it more. The fire crackle became a part of our conversation.

I leaned over to see what he was looking at. The light from the fire illuminated his side profile and his eyes were what caught my attention. The last time I saw someone with those eyes was Mom. The way they both looked at the stars. Their heads were tilted a little high and it seemed like they never blinked. It added another level of comfort.

"Thanks..." I tried to sound grateful but ended up sounding flat. More silence caved over us.

There was a ton in my mind at the moment. The sound of the rain and starry night made my heart more vulnerable. There was so much to think about that my mind couldn't pinpoint what to think about. All I knew was that I was a monster. I tried to embrace what I was, but I realized how many people I was affecting because of it.

The minuscule feeling of my tears started to run, leaving trails of moisture on my face. My voice started to be taken over by the dam that kept me from bursting out in tears.

"Whoa!" He quickly turned around and saw me in my own storm of despair. This wasn't the sparks anymore. This was something completely different.

He thought for a second if he should come within my storm. He stood up from his chair and embraced me, trying to calm the storm. My body felt weightless in his arms. I softly embraced him back, leaning on him for moral support.

"It hurts. I can't make it stop." My voice was enveloped in tears and pain. It felt like it was never going to stop. It's like an itch that never goes away, no matter how many times you scratch it. I started to hug tighter.

"I'm sorry..."

He put his hand over my head, as to say everything was going to be okay. I really wanted to believe that he understood what I was going through, like he understood me down to every detail. But he didn't. He was an extremely nice boy that happened to run into a girl that didn't know who she was anymore.

"It's okay to hate ourselves once in a while."

Those words cut deep, deep into a place that I've never explored. I didn't hold back my tears. The dam was completely broken and so was I. Babies would be jealous at the magnitude I cried at. I wanted to hit myself more, but my whole body was too weak with emotion to continue to pound myself. I let it all out, in the middle of the forest.

When I pictured my situation in its entirety, I realized how rock bottom I was. Crying in a stranger's arms, in the middle of the forest, the rain pouring harder than ever, and here I was more of a mess than all of those combined.

There wasn't a specific thing I was crying at. Now that I think about it, it was probably everything combining into one ball.

A few more minutes of silence caved over us. We kept embracing each other until the waterworks turned off.

"You okay now?"

"Yeah, I did all I could." I sniffled a little, hugging him less tightly. "I'm fine now," I said in full honesty.

"I'm gonna head inside to sleep." He held my shoulders secure. He looked me in the eyes. I was too weak to return the favor of eye contact. "Don't stay out too long." He said in a raspy voice before letting me go.

I stayed leaned up against the wall for some time. If someone told me that three hours went by, I would believe them. There was a lot on my mind. Thankfully, my emotions were calmed now. Whenever I had a moment to contemplate life, it would fill me up with strong emotion and I would feel like breaking something. When that feeling comes over you, your hands feel destructive. You could literally envision punching a hole through a wall. But at that moment, I didn't feel any of that. Once again, this was completely different from the sparks.

I put out the fire before going back inside to sleep. The sound of the rain still filled the room with ambiance. He was on the bed, facing away from me. I laid down next to him, putting the covers over my body. Our backs were touching and our body warmth started to exchange. The sound of the rain still filled the room with ambience.

"Are you awake?" I called out.

"Yeah, can't sleep?" He asked. He shuffled around and I felt his back movement rub against my back.

"Yeah."

I sat up and turned on the mostly dead lights that this cabin had. My bag stared at me from the other side of the room.

My body tensed up, knowing what I was about to do next. Future Lilith, or whoever is reading this, please forgive me for what I'm about to do.

"Can I... can I ask you for one last favor?" I asked.

"Yeah, sure." He said, unconfidently. I've put this boy through a lot. I don't blame him for sounding unsure.

I walked across the room and grabbed the bag with (almost) everything I cherished in life.

"I want you to have this." I held the bag up to his chest and almost shoved it into his arms. "This isn't a gift, it's just... something that I can't have anymore." I plopped the bag in his hands and he just looked at it like how a monkey looked at a phone.

"What is this?" He put it down and opened the zipper. Mom's journals, my diary, and the photos, all held together by the bag's material and a zipper.

"Something that I need to get rid of, *or else I can't move on*," I said under my breath. This time, I was sure it couldn't be heard by anyone else. "You can do whatever you want with them. You could throw them away, use them for scratch paper, read them, burn them, literally whatever you want." I pretended that none of this bothered me. I crossed my arms and tried to sound like I was barely paying attention.

In reality, I was starting to hate myself again. Seeing all of Mom's journals and knowing that I won't have them anymore started to activate some sort of hatred. I fought against that hatred. My goodwill knew that this was for the best. I clenched my fists to shove those emotions aside. All I wanted was for those burdens to be out of my possession.

This boy was literally saving my life in more ways than one. I wish I had the guts to communicate that to him.

"Are you sure you want me to have these? These seem important." He asked. He picked up one of the journals and felt the cover material.

"I'm sure," I said as I climbed back into bed, trying to pry my eyes away from that bag.

Mom's charm started to be noticeable again. I took it out, stared at it for a few final seconds, and tossed it in the bag. If this was a movie, then this was a goodbye scene and the main character would be too broken up to look at their lover. But the lover was literally a children's toy.

After tonight, I plan on never talking to Tess in the near future. When I get my new phone, I won't bother even adding her number. That idea deeply pained me, more than I could describe. A little part of my heart was bitten off by the monster inside of me. That same monster was driving me into the ground.

The bad part was that I was sacrificing people to make myself feel normal again, regardless of who it benefited. Tess, this boy, and, most bitter sweetly, my own mother was being tossed in the fire to make my monster go away. Once I end this diary entry, I will hopefully feel free. Goodbye boy. Goodbye Tess. Goodbye Mother. And goodbye monster inside of me. All four of you will be missed.

Mark: December 10

There was a lot to think about over the course of five days. All I can say is: What the fuck was that? It took me a couple of days to convince myself that it all *wasn't* a dream.

That night, it was really damn difficult to fall asleep. No matter how physically exhausted I was after running around in the pouring rain, my brain wouldn't let me sleep. When I eventually *did* fall asleep, the girl woke me up around sunrise to tell me she was leaving. The heavy rain had ceased by then. She gave me back my coat and just took off. *There was no way someone this unexplainable exists on earth.* I thought to myself.

As for the notebooks I received, she said I could read them if I wanted to, but that felt like an invasion of privacy. These were probably diaries or something really personal to her. I could tell by the way she started tearing up when she lent them over to me. I just left them on my dresser, not really knowing what to do with them.

After school, I met up with Nicole and the others at her house. Apparently, they've been doing a lot of planning and tape watching while I was gone. Damien snuck out of the house to help the girls out. Apparently, he was grounded since his dad found out that he took the guns and didn't tell him. If you ask me, though, he definitely deserved it.

The good part was, he seemed as invested in this investigation as Nicole was. Granted, that was probably because he still loved Avery, but hey, any motivation is good motivation.

"Mates, should we tell Mark the plan?" Sky asked the group.

My eyes widened, not knowing we had a plan already. Nicole and Damien agreed.

Damien stood up and all of our attention went on him. He seemed to take up the role as leader while I was gone. When everyone was watching the security tape and discussing, it was usually him that talked over everyone. It wasn't a bad thing since he seemed to have the most information.

I'm gonna be honest. It was really hard to pay attention and not space out during all of this. I was present, yes, but I wasn't really here... if that makes any sense. My priorities should be on this since this is probably the most important thing I've ever worked on, but my mind was everywhere else.

Sky kept occasionally looking up at me and smiling, probably as a friendly thing. My head would always be angled down, so I wouldn't notice it until it was awkward. It made me self-conscious about how lost I looked.

"Is it okay if I step out for a bit?" I blurted abruptly. Damien was talking, then everyone seemed to all turn their heads to me. Nicole looked at me like I wasn't the same person, which both equally stung and confused me. "I just need some fresh air," I added.

"Sure, go on." Sky being the first one to say anything.

Whenever anyone says they want 'fresh air', they just want a viable excuse to leave the room. I was trying to tell myself that being outside would help me get my mind straight, but I kinda just wanted to be alone.

I went to Nicole's backyard and sat on one of the wooden benches she had. The sun was just starting to set, so there weren't any stars to gaze at. I just kicked my feet around like a little kid and let my brain air out a bit.

From down here, I could hear everyone discussing upstairs in Nicole's room. I felt bad that I was down here, doing basically nothing, instead of helping out and getting caught up to speed. But if I forced myself to stay up there, I wouldn't be able to grasp anything.

After a bit, I noticed that the sun started to set. The weird thing about sunsets is that you don't really notice them until it's too late. I didn't notice how much time had passed until the sky was completely black. My eyes felt dry from how much I just wasn't blinking.

"You're still out'ere?" I didn't hear Sky open the backyard gate. I had to blink three times to fully remember where I was.

"Yeah, are you guys finishing up?" I looked at my watch and it had been a little less than two hours. I wasn't as surprised as I would normally be.

"Yeah, Damien just left. Nicole said we can leave whenever." Sky slung her bag over her shoulder, probably with some of the security tapes in it.

Sky awkwardly sat down next to me. The bench was long in length, but it felt suffocating with one more person. My hands felt particularly awkward, so I put them under my thighs.

"You want one, mate?"

I looked to my left and Sky pulled out a small-ish box of cigarettes. I had to double-take to make sure I wasn't seeing things.

"You smoke...?" I questioned.

I tentatively pulled one out of the box and she lit it for me. She held her cigarette between her lips before lighting it. The flames illuminated us both, even though it was very small.

"Yeah. When I used to live in Australia, me and my friends used to do it a lot, but when I moved to America, I sort-ah just dropped it. But every now and then, it's nice to unwind with one." She said, reminiscing on her own memories. Her accent thickened more than I've ever heard.

I can tell being homesick was an often repeated theme for her. To my knowledge, she's been away from home for almost two months. She even told me she wasn't even going home for Christmas. That had to have a weight on her shoulders.

She took a small puff and slowly released the smoke from her mouth. We both watched the smoke disappear in the direction of the wind.

"You probably never smoke at home, do you?" I asked.

I faked laughed to ease how uncomfortable that sentence was to say. The second the sentence left my mouth, I kind of wanted to die.

"Yeah, my parents would kill me..." She also uncomfortably laughed. Our cigarettes were already dying out.

I stopped staring at the flame and just took a puff. It was very bitter. Like black pepper and Pop Rocks. I didn't know how appealing this was, but it was calming me down.

"Hey, can I ask you something?" I asked out of thin air.

"Something bothering you, mate?" Sky asked back, probably seeing how uncomfortable I looked today.

"You remember when you encouraged me to go to the star festival, right?" I brought up.

"Well yeah. It was only a week ago." Sky said, followed by a disconcerting laugh. I looked over at her and she slowly put a piece of hair behind her ear. "Why do you ask?"

"I was hoping to use that to try and convince you to go back home." I took another puff from the cigarette.

I looked her in the eyes, but she didn't have the courage to look back. She just stared at the tip of the flame.

"You told me I've been doing a lot for the investigation. But look at you." I spotlighted Sky. "You've been a guardian angel to Avery since the night of the party. I'm pretty sure even she won't mind if you go home for a bit. You need to see your family mate." I said, throwing some of Sky's words back at her.

Sky really thought about it for a few seconds, not really saying anything. The flame danced between her fingertips. Even though it was very subtle, the flame slowly ate away at the cigarette as her silence grew.

"Yeah, maybe you're right." Sky tossed her cig on the floor and stomped the flame out. "Avery has been telling me to go visit my family, but I didn't think I needed to until recently. " Sky admitted. It was probably refreshing for her, finally realizing something she knew this whole time.

"So are you going home?" I asked excitedly.

"Yeah. After we follow through with the plan, I'll go home for a bit." She smiled before she ended that sentence. Her joy was infectious.

"Yes!" I celebrated. I was over the moon. At that moment, I was the happiest I've been since coming back from Atlanta.

"Thanks, Mark." Sky managed to say. Before stepping away, I took the last puff out of my cig and put it out.

"Come inside, I have to lock all the doors," Nicole commanded. Sky went to pick up the car and told me to wait for a bit.

I walked inside, where every light in Nicole's living room was turned on. My eyes hadn't seen light for the past two hours, so it was harsh for a few seconds.

"Shouldn't you explain the plan to me now?" I reminded Nicole.

I forgot the reason I was supposed to be here. But on the dinner table was one of the security tapes. Then I remembered there was a supposed plan.

"Okay so, next-next Friday. There's gonna be two big parties near the college. Damien thinks the biggest chance we have of catching him is finding him at one of the parties." Nicole explained while putting plates in the dishwasher.

"What are you suggesting? That we go to those parties?" I asked.

"Yes sir. We're gonna have to split us up into groups of two. The goal is just to look for the guy. If we happen to find him, then keep your eyes on him and wait for the other group to arrive, and ideally, the police."

My first thought was: *Fuck, another party?* Every party I've gone to as of recently has gone to shit, one way or another. And this plan seemed like a situation of What *can* go wrong, *will* go wrong. I knew I was being pessimistic, though.

"Is any of this legal?" I asked, scratching the back of my head.

"I'm gonna be honest. Probably not, but we're doing it for a good reason. Just don't flaunt your gun and we're fine." It bothered me how casually she said those words.

I hit the bed as soon as I got home. I wasn't sleepy exactly, but being in my own head all day left me pretty energyless.

While I was in bed, the bag that the girl gave me was calling me. I tried to ignore it, but it acted like a beacon in my pitch-black room. This has been happening for the past couple of nights, ever since I got back from Atlanta. I could swear that the bag literally glowed across the room. This time, I couldn't fall asleep until I did something with the bag.

I groaned, turned on the lights, and walked across my room where the bag was sitting.

The bag was old. The zippers barely opened and there were rips and random color splotches everywhere. Even the feel of the bag was old. When I touched it, years' worth of existence poured into the nerves of my fingertips. The contents weren't all too different, either. I knew there were notebooks in here, but not what they looked like. I picked up a random notebook to see what it felt like. The tips of my fingers gripped the leathery cover of the book. The frills of the beaten-up leather indicated this was old as dust. I thought that they were bibles for a second.

I opened it up to see the contents. To my surprise, it had human handwriting, not computed. It was written in extreme cursive. A lot of the letters were hard to identify. I caught myself squinting at certain words and letters. The pencil marks were very dulled out, either due to time or a bad pencil. I could probably erase some of the writing with the oil of my fingers.

In my mind, there was no way this was the girl's handwriting. There were dates on these pages. Aug 5, 1991, May 1, 1992, Sept 8, 1992. These were someone else's journals. I put down this journal and flipped through the other ones.

One of these had to be hers, right? Or was this the elaborate prank that I wanted to believe?

Finally, I found something different. The front cover had a different material and color different from the other journals. It had new leather, fresh paper, and recent pen markings. *This is 100% her journal.* I thought.

I was curious, too curious, to find out any information about this girl. She was so God damn mysterious. I wanted to know more. My hands rested flat on the journal, shaking at the decision to read what was inside. I knew that once I started reading, I couldn't go back. A feeling of guilt came over me, but I ignored it fully this time.

Mark: December 18

I haven't really talked about school in a long time or school in general. Today was the last day of school before the break. I didn't think much of it, since lately, none of us have really been paying any mind to school. And by us, I mean me, Nicole, Damien, and Sky. Almost every second during finals, I was thinking about the investigation or the girl's journals. Both are equally attention-grabbing. I basically half-assed my finals. I ended every class with a B, except math with a C and an A French. The French final was incredibly easy to cheat for since some TA leaked the final online.

Nicole texted me to remind me that today was the day that the five of us were going to the parties. We all met up at Damien's house to go over any last-minute plans. The emotions in the room were heavily mixed. No two faces looked alike, in terms of what emotion they portrayed. Nicole was her usual peppy self. Her energy, combined with Damien's attempts to be the leader of the group, created all the energy in the room. Sky was nervous, which was to be expected. In a few hours we were about to be makeshift undercover cops.

Damien arranged the groups, and it was supposed to be Nicole and me at Party one, and Sky and Damien at Party two. Then Nicole pulled me aside and asked if Sky and her could swap so she could be in a group with Damien. She treated this like a fucking school project. I supposed that swapping Sky and Nicole wouldn't do much harm. Also, a little part of me hoped that I'd be in a group with Sky.

I really didn't fully take in what we were doing tonight until right now. I had eight days to realize what we were doing, but it only hit me right then when Damien took us into his shed that afternoon.

He opened two large brown crates, similar to the ones back at the abandoned building.

"Why are we here?" Nicole asked. All of us would've asked the same question if Nicole didn't say anything.

"See for yourself." Damien pointed at a big brown crate. I opened both crates, and they had pistols, ammo, and bulletproof vests.

"Whoa."

"What the fuck."

"Mate, what the fuck are these?"

All of us reacted. Damien just laughed like a maniac when he saw our reactions to seeing literal weapons.

"How did you get these?" I asked while picking up one of the vests. It was *heavy*. I couldn't imagine myself wearing this.

"My dad is into weapons n' stuff. That's why he grounded me when he found out I took them. He would get his gun license taken away if the police found out I took them." Damien explained.

"Your dad is a bad-ass," Nicole commented. She picked up one of the pistols and started using them like a toy. She aimed it at a wall and made *pew* *pew* sounds while she aimed it in different directions.

The way she held the gun screamed inexperience. You might think that holding a gun is straightforward, but it's more complicated than it seems. The reality that Nicole might have to shoot it, and not kill herself with it started to settle in.

"Why do we need these? Isn't this a lil' overboard?" Sky asked concerningly. She also picked up a gun, but then put it down immediately after she gave a scared impression.

"Nicole, you said the guy had a gun and knife, right?" Damien asked to confirm.

"Yeah." She responded.

"So yeah, we might need these." Damien insisted.

"Is this even legal?" I asked, still examining the gun.

Feeling the material of the gun was enough to send chills down my spine. I put the gun back in the crate, even though I knew I would have to pick it up again in a few hours.

"Yeah, as long as we're eighteen or older, we're fine."

"We're not eighteen." Nicole and I said in unison. Nicole and I just turned seventeen this summer.

"Sky, how old are you?" Damien asked.

"Twenty," Sky responded.

"See, fifty percent of us are above eighteen. So, it's only half-illegal!" He joked like it would make the nervous people feel any better.

Damien suggested that Nicole go home and find some big winter coat for her to wear. Nicole was the smallest one out of all of us, so the vest didn't really blend in unless she wore something big over it. So, she quickly drove home.

The rest of us got suited up and loaded our guns. As serious as this was, we felt like power rangers or some other cartoony crime-fighting show. *We're really doing this, huh?* I thought to myself. I tried not to imagine things going south, but that was hard to believe, considering how bad my luck was with these things.

We had a couple of moments to relax until we had to leave. I had a chance to look in the mirror to see if my gun and or vest stuck out at all and surprisingly, they didn't. We all had jackets with deep enough pockets and had big enough frames to hide everything.

While everyone was hanging out, doing their own thing. I sat in a corner, reading Lilith's diary. In the process, I discovered that her name is Lilith. This whole time, she was just a nameless girl to me. That made me realize she probably didn't know my name.

I haven't read that much of it since a lot of the guilt had been catching up to me. But I've read a *decent* amount. The stuff I've read so far has been very emotional. Sometimes I've mentally struggled to turn on the next page. A lot of stuff about her dead mother and her alive brother. This all made Lilith more *human* in my eyes. There was finally a relatable, yet not-relatable, person behind the craziness.

There was one particular thing that was bugging me, though. That Taylor guy. The way Lilith talked about him was so vague, maybe purposefully vague. I couldn't wrap my head around why I found that person so intriguing. She talked about him on page one. And from what I've learned from reading books, nobody unimportant is talked about on page one.

The more I read, the more questions I had. I thought for half a second that he could be a suspect of ours. I realized how unreasonable I was being and dropped the thought. I was getting a little too 'on-my-toes' about this whole thing. I was suspecting people that probably had nothing to do with this.

"We're playing Monopoly in the kitchen. Do you wann-uh join us?" I looked up, and it was Sky standing in front of me. I didn't even hear her footsteps approach me, similar to what happened the other night.

"No, I'm good. Thanks though." I said blandly, looking back down at the journal.

"What are you reading?" I had to scoot over so she could sit down next to me. She just took out her phone while I *pretended* to read.

"Some book I picked up at the library before the break." I blandly explained and lied. I haven't told anyone, even Nicole, about these journals.

Damien and Sky got us food before we all left. That forced all of us to eat at a table together. Normally, I would be all about socializing with any group of people, but I really wasn't feeling it. Even though I wasn't reading the journal, it continued to bug me outside of its pages.

"Are you guys ready?" All of them were done eating by that point. Meanwhile, I had only taken a few bites out of my burger. It seemed like before I sat down to eat my hunger was being sucked away.

"Ready as I'll ever be." Sky said with little to no energy. Her nervousness started to take over, as well as mine. I convinced myself that the source of my quietness came from being nervous, which wasn't exactly right or wrong.

"Yes! Let's get this show on the road!" Nicole shouted. I don't think I've heard that expression outside of movies.

Nicole managed to get the vest on her body. She wore about three or four layers over it, including a scarf, for a chance to make it look natural on her body. It was like a little kid wearing her mom's clothes, except this time, it was a fucking bulletproof vest.

Nicole and I got in our car, and I was responsible for driving Nicole to her party. It was basically pitch-black outside by this point. The night mood *really* settled in, and really quickly. This time, it was the bad, awful, terrible night mood.

"How do I look?" Nicole's torso could barely move with the number of jackets she had on. I was worried she might just tip over from the sheer weight.

"You're gonna burn up with that many jackets," I warned. My attention was still on the road. From what little attention I had left *not* reserved for other things.

"Eh, I can remove one or two layers if need be. I just wanted to sell the look." I stopped paying attention after I stopped speaking. I couldn't stop thinking about the diary. The thought of it was latched onto my brain, even though I thought I dropped it.

"Hey!"

"What?" I yelled. I didn't realize I was spaced out, driving on the highway until now.

"Are you okay?" Nicole asked, subtly concerned.

"Yeah, why?" I responded, very defensively. I kept my eyes on the road, so she couldn't see an inconsistency in my eyes.

"You seem off. Like the other night at my house." I rushed to think of something to say.

"I'm just tired, that's all. I didn't get much sleep last night. Also, holding a gun in my pocket isn't helping anything." I explained, half honestly.

"Okay, good. I was worried because you *just* missed the turn."

"Huh?" Nicole started laughing up a storm to my right.

It's gonna be a long night. I warned myself.

I dropped Nicole off at her party and went to mine. I made sure to pay attention to the road this time, instead of spacing out. I legitimately had to try to not autopilot. The night mood was fully set and stone. This forced my brain to think of the worst possible scenarios. One of us could get shot, caught with a gun, and do other horrible things. Before getting out of my car, I did a little prayer to *some sort* of God. I wasn't religious, but I was willing to kneel before any God to ensure our safety tonight. I gripped the gun one more time before sealing it in my back pocket.

"Ready mate?" Sky was waiting outside my car. She tried her best to look cool by leaning on the door of my car with a cigarette between her two fingers, but her eyes were telling a different story.

"Ready as I'll ever be," I said apprehensively.

We both went inside. Immediately, I felt like I didn't belong. Even though I was taller than most of the people, I still felt little compared to everyone. Nothing crazy was happening so far. People were just casually drinking, playing board games, talking, anything a normal party would have. Sky immediately jumped into the action and put on her best party facade. I watched her as she ran towards a group of people drinking and started to blend in with them. She suggested that I'd do something to blend in, but attempting to do anything would draw attention to myself. But at the same time, doing nothing probably drew a lot of attention. I felt a spotlight follow me everywhere I walked.

I walked around and looked out for anyone with the traits that Damien told me. Skinny frame, brown hair, and a small mole. I definitely looked like an undercover cop, walking around, swiftly looking at people, and then walking away. It didn't help that I was always putting my hand in my back pocket, making sure my pistol didn't fall out or anything.

"Hey bro!" I turned around and a typical college dude-bro called out to me. At first, I hesitated, thinking he was calling out to someone else. I saw that he and a bunch of his other friends were directly looking at me.

"Yo, what's up?" I yelled back, trying to sound like one of them. All of them wore some form of a college tanktop and sat down in the same way. It was like looking at ten of the same persons, just with slightly different hair.

"You wanna join us? We have some beers." He offered.

At first, I thought he was making fun of the fact that I looked like a kid who lost his parents at the mall. But I realized he was probably drunk. Dude-bros are pretty much the same, but what separates them is: 1) What sport they played in high school and 2) How they act when they're drunk. More often than not, they're cool and really inviting. But sometimes there are the ones who try to make chaos. That could mean fighting people, breaking things, hurting themselves, etc. This guy seemed to be in the cool and inviting category.

I accepted his offer and sat down with them. I still felt like I stuck out a lot, but at least the feeling was toned down. They continued to talk about whatever they were talking about before, which happened to be football. Nothing I didn't expect. It definitely made me less tense, listening to their casual conversation.

"Hey kid, you want a drink?" The same guy asked, finally acknowledging me after what *felt like an* hour. He held up a bottle of beer to my face

"Nah, I don't drink. Thanks though." I said softly.

"Aww come on. Are you a mormon or some'n?" He joked. That joke was barely funny, but somehow everyone laughed.

"Nah, man. I have to drive me and my girlfriend home, so I can't drink tonight. Designed driver y'know?" I said as an excuse. I realized I could basically say whatever I wanted to these people, knowing that I'll probably never see them again.

"Yo, who's ya girl?" Another guy asked. I pointed across the room where Sky was drinking with some other girls she befriended.

"DAMN! SHE SPICY!" another dude shouted.

"Hey kid, where you from?" The original guy asked me once everyone stopped admiring Sky.

"Uh, southern California." I blurted, continuing the lie.

"Oh, sick! You're from so-cal? I would've played there if their teams didn't suck."

I got a text from Sky telling me to meet her inside. I had to slowly drift from the group. Not like I was that attached to them in the first place. I was basically a spectator in their entire conversation. I would've gone on my phone, but that would've been really rude.

Sky was sitting by herself in an isolated room with a beer. I looked over to where she was sitting before and all the girls, she was with had dispersed.

"Everything alright?" Her face seemed to be burning up. The alcohol made her face turn four shades redder. She didn't *look* to be drunk, though. Her eyes looked normal.

"Yeah, I just wanted a break. Talking to those college girls is such a pain." She complained, taking another swig of her half-empty beer bottle. "All they talk about is boys and boys and boys and *boys*."

"Lucky you, all my guys just talk about football and basketball. At least your girls talk about living things." I joked. I sat down next to her and just stared at the ceiling. "How much beer have you downed?" I asked.

"Four bottles? This one being my fifth." She took another swig after she stopped talking like drinking was how she kept herself alive.

"Jeez, why so much?" I asked, not having anything to drink myself. Believe it or not, I've never had alcohol before. I'm not particularly against it, it's just not in my best interest, I guess.

"My parents don't allow me to drink, even though I turn twenty-one sooner rather than later." *swig* "So I can take what I can get." *swig again*." I keep forgetting Sky isn't my age.

"Are you gonna be able to stand on your own two feet tonight, in case something breaks out?"

"Yeah. My alcohol tolerance is pretty strong. I got that from my dad. I basically only feel tipsy." She said as she touched her face. "Hey, Mark?"

"Yeah?" She looked up at me, with different eyes this time. They looked vulnerable. Eyes that no one is used to seeing.

"I'm not saying anything is gonna happen to us, but if something *does*, just know that you've been a good friend to me." She sounded drunk, but that only meant she was being honest. I just smiled and left it at that.

She took out her gun and started staring at it. That definitely made her previous words dig deeper.

"Yo!" I yelled after a short silence. "Put the gun away, we're at a fucking party!" I yell-whispered.

"Fuck! Sorry, I forgot we were out." She put the gun away. I was afraid for a second, she was going to shoot it randomly. My heart skipped a few beats, waiting for something to happen.

Both of us suddenly got a call from both Nicole and Damien. Nicole called me and Damien called Sky. We picked up at the same time, breaking our awkward silence.

"Hello?" we said at the same time.

"Mark? Can you hear me?" Nicole was whispering. That made me worried that something had happened to her. I tuned out Sky and Damien's conversation to my right.

"Loud and clear, what's up?" I talked quietly alongside her.

"You and Sky need to come here, now! We found him, we're just waiting for you guys." Sky and I looked at each other with worried eyes.

"Okay, on our way!" I said after a processing second of silence. Both of our calls hung up at the same time.

"Ready to go?" I put on my jacket, already preparing to leave.

"Hell yeah, I am." Sky said with an immense spirit inside of her.

I've felt this feeling of pre-adrenaline before, recently actually, but it never feels old when it first strikes.

We both left the house without saying bye to anyone. I got in my car and Sky got in hers. She shot me a two-fingered wave, and we both drove off.

I double-checked to make sure the gun was in my back pocket. Update: It was. The reality of having to use the gun started to settle in even deeper and made my heart feel heavier.

I raced on the highway, going over the speed limit. Normally I drive very calmly and carefully, but I had to drive like a teenager today. I was cutting people off, changing lanes all the time. It being pitch-black outside didn't make anything easier. All the cars aggressively honking at me sent lots of guilt and adrenaline down my spine.

I arrived at the house. I could already tell this party was way more chaotic than the last one by the sheer number of cars and the noise coming from inside the house. It gave me flashbacks of the Halloween party, which is never a good thing.

When I first entered, everyone was already drunk, which was a regular sight for me by this point. This made the last party seem like a Bible school in comparison. I got a call from Damien.

"Are you here?" He yelled over the phone. I could barely hear him over the loud music and people.

"Yeah, I'm downstairs. Where are you guys?" I asked.

"Upstairs. Hurry, please." He said, forcing his words between his teeth.

As I ran upstairs, I tried to theorize what I was about to see, also making sure that no one was watching or following me. At this point, the possibilities were endless. The guy could be in a clown costume and I wouldn't think twice.

"Mark! Over here!"

Damien's voice yelled out to me as soon as I stepped foot on the top step. I turned around to see Damien waving his arms at me. The whole upstairs was pitch black, and I could only see his darkened silhouette. It didn't help that he was dark-skinned, and I had to squint really hard to see him. All of this creepy isolation was giving me flashbacks of the Halloween party. Once again, that's never good.

"What's happening? Where's Nicole?" I asked.

I walked over to Damien and the room he was standing outside of. Damien gave me a hand motion to look in the room, and my eyes were not prepared to see what I was about to see. They widened the millisecond I saw it.

The guy sat down on the floor, hands behind his back. Nicole had her pistols two feet away from his head, waiting to be shot at any moment. When I arrived, the guy looked up at me and just smiled.

"Motherfucker..." I whispered to myself, loudly. The thought of what this guy did to Avery shot up in my head, spreading anger through my body. I ran up to him with a prepared fist, willing to connect to his face. Nicole and Damien had to hold me back. If they didn't I would've fought that guy even if it killed me. The guy barely flinched.

"Mark, stop!" Nicole yelled, trying to push me away while maintaining gun control. I was like an angry dog. The way my eyes opened wider and my teeth bared in his direction was instinctive.

"Mark! It's not worth it, we already have him pinned." Damien pulled around my shoulders, stopping me in my tracks. His words and the guy's lack of expression got me to calm down.

"Yeah, sorry," I said calmly. The two of them removed their hands from me and my breathing became steady again. I didn't want to look at him any longer or else I would get angrier.

"Hmf, you bitch." He whispered deeply, loud enough to reach my eardrums. His voice was enough to get the anger flowing.

"What did you say?" The audacity caught my emotions again.

"Mark!" Nicole and Damien yelled at once. I stopped myself before they put their hands on me again. Everyone held a breath as the room froze, trying to contain my anger, including myself. I loosened up and everyone let go of their breath.

"Come on Mark, let's go." Damien guided me outside. He made sure that I didn't look at him more than I had to. The sight of him disgusted me. I looked back at him for a second, out of curiosity. Nicole put her gun a few inches closer than before, so that he got the message. She made sure that he didn't say anything else.

"You okay, bud?" Damien asked, looking at me like I was crazy, which was deserved.

"Yeah, I just lost my composure. You, out of all people, should understand, y'know?"

"I get it. It was hard not to sock him in the face when Nicole and I first saw him."

"How did you get him up here in the first place?" I asked, trying to change the focus a bit.

"Nicole and I were exploring upstairs when we found him sitting in that room. We recognized him instantly and pulled out our pistols." He said, impressed with himself as well as Nicole. I would've been too if I was in his position. That's the kind of stuff you see in cop movies. I wish I was there to see it. The satisfaction would've been immaculate.

"Wow. Do you know what he was doing up here?" I asked.

"He was planning to meet a girl up here. We grabbed his phone, and he was talking to an underage. Disgusting." He said irritatedly.

"Fuck. Really?"

"I know, right? This guy doesn't stop. I wonder how many times he's gotten away with this stuff."

"Probably a lot, now that I think about it." I contemplated out loud. "Should we call the cops or what's the plan?"

"We can't call the cops in the middle of a party, dude. That's like rule number one." He said.

I momentarily forgot we were at the party. The loud music became more of an ambiance compared to the sound of our current situation.

"We're just gonna wait till the party ends."

"Seriously, that long?" I complained, knowing that the party will last for a few more hours, if not till morning.

"We really don't have another choice. As long as we have one gun pinned to his head, and if no one walks in on us and causes a scene, we should be fine." I was on the edge about that last part. If someone stumbled upstairs and saw *three* teenagers holding *one* guy to gunpoint, they'd probably think we're the incriminating ones, not him. I complied nonetheless; not much else we *could* do.

We went back to the room and kept an eye on the guy. Nicole was tired of holding up a gun to his head since she's been doing it for God knows how long, so Damien offered to take over. Now it was Damien who was on gunpoint duty.

Everyone advised me to face away from him since he was willing to make me angry again, but I knew I could contain my emotions this time. I even plugged in my earphones to tune him out if he said anything.

"God, it's so fucking hot in this thing." Nicole plopped on the bed and removed three of her layers, revealing only her bra and her bulletproof vest. She let out a relieved sigh.

"You know we're not exactly in good company? I recommend you put your clothes back on." I suggested. I didn't look up at the guy, but I already knew he was eyeing down Nicole based on his... desires. *It felt weird writing that.*

"It's fine, he can't touch me. Besides, he deserves to be teased, anyway." Nicole started to subtly taunt her body. I could tell Damien wanted to say something but chose not to. He and I just looked at each other like lost animals.

"It's fine. It'll give me a nice sight before y'all fuckers take me to jail." The guy responded. His plain voice was gritty. None of it resembled a teenager or young adult. His voice, when calmed down, was mostly air and breath, which I wasn't used to hearing.

"Shut up, bitch." Damien slapped him with his left hand while maintaining gun control with his right. The guy barely reacted and just started subtly laughing to himself. All of us felt the same amount of disgust. Nicole put one layer back on wisely.

"Wait, where's Sky? Was she riding with you, Mark?" Nicole asked.

"No, she was in her own car," I responded.

"Where is she then?" Damien asked.

Uh oh.

"Uh, she was driving a bit slow, but she should be here by now..." I checked my watch to see how much time had passed. Thirty minutes. "Yeah, she should definitely be here by now," I confirmed. A worry seed was planted in my mind.

"Didn't you call her, Damien? Around when you called Mark?" Nicole asked.

"Yeah, I did... But she said she was coming." Damien responded.

Everyone's voice got concerningly worried. I was probably the most worried, considering I've been keeping a keen eye on her as of late.

Damien and Sky looked away from the guy, and we all stood in silence. Their pistols started moving away from his head. In the corner of my eye, I saw the guy reach into his back pocket.

"Stop!" I yelled. Before I could process any words, he pulled out something small. In the dimly lit room, it was hard to see, but it was something brown. Everyone turned around and Damien yelled out, "HEY!" and the guy threw something on the floor.

BOOM

CRASH

BANG

"AHHHHHHHH!" Damien yelled out.

There was smoke in the air. I couldn't see anything. The sound of the explosion kept bouncing off the walls... The chambers of my ears were ringing.

The smoke became see-through. Damien was coughing profusely, being at the center of the explosion. When I opened my eyes, the window was broken, and the guy was gone.

"Damien! Are you okay?" I called out. The sound was beginning to calm down, and the smoke cleared.

"Argh, yeah I'm fine." Damien was on the ground on all fours, writhing in pain. The explosion blackened his jacket.

"What was that?" Nicole yelled.

"A homemade bomb. A small one." Damien responded. Even though Damien was right next to the explosion, he seemed okay.

I ran towards the window and the guy was running towards his car. My fight-or-flight reactions started kicking in.

"We need to go after him! Let's go!" I started running out the door.

Nicole and Damien paused before running out the door behind me, storming through the party. We all bumped and ran through a bunch of people. We tunnel-visioned out the door. Once we got out. We saw and heard the guy's car racing down the street. The lights of his car started dimming as he got further from us.

"Get in your cars!" Damien commanded.

The three of us took less than a second to react to his words before we started booking it towards our cars. I literally hopped into the driver's seat. My head grazed the roof, but that barely affected me.

I shoved my keys into the keyhole and revved my car. Next thing I know, I was on the residential roads at 60+ mph. I *barely* saw the tail lights at the end of his car. He seemed so close, yet so far. I had to resist the temptation of slamming the gas any harder than I already did.

"Wait, Damien!" I called out to him. I looked over into his car, and he was trying to find his keys. I couldn't see Nicole, but she already had her engine started and was ready to go.

"What?" He quickly shoved his keys in and looked at me.

"I know it's a long shot, but can you go find Sky? Nicole and I will chase him!" My mind was so rushed at this moment that I couldn't tell if this was a good idea or shit idea. None of us knew where Sky was and that honestly was one of my biggest worries.

Damien blankly looked at me, like time had frozen over. Every millisecond that was passing by was time that the guy was getting further from us or time that Sky could be facing danger.

"Come on! Let's go!" Nicole honked her horn, getting impatient to leave.

"Y'know what? Fuck it! Sure." Damien swiftly fastened his seatbelt.

Not a second passes and I hear Damien's engine rev and take off in the other direction. Nicole is already on the road, and I try my best to catch up.

Suddenly, Damien called me on my phone. I had to fish the phone out of my pocket while driving to answer it.

I made a sharp right turn to get out of the residential roads. The guy ignored the existence of stoplights, so I did the same. I heard the rubber of my tires scream as I made jolt-like movements. This car was too old for this kind of driving and it showed. I don't think the gas pedal on this car has ever been this far.

I started hearing gunfire behind me. I looked in my side-view mirror and Nicole was shooting his car. Some of the bullets were ricocheting off the roof of my car. It was hail but with more consequences.

"NICOLE! STOP!" I opened my car window and yelled as loudly as I could. I had to peek my head out the window while driving. Death was staring me in the eyes at that moment. She still continued to fire. The sound of the gunshot was pounding my ears and definitely echoed through the neighborhoods.

The guy made a turn onto the freeway. *Fuck.* I hesitantly followed as well, having Nicole as backup. She eventually ran out of bullets, which relieved me a bit. It seemed like this guy's car was always faster than mine. Whenever I sped up, he seemed to speed up even more than I could match. It was getting really frustrating.

Suddenly, my phone started buzzing itself. My phone was in my cup holder so it vibrated inside of it, making a noise I couldn't ignore. I looked over for a second to see who it was.

Damien. It was hard to both look at the phone and pay attention to where this guy was going while driving 80 MPH.

"Hello?" I yelled over the phone. I don't know if he could hear me by how fast I was going. I tried closing the window to cut the sound of the wind, but the car was doing enough to mitigate any sound.

"Mark, I found her location!" Damien yelled. His words were cut by the wind, but I heard the words, *found* and *location.*

"Where?!" I jumped forward in my seat to yell at that.

The guy kept changing lanes the faster we got. There weren't many cars on the road with us, but the few we came across honked their horns aggressively at him. I was almost starting to expect the police to come for us.

"On the highway! Her GPS isn't moving!" Damien yelled as loudly as a human could.

"What is she doing there?" I yelled between my teeth.

The guy started to throw more of his bombs out his window, momentarily blocking my car window. I almost lost control of my car, but I held on.

Nicole was getting impatient and started speeding ahead of me. We were going 90 MPH by this point. I wasn't looking at my speedometer, but it definitely felt like way more MPH more than what should be legal.

I tried speeding ahead of Nicole to make sure she was behind me. My worry was that she was gonna do something dumb. The sound of her coming up on me made my body shake.

"Should we turn back?" I asked. Damien wasn't saying anything. The sound of his engine and mine combined into a sound of pure intensity. "Damien!" I grabbed my fucking phone and yelled into it.

BEEP Damien hung up.

"Fuck!" I slammed down my phone on the floor of my car. After that, I had a strong urge to punch my window next to me, but I barely suppressed that emotion.

I realized quickly that I'd have to make some sort of decision. My instinct was to either keep going or turn back was split right down the middle. 50/50. 1:1. Left and right. My arms shook at the decision to turn back. All it took was one swift U-turn to turn back. That's all it needed. We were about to hit the highway. There was a voice in my head saying to persevere and keep going, or be smart about this and turn back.

"Fuck it," I said to myself.

I made the sharpest fucking turn to exit the highway. The rubber of my tires screamed the loudest it could scream, making that turn. Cars around us honked as I cut them off. I bet one of them was Nicole as well. I didn't bother to look back to see if Nicole followed me or continued to chase. There was no way I was going to catch him on the highway. The instinct to turn back took over my body at the last second. The idea of Sky being in trouble was an overpowering feeling.

I heard two honks behind me. In my rear-view mirror, Nicole waved her hands out the window for me. I smiled with confidence for a few seconds. *Sky, we're coming.* I kept thinking to myself.

Damien called me again to guide me to where we were going. I was basically disregarding all the other cars on the highway. I mindlessly cut lanes until I had free space. I kept hearing more honks behind me, as well as the ones Nicole was making, trying to keep up with my speed.

"Damien! Are you sure she's here?" I yelled, hoping my words would travel to his ears. I kept breathing in and out as I spoke, but I didn't necessarily feel tired.

"Yeah! She's definitely here! She hasn't moved!"

Why wasn't she moving? We literally left at the same time. I thought to myself.

"Mark, hurry!" Damien commanded, with his tracker in hand.

I swerved my car left. That wasn't my brain's doing. My brain was barely in control anymore. Everybody part had its own consciousness.

"There!"

I looked to my right to the side of the road and there was a crashed car. The car's light kept blinking and beeping. My mind didn't make the connection until a few seconds later.

"Oh fuck!" I let out.

The three of us parked our cars on the side of the highway. This part of the road had little to no lighting. The only lights that illuminated the area were the headlights of the group of cars that pulled over to see what happened.

Nicole, Damien, and I all got out of our cars and ran up to her car. The car was in more despair when seen up close. Waves of smoke came out of the engine. *Not good.*

The three of us ran over to see what happened. There was a crowd around Sky's drivers' seat and sounds of commotion entered my ears.

I bursted through the crowd of people in a state of panic. Nicole and Damien followed me. I held my eyes shut in fear that Sky would be unconscious or dead. When I opened the door, Sky was still conscious, but her eyes were beginning to lose themselves. Seeing that kind of stuff made me want to vomit.

"Someone call nine-one-one please!" Nicole yelled out. Her voice was beginning to sound desperate.

"They're on their way." A middle-aged woman came up behind us and informed us.

Sky looked at me with her uneasy eyes. Her voice was shaky, like she was about to pass out any second now. They kept rolling from side to side. *We're losing her.*

There were streaks of blood running down her cheeks from the shattered glass that ricocheted back at her. There were shards of glass all over her car.

"How long until they get here?" Damien cried out.

I looked at him for a quick second and tears were rolling down his face. Damien was one of those people you couldn't imagine crying ever. So, seeing this up close was shocking to me. It made my heart sink a few inches.

"A few more minutes!" The same woman responded.

Damien and someone else were trying to pop her shoulder back into place. I took a quick peek and her back shoulder was all fucked up. I didn't even know a shoulder could do that.

How long has Sky been here? I asked myself. I started to blame myself for not worrying about this type of thing earlier. I knew she was drunk, and I knew she wasn't in a state to drive herself. Why the fuck did I not offer to drive her, or tell her to stay behind? This all could've been avoided, I felt like.

It seemed like the world was crashing all down on me at once. I wasn't having a panic attack, but it certainly felt like it. My body didn't know how to react to things like these. It seemed like I could only watch and be a spectator. I was frozen. If God gave me the option to disappear, I would take it in a heartbeat.

"It's here! Get her in the ambulance!" Damien commanded.

Damien and another man quickly lifted Nicole above their shoulders, like fucking cinderblocks. Three men ran out of the ambulance and helped them. I blinked, and the ambulance took off as quickly as it got here.

Mark: December 19

None of us could sleep that night. After everything had calmed down, Sky was the only thing on our minds. All I could think about was her eyes that could be compared to a zombie's when I opened the door. That kept me awake for longer the whole night.

The thought that Sky could've died scared me to death. *What the fuck was I thinking?* Letting her drive by herself in the dark of night while she was drunk. I didn't even bother making the connection. When she randomly took out her gun, that should've been a sign. I was tempted to break open the window next to my bedside. Avery almost broke down when I told her about the news. And the *last* thing I wanted right now was for Avery to lose herself again.

I knew I couldn't sleep, no matter how tired I was, so I picked up Lilith's diary. I thought that reading more about death (in the form of Lilith's mom) would fulfil me in some way. That's what depressing thoughts do to you. It invites more in. I knew that too, but I couldn't help myself. The way Lilith writes about her mom is so specific. How someone describes someone after they died was interesting to me. It got me to keep turning the pages, that's for sure.

In between all that, though, she started talking about her brother more. From what I could tell, they are very distant, for a reason she doesn't name. That always bugged me about her diary logs. She wrote about things so... inexplicably, if that's the right word. I mean, to be fair, these are *her* diary logs. They were meant for *her* eyes only, but I feel so led astray after reading some of these pages.

Lilith talked about this charm necklace of her's that her mom used to have. I vaguely remembered something like that in the bag that she gave me. She described it as: <u>The charm was made out of plastic wires that were woven together. The colors of the wire were black, white, and purple. There was a little star engraving near the bottom of it, signifying it was, in fact, Mom's.</u>

I smelled it, yes, I smelled it. It smelled like Mom. How does Mom smell? Not-so-strong perfume from the 1990s.

I jumped out of bed and looked in the bag. It was there, exactly how she described it. *Why was it there? Why would she give up something so precious to her and her family?* I thought to myself.

It reminded me how mysterious and unexplainable this girl was. This felt more sacred than all the journals combined. She wrote about it like she was obsessed with this thing. I almost didn't want to touch it. I did though. I wore the necklace like it belonged to me. When I looked myself in the mirror it looked all wrong. I felt like everyone in the world who saw me wearing this could tell it wasn't mine, but I didn't take it off. It felt a little wrong to use it for my own 'benefit', but I wanted to give it use instead of just sitting in a dirty bag.

Later in the log, she admits to putting security cameras in her brother's dorm room. Once again, she doesn't explain why. This instance bugged me the most since it's the one that conjures the most questions. She wrote it like she *had* to do it, or something else would happen. She doesn't say what that something is, though.

One thing did stick out at me, though. The way she described his brother. Messy brown hair, very skinny, noticeable mole. I searched my mind to remember how

Damien described the guy. I also tried to remember what he looked like from last night as well. Last night was the first time I got a good look at him.

The traits were very similar to how I remember him. My brain really wanted to believe that Lilith's brother was *somehow* the guy we've been trying to catch this whole time. My mind was becoming desperate. But after a while, I realized how farfetched that theory was and just stopped thinking about it.

In the morning, Damien called Nicole, and me and asked if we were busy. He called us at six in the morning, on a weekend, so I knew he didn't get any sleep. Nicole picked up the call, and knowing Nicole, she wouldn't be caught dead being awake at six on a weekend, so I knew she didn't sleep either.

After saying we weren't busy, Damien asked us if we could visit Sky in the hospital as soon as the visiting hours opened. Apparently, Avery called Sky's parents last night to tell them what happened to their daughter, and they dropped everything and came over. Avery told us that Sky had to stay the night in the hospital.

We all agreed to meet up in an hour at the hospital. Even if we were somehow busy, we would drop whatever we were doing to see Sky. We were all worried about her the entire night.

Avery and I arrived before visiting hours for an excuse to leave the house that I struggled to sleep in for the past five hours. Avery's house felt so empty and lifeless without Sky bursting into my room every morning. When I went to wake up Avery this morning, her eyes were wide open like they hadn't been closed for days. I slowly exhaled, knowing that this situation was creating another burden over her that she didn't need. I could tell she felt guilty, even though she had no reason to be.

I thought Avery and I would be the first ones there, but Nicole and Damien were early as well. I took a good look at them and all of our expressions were identical. Our eyes were heavy from not sleeping. Nicole didn't have any makeup on like she usually did to cover her eye bags. We all awkwardly placed our hands in our jacket pockets. It was generally not a good time. We managed to fake a smile and wave at each other, but other than that, it was silent.

We didn't say a word to each other. It wasn't awkward like I expected, it was a much-needed silence. Emphasis on the much needed.

The air around us wasn't tense, but it was solid. There was an aura of pain surrounding the three of us as we stood next to one another. Nothing could penetrate the aura. It was that strong.

After a long time of sitting outside the hospital, the doors opened up, and we were allowed in. The desk lady noticed how distraught we looked. She thought about waving and greeting us but chose not to last second. I don't know if I had the energy to wave back if she did.

"It's room eight-o-five," Avery said softly, telling us what room Sky was in. Those were the first words spoken between us this morning.

I was petrified to step foot in the room. I wasn't sure if I was able to look into Sky's eyes if they were in front of me. Her parents were probably there in the room with her. Once I stepped into the room, with small, slow steps. I saw her parents sleeping on the hospital chairs.

"Oh shoot." The dad woke up when he heard our footsteps. "Babe, wake up." He woke up the mom as well.

"Hi, Uncle and Aunt Dezel." Avery greeted.

All of us looked sheepish. Nicole hid her body behind me like I was a pillar.

"Hey, you guys." Mrs. Dezel said, rubbing her eyes to wake herself up.

Both of them stood up and fixed themselves. Both of them had Australian accents.

"Hi..." Nicole and I awkwardly said.

I was half-expecting them to have ill will towards us. I kind of wanted to get scolded by them, since it's kind of our fault their daughter got hurt. But they smiled and greeted us nicely. I couldn't tell if they were faking it or not.

"We'll leave you four alone."

I watched as they stepped out. I realized that this was the first time Sky was seeing her parents in quite a while. I couldn't imagine what any of them were feeling. Your daughter has been across the state for months and one day you get a phone call at three in the morning that she got in a car accident. *What a cruel reunion.* I thought.

Sky was reading a book on the hospital bed, looking seemingly dead inside. I avoided looking her directly in the eyes for the sake of my composure.

There were multiple vertical cuts that appeared across her face, probably from the glass. The only thing that relieved me was seeing her shoulder back in place. But there were random bandages all over her body.

"I heard what happened." Sky said monotonously, speaking about what happened to the rapist. Sky didn't bother looking away at the book.

"We're super sorry Sky," Nicole said endearingly. I looked over at Avery, who was at a loss for words. I put my arm over her shoulder for an attempt at comfort. Her shoulders were freakishly tense.

"It's not y'all fault. Please don't blame yourselves." She placed her book down and sat up. "I still can't believe I allowed myself to drive while I was drunk." Her accent became very noticeable when she seemed depressed.

"Please don't blame yourself, Sky." Avery pleaded. I heard her try to fight back the tears.

"I should've been more alert. That's all I'm saying." Sky clenched the book's spine as some sort of anti-anger mechanism.

"Are you gonna be okay?" Damien asked.

"Yeah, don't worry about me, mate. My doctor said I could be out of here soon."

Everyone in that room smiled at those words, including Sky, but excluding myself.

"Mark?" It took me more than half a second to respond to her.

"Y-yeah?" I responded.

Sky probably saw how non-responsive and spaced out I was. I didn't realize I was like that until everyone looked at me.

"Everything okay mate?" Everyone started to realize that I haven't said a word yet, which didn't seem like that much of an issue till now. I was surprised that Sky paid any amount of attention to me since she was the one who should be receiving all the attention right then.

"Yeah, I'm just beating myself up right now. A lot of what went wrong last night was my fault."

I didn't look up at anyone, rather staring at Sky's bandaged hand that held her book. The tip of her index finger sat between the pages she was reading. It gave my eyes something to look at other than a set of human eyes.

"I should've kept track of you after we left our party. I could've pulled you out of the grenade, Damien. I was the one who saw him pull it out and didn't say anything until it was too late. I was the one who turned the car around, letting him get away." I was spilling my guts here. I couldn't wrap my mind around why no one seemed to be mad at me for one or multiple of the reasons I said.

"Mark..." Damien uttered, probably at a loss for words.

"Mark, you probably saved our asses last night. If you didn't turn around, we could've gotten ourselves killed." Nicole put her hand over my shoulder and talked to me like this was a pep-talk. "I'm being serious."

"Yeah, he's right." Avery and Damien said simultaneously. Then they looked back at each other and awkwardly smiled. I forgot those two have a history. That didn't matter today, though.

"Thanks, guys." I was warmed by their words, but the warmth was very temporary. It was like turning on a small heater in Antarctica.

We all hugged, including Sky, who was sitting up on her bed. The nice hug was telling everyone that the troubles were over. The joy of the holidays was telling us that as well. A lot of signs pointed to this being the end of it. We saved the girl's life in a dramatic end scene and the main characters are alive and well. It all seemed too perfect, like a storybook ending. But there was a little speck of discomfort in my heart, knowing it wasn't over.

We hugged for a long minute until Sky gently pushed us away. Everyone was in genuine, wide smiles. I haven't seen a smile that wide from everybody, including Nicole, in a long time. I forced myself to smile back. I should be happy. Therefore, I tried to be.

"Mates, I need to sleep. My doctor gave me some strong sleeping medicine this morning. I'll text you guys when I'm out of the hospital." Sky gave Damien a large pat on the back.

We all left the room with seemingly smiling faces. I say seemingly, because Nicole and Damien were happy, while I was indifferent. There was still unfinished work to be done. How are they content with everything? We can't just end everything like that, right?

Even if my mind was playing tricks on me. It kept forcing me to think of him, and him only. I was trying to tell myself that it wasn't him. My obscure sense of justice was pointing in his direction. It's the most far-fetched thing in the world, but it was the only direction that seemed to fit.

Sky's parents waved to us as we left. I assumed they were gonna stay in the hospital until Sky was discharged.

"Mark," Nicole called out to me. I was spaced out again like usual.

"Yeah?" I looked up at Nicole for once. These were the first set of eyes that I actually focused on today, instead of looking away.

"The three of us are gonna get some breakfast. Do you wanna come with?" I checked my watch. It was barely eight in the morning.

"Yeah, and maybe, we can drop some off to Sky." Damien added.

"Nah, you guys go'on ahead. I'm gonna catch up on some sleep. I didn't get any last night, y'know?" I responded.

"You sure? We're going to Nico's. Nicole told me that's your favorite place." Avery mentioned.

"Yeah, you sure?" Nicole added. I was slightly overwhelmed by these sudden episodes of attention.

"Maybe next time, when I'm not on zero hours of sleep." I joked, trying to make my mood seem a little lighthearted.

"Okay, see ya man." The three of them took off.

Mark: December 21

Sky texted us this afternoon that she was let out of the hospital. That text took a lot of weight off my shoulders. If something was *really* wrong with her, I wouldn't know what to do with myself. Though the scars and bruises on Sky will always be a reminder.

After I got home yesterday, I ended up taking a full sleep rather than a nap. All the exhaustion from everything that happened caught up to me and I passed out for twelve hours. My mom asked if I got drunk or something. I had to use Nicole as a testimony for my defense. Although, I would rather admit to being drunk rather than admitting what we did that night.

Even though I basically inverted my sleep schedule, it gave me a chance to read more of Lilith's diary. I've read it enough to the point where guilt doesn't even enter my mindscape anymore. It felt like I was reading an actual book, except the characters felt more real than anything.

Whenever I watch a movie or read a book, I constantly remind myself that the situation/emotions aren't real, because they're made up for story purposes. This diary is not. It is real human emotions written by the person feeling them. It was hard to wrap my mind around.

I read the diary the entire night, very slowly, to pick up every subtle detail she left. The part about the cameras in her brother's room still bothered me a ton. There was definitely more to why Lilith did that. Reading between the lines didn't answer that question for me. I'm pretty sure I read those sets of paragraphs nine times over until I gave up trying to figure out a reason.

What the fuck is going on? I thought to myself. There was no theory in the book that could excuse putting fucking security cameras in someone's living quarters. Did Lilith work for the FBI at the age of seventeen? You need to be at least twenty-three to work in the FBI. Was she lying about her age and only *pretended* to attend high school? That was the only semi-logical theory I could come up with.

I kept reading and continued to read between the lines. A puzzle was unfolding right in front of my eyes, but I couldn't see or feel the pieces. A few chapters later, it all unfolds for my brain. Lilith and her dad get into a heated argument about Taylor. <u>"HE'S FAMILY HUH? DO YOU KNOW WHAT FAMILY DON'T DO? THEY DON'T RAPE THE ONLY PERSON THAT HAS EVER UNDERSTOOD ME RIGHT IN FRONT OF MY EYES!"</u>

I read that line over and over and over until I randomly slammed the whole notebook shut, making it fall off my bed.

I fucking knew it. At that moment, you *couldn't* convince me that Taylor wasn't the guy.

I almost couldn't believe it for a second. That the sister of the guy we've been hunting down *happened* to be Lilith. And I *happened* to see her in Atlanta at the star festival and she *happened* to give me her notebooks that had the answer on the 48th page of her diary. It was all too perfect.

I had a hail mary plan all thought out in my head. I sat in bed, eyes parallel with

the ceiling, thinking it all out. It wasn't complicated, but it would cleanse me of my suspicions. Either confirming or debunking everything that I've said about Taylor. I was desperate to have all or any number of questions answered.

That afternoon, I left the house, preparing myself to do something incredibly stupid. I sat in my driveway for a while, trying to mentally prepare myself. I eventually stepped on the gas and there was no turning back. basically. I was on my way to Lilith's house. I had to search the diary for Lilith's last name and then search for where she lived. Creepy, but necessary.

I parked a house and a half away from Lilith's house. Her house almost glowed at me when it was in my field of view. It was like in a video game where the checkpoint would be outlined by something. I took another breath before stepping out of my car. I couldn't believe what I was doing, but I was doing it, anyway.

I went around the exterior of her house, trying to locate her room. I was scared her neighbors would see me, so I tried to not look suspicious. But peeking through someone's window definitely looked suspicious. I specifically remembered what her room looked like based on what she wrote in her diary.

"Mine was painted a very light pink which wasn't noticeable at first, but after being in the room for more than three minutes, I felt like I was surrounded in a very chewed bubblegum."

I squinted through every window, looking out for a pinkish room. There were definitely people in the house, so I had to be on high alert. I found the pinkish room, eventually. After looking at it from multiple angles, Lilith wasn't in her room. Seeing a pink room gave me a confidence boost.

I took a deep breath, and I opened her window from the outside. Almost all the houses in Macon have a surprising amount of security weaknesses, including the windows.

Luckily, this town was pretty much crime-free. I definitely wasn't helping that cause, though.

I softly tiptoed around her room, trying to find her laptop with all the footage on it. According to her diary, all of her security cam footage was living on her laptop. I looked under her bed, at her desk, and all around her room. My chest was pumping like I shouldn't be here. My chest was tight, but my brain knew I was doing this for a good reason, and that's all the justification I needed.

I looked at Lilith's door and it was shut on itself. If that wasn't closed, then this whole thing would be way harder. I found the white laptop in her closet. That was the spot I would've least expected. I figured she wanted to hide it since her dad shamed her for its existence. I grabbed it and then tried to make a run for it. Suddenly, I heard the door behind me open. I cringed inside when I heard the doorknob crack itself. My whole body froze.

"What the fuck? What are you doing here?" Her voice-activated so many emotions inside of me. That same voice had so much mystery behind it. It sent a familiar void-like feeling down my body like a wave.

Lilith walked in with a bowl of fruit and one of the pieces of fruit in her hands. She dropped that one piece of fruit on the floor when she saw me.

My body was frozen. I could've easily made a run for it. The window was open. Lilith and I held a breath to ourselves while looking stunned at each other. The laptop was firmly in my hand. Time stood still for a few seconds. The tension around us was tight. I could cut it with a knife.

"What I should've done long ago..." I said softly. I exhaled with authority.

I broke our eternal staring contest. My body released itself from being frozen, and I made a dashing attempt out the open window.

"Wait!" Lilith pleaded.

She stepped one foot forward and reached her arm out towards me. I had one leg out the window as well as the laptop. I was half free, but the other half took control and made me freeze again. There was nothing I could do to unfreeze, so I turned around to see Lilith not making any attempt to stop me. She didn't grab me or anything. Our eyes locked again. Seeing her up close installed more emotions in my system. It wasn't good or bad.

"Stop him, please," Lilith uttered in her words. She looked at me dead in the eye, but it wasn't exactly intense. It was intense without leaving me on the edge of my seat.

My mind had to double-take to process what she meant. We had another staring contest, with our breaths on hold. When I figured out what she meant, all I could do was smile and almost laugh.

"You have my word." I closed with that. The other half of my body leaped out of her window. I made sure to not look back. I kept the smile on my face as if Lilith planted it there herself.

When I got in my car, I opened the laptop immediately. There was no password in there, thankfully. It was like Lilith wanted someone to get inside of this thing. I opened the program which the footage had. The first thing I saw was Taylor's face. His sick, disgusting face. It was low quality, but it was incredibly clear to me who that was. Nothing disgusted me more than seeing that man walk on two legs and live a normal life. There was no doubt in my mind that I found what we've been looking for.

Mark: December 24

It never snows around here in Georgia. The cold weather was enough for everything to feel festive, though. The best thing about cold weather is that you somehow wake up feeling incredibly warm and you never want to leave the bed. I guess that was the added effect of having no school, but it all leads back to Christmas. Last night I took an amazing stroll around some plazas just to admire the decorations. I was able to surround myself with festive energy. The colorful decorations, the prop up snowmen, God I love them.

On the contrary, I felt unsafe walking alone at night. I almost felt forced to bring a knife with me when I went out. I've never felt unsafe in my own town. I guess that was the price to pay by involving myself with dangerous people.

Sky called me the other day and told me she wanted to spend Christmas Eve with the group, so her parents drove her back to Nicole's place for the day. I already expected for Sky to not return to Macon to be with us, either because of her injuries or her parents, but hearing her enthusiasm to come back made me both worried and relieved. It was definitely a surprise.

Nicole told me that everyone was just going to buy a gift for one person, so each person would get just one gift. I was told to buy a gift for Damien, and I'd be receiving a gift from Nicole. I remembered seeing a lot of Lego sets in Damien's room, so I went to the Lego store at the mall and bought the first thing I laid my eyes on. It was a mini Death Star set.

Everyone was in Nicole's room when I arrived. I didn't get the memo that we were all arriving early, like when we visited Sky at the hospital. As soon as I walked, everyone seemed happy to see me. The sudden mood change of everyone was extremely refreshing. I was always happy to be around these people, but when we're together, the subject is serious. This time I was happy.

It was definitely awkward to face Sky a bit, though. I was still surprised she showed up on her parents' terms, let alone her terms. I told myself that her hospital episode was over and done with, but it still had an effect on my ability to look in her direction. It was like our faces were magnets and we both happened to be positive.

I was very happy to see Sky in good shape. Honestly speaking, I was just happy to see her in a *shape*. The cuts on her face were slowly fading, which only meant healing.

The smile she gave was legitimate, too. There was always an underlying bad aftertaste to her smiles. I've noticed that for a while but never thought much of it. This time, it was a legitimate smile. It's a Christmas miracle, as Damien called it.

Our friend group started to feel normal. It was the most harmonious thing in the world, seeing everyone enjoy themselves. Every laugh and joke someone said made everyone's happiness bar go up, even if the joke wasn't all too funny. It was like we made a friend group through normal means. No one even hinted or mentioned anything relating to the parties or the rapist (Taylor. I have to get used to calling him that)

A few hours in, I started to phase out. I started to deeply ask myself if this was the end. I remember this exact feeling when I was leaving Sky's hospital room. Everything in the room was surrounded by pure happiness. Nicole's room was decorated with red and white Christmas decorations. There was a little fireplace decoration in her room that added more than just warmth. And everyone was in some sort of festive and cute outfit. It was all perfect, too perfect. I could literally envision our situation as a story ending in a movie or something.

It seemed like everyone was happy with the idea of things being over. I haven't mentioned anything to anyone, but if I did, I would find myself being some sort of odd one out. I looked up at everyone as an individual. Nicole was her old, peppy self that I always knew. Damien was happy to see Avery, being the obsessed ex-boyfriend and such. And Sky survived their circumstances in movie fashion.

The laptop I stole from Lilith. Did that mean anything? Or was I just trying to edge to force the ending *I* wanted? Instead of accepting the ending that everyone earned. Our story could end right here and it would be an amazing story. An amazing story I could tell to my children and colleagues. But not amazing to me. I started to question if I should call it quits myself.

"I'm gonna step out real quick. I need some fresh air." I said quietly, interrupting Nicole. Everyone shut up for a second and it allowed for my words to echo. *This feels familiar.*

It was getting increasingly difficult to stay happy in that room with the mindset that I had. I wanted to experience happiness like everyone else, but the story-ending narrative was too overpowering.

Still questioning everything, I went into my car and pulled out Lilith's diary. I hoped that reading it would give me an affirmative answer on whether or not to accept this ending. I was viciously flipping through the pages, hoping to read some drama involving Taylor. Any dirt on him would give me a sign. I was taking a shot in the dark. There was nothing.

In a rush to find something, anything, I fished out Lilith's laptop. Watching Taylor would give me something to reaffirm myself.

"Yo Mark!" Damien started knocking on my car window, which scared the daylights out of me.

"What are y'all doing out here?" I opened my window to see everyone outside.

"I forgot that a bit of my family was coming over in a few hours, so I need to ask y'all to leave soon," Nicole informed me.

Hey... what the hell are you watching?" I looked to my left and Damien was looking straight into my window, in view of the laptop.

"I managed to find footage of the guy we've been looking for. I've just been studying it to find any clues." I said, trying to pull up the footage.

I didn't think to sugarcoat or even straight up lie to his face.

After I said that, the both of us paused in time. I continued to stare at the footage while Damien stood speechless for a couple of seconds.

"Dude... Why are you doing this?" Damien shoved his hands in his face in disbelief.

"What do you mean? *Why are you doing this*? Our job isn't done yet." I said, extremely defensively. It felt like I was defending everything I represented, along with the investigation.

"Mark, get a clue! I got rid of the tapes the other day. We're fuckin' done with dealing with that guy." He looked at me like I haven't lived a day on earth.

"What's goin' on over here?" Sky ran over when she heard Damien and me arguing.

"Mark is planning our next suicide mission, trying to get one of us killed." Damien walked away from my car in disbelief.

"Mark, what does he mean?" Sky asked, unaware of what we were arguing about.

"I have live security footage of the guy, so we can try catching him more effectively this time." I slammed the laptop shut out of frustration.

"Mark, *please* tell me you're kidding," Nicole said in disbelief.

"We had that guy *pinned* last time. If it weren't for Sky, we would've had him. That won't happen next time." I said firmly. I said, as if Sky wasn't standing right there. When I glanced at her, she looked as if I slapped her in the face.

"It won't happen again because there *won't be* the next time. We're not risking that no matter what kind of footage you have." Damien interjected.

"What do you mean? He's still out there! Probably planning his next victim. He's raped before, he'll do it again! We have to keep trying!" I yelled out of my car. I wanted to smash everything around me at once.

"MARK!" Damien yelled, grabbing my shirt. "Have you not been paying attention to anything that happened? Sky almost got killed! And you're saying you want to risk that shit again? Are you fucking insane?"

I shoved his hand off my shirt. He tried to knock whatever sense he had into me, but I wanted to be stubborn.

"If we just plan better and use the footage-"

"No Mark! You're on your own on this one! The three of us are not willing to risk our lives for some sort of goose chase."

I looked over at the girls and they seemed to agree with him. They were looking into my eyes with confusion instead of Damien. It pained me to see Nicole on the other side of things. It took so long to get her on board with this thing, and it was that easy for her to leave. She was willing to forget it all.

"The heroes don't always win, Mark. You have to accept that." *Heroes don't always win, my ass*. I thought to myself.

I clutched my gear and backed out of Sky's driveway quickly, filled to the brim with frustration. I felt my car roll over a bump on my left tire, followed up by Nicole yelling out in pain. I ran over her foot.

An instinctive wave of guilt came over for half a second, but I was reminded of my frustration. I drove off without looking back at them. I was done hearing what Damien had to say. We weren't listening to what each other had to say, we were just stuck by our opinions like glue. I was convinced that I was the right one in this argument. Their sense of justice and determination was all gone. My respect for them, including Nicole, went down with it. All this proved one thing, though. The story isn't over. It's just getting started. I'm getting the ending that *I* want.

Mark: December 25

"Hey, Taylor."

"Merry Christmas Lilith."

Taylor texted back within five minutes. My heart skipped a beat when I got that text notification on her laptop. Even sending a message gave me chills. It made so much sense and such little sense that Lilith and Taylor were siblings.

"Merry Christmas dude."

I just realized Lilith probably doesn't say things like 'dude'. This made me realize how hard catfishing online might be. Pretending to be someone you aren't, let alone someone of the opposite gender, is almost impossible in my eyes.

"What do you need?" He asked.

I didn't have a plan going into this, to be frank. I just felt like using the anonymity of texting would be the only way of talking to him.

"Are you coming over for Christmas?" I asked, for the sake of conversation. I remember reading that Taylor lived in his college dorm.

"Dad invited me over, but I declined. I wasn't sure if Mason is ready to see me, and you probably aren't the biggest fan of it either." I felt offended for Lilith, but it wasn't aimed at me. Mason was their younger brother, if I remember correctly.

"You should come over. Maybe when Mason goes to bed, but I think it's okay if you come." I couldn't believe how either convincing or unconvincing I sounded as Lilith. Either way, I was proud. I was obviously bad at this, but I read enough about Lilith to know deeper parts of her life. "*Are you sure? I haven't visited in four years, it would be kinda awkward.*" FOUR YEARS?

For a second, I started to feel bad for Taylor. He hasn't visited his family in four years. On top of that, he has a dead mom. It all made him more human-able for a few seconds, reading that text and such.

It was similar to how I felt when I read Lilith. I quickly snapped out of it though. What Taylor did was unforgivable. No amount of dead family members can justify that.

"Me and Dad think it's fine. I just asked him. When do you think you can come over?" I asked.

I was digging myself in a hole. *Fuck.* I wish this was like a video game, where I could press some sort of restart button on this conversation.

"I can come at 11:00 PM at the earliest. I still have some to do some essays, so I can only be there for a bit." Why did he seem so regular? He texted like he didn't rape people.

"I'll tell Dad."

"Thanks, Lilith."

I slammed closed the laptop out of stress.

I forgot to mention that I was allowed to come home for Christmas. Claire called me last night and convinced me to come home. She tried to convince me to come home permanently, but I only agreed for Christmas day.

I wasn't feeling particularly homesick or anything, but when I heard my mom's voice in the background, I had some sort of sudden urge to just *be* home. Her voice-activated some sort of primal instinct to be around family. It didn't matter though, since I would go back after tonight.

Claire picked me around dinner time to come home. When I walked through those doors leading to my house, it was so... surreal. Even seeing my house from the outside was bizarre.

"Welcome home son." My mom greeted me as I walked in. I hated how formal this was. Why was this more awkward than it needed to be? My dad was just standing behind her, wanting to say something, but holding back. We made eye contact, but that was about it.

I just said my hellos and gravitated towards my room.

Stepping into my room was also weird. Everything was weird. You know how you never really smell your room because you're so used to it? Yeah, I think for the first time I actually smelled my own room. It was exactly the same as how I left, except for the shattered monitor part, that is. *I wonder who cleaned that up.*

Later that night, Claire came into my room and yelled at me to come to dinner. I forgot that a bunch of my extended family came over for Christmas. I hope none of them know that I was basically a runaway for the last few months.

I noticed that all the Christmas spirit kind of died out after we all left Nicole's house in a bad mood. Christmas just seemed like a necessary chore instead of a holiday. I was too focused on everything else happening to embrace the holiday.

Avery texted me last night, hearing about Damien and I's little argument. I was glad she wasn't involved or heard anything that was said. She's the one person that shouldn't have to hear anything about Taylor. I was still pissed after everyone resented me for trying to do the right thing. Or at least, it *felt* like the right thing.

Claire pulled me out of my room and I was basically forced to eat dinner with my family. To be frank, I wasn't hungry in the slightest. I just poked at my food, occasionally picking up a small forkful of food to give my mouth something to chew on. I felt like I was rotting at the dinner table.

In a few hours, Taylor is going to show up at Lilith's front door. I was gonna have to do something. *Or was I overthinking it? Did I really have to do something?* My mindscape was a mess. It was the only thing I could hear. The sound of my family and relatives talking drowned itself out.

"Dad," I called out to him. He sat across the table from me, so I basically interrupted everyone's conversation. I couldn't care less.

It was the first time I talked to him in a while. There was tension when we locked eyes.

"What's up?" He took a swig of his water.

"Can we talk in private for a second?" I said, grit in my voice. Mom and Claire looked at me with concerned eyes. I think they knew something was coming.

"Sure...?" I walked him into the living room with him. He tried to hide the fact he was irritated by me interrupting dinner. "Is everything okay, son?" I dragged him to the living room. There was a fixed frown on his face.

"Do you have work tonight?" I asked, ignoring his question. I didn't care about any sort of greeting.

"Uhh, no? Why do you ask?" I started to worry that he was connecting the dots in his head.

"Wait then, who works on Christmas then?"

"I have a tenure so I can choose what days I have off before the other workers. I made sure to check off the holidays." He explained.

"Is there any way you can like..." I paused for a second, trying to find a way to word my question as unsuspectingly as possible. "Come with me somewhere in your police uniform? With some handcuffs and a gun preferably." He paused for a second, trying to process the question, checking if he's dreaming or something.

"Mark. What's going on dude?"

When my dad says 'dude', something is wrong. He uses my language to get to me. A father tactic.

"This is the first time you've been home, and that's what you asked me? What's going on?" He asked, more aggressively than the other time.

"I-I." I paused. "Nothing," I said ashamedly. I prepared myself to receive some sort of scolding for the shitty response I gave. It was the only response I could've given. Once again, I had nothing planned, and some cracks were showing.

"Then no, I'm going with you anywhere. End of conversation. Go enjoy Christmas with your family."

After he left, I just realized there was festive Christmas music on our speakers. In any other situation, I would absorb the happiness of the music into my soul. This time, there was no happiness to be sucked. Jingle Bell Rock, Winter Wonderland, Sleigh of the Bells, it might as well be funeral music.

I poked at my food for a few more minutes until I couldn't take it anymore. I started to actually feel sick. Even my stomach was telling me that this isn't how things are supposed to be.

"Mom? Can I go to my room for the night? I think I ate *something* earlier, but I don't feel well." I asked my mom. Once again, in front of everyone.

"What did you eat?" my mom asked concerningly.

"I think I tasted a little undercooked chicken earlier." I surprised myself with how convincing that lie was.

"Okay, you should head in for the night then. Good night sweetie."

Everyone in my family said good night to me and put a queasy look on my face before walking to my room. I didn't dare look in my dad's direction, in case he was shooting me death stares. He probably saw right through me but didn't want to make a scene in front of everyone. If the family wasn't here, he'd definitely say something.

I laid down on my bed, head parallel to the ceiling, stuck in thought. What was I thinking about? I couldn't tell if my mind was blank or moving at one hundred miles per hour. My room was pitch black. The only thing illuminating it was the cracks of moonlight that shined in between my blinds.

I looked at my watch. It was 10:30. It felt like 6:30, though. Time was crucial, yet it felt so unimportant. That meant I was losing determination. The last thing I needed. Out of desperation, I picked up Lilith's diary. It was sitting on my nightstand from past reading sessions with it. I opened it to a random page. I split it down the middle, actually. *"YOU WEREN'T THERE DAD! THREE YEARS AGO! YOU DON'T KNOW WHAT IT FELT LIKE WHEN I WAS GENUINELY WORRIED I WAS GOING TO DIE THAT DAY! TESS DIDN'T DESERVE WHAT TAYLOR DID TO HER!"*

I read that line multiple times. Lilith's yelling voice echoed throughout the chambers of my brain. *How powerful.* I thought. I didn't know the context by any means, but I felt the emotion through the fibers of the paper.

I couldn't sit still, knowing that my ending was out there, calling out to me. I started to feel claustrophobic in my own house. The walls were closing in on me. There was a timer ticking down in my head.

I dashed out of my room. My dad's office called out to me. I ran to his room as well. Suddenly, I remembered his gun. My dad always kept a pistol in his drawer in his office in case of a break-in. He always warned Claire and me to only use it if absolutely necessary.

I left the house, heading towards Lilith's, gun in pocket. I snuck out through my window, the same way I left Lilith's house. There was still time until Taylor was supposed to arrive. Even now, I still didn't have a thought-out plan like I usually had. That was the type of behavior that could get me killed, but I was ready to die. My blood flowed like this was my last on earth.

I texted the group chats with everyone. I'm surprised Damien, the person who started the chat, hasn't removed me by now. Nonetheless, I told everyone that I was finishing this once and for all. I sounded dramatic, but that's how I felt about what I was about to do. The idea of being a lone wolf motivated me rather than discouraged me.

My hands held the gun. I held it firm, with a smile on my face. The feeling of the gun in my hand was powerful. The freezing cold steel of the gun provided me with a sickening warmth. This is what true power feels like, not running away from anyone or anything.

Mark: December 26

"The jig is up buddy."

My voice was shaky as all could be. Taylor's headlights illuminated the front side of my body. It felt so badass. Holding the gun towards his face and looking at his stunned face. Fear and satisfaction entered my body in this mutated form.

"Wait, how did you know I was coming here?" He shoved the hair over his eyes.

aside. His voice sickened me to my core. Seeing his face had the same effect, but hearing *that thing* speak human words with his human voice disgusted me.

"That's none of your business. All that matters is that you have a gun straight at your head. Now put your fuckin' hands up." I said firmly. I made sure he stepped out of his car before I ran upon him. I was not willing to participate in another car chase. He puts his arms straight in the air.

"Where're your fuckin' friends at? Isn't there like four of you guys?" He asked with defeat in his voice. That was enough to put some confidence in my heart.

"Not here." I awkwardly gulped. "I can do this by myself," I said with an unnecessary amount of pride in my voice.

"They abandoned you, huh?" He made the slightest grin, slight enough to piss me off. "I guess that makes sense." The grin grew like he was proud of what he accomplished. His lack of fear in his voice made me tense. I tightened my grip on the pistol. That didn't seem to faze him though.

"What do you know?" I tried to sound tough, but it sounded incredibly artificial. The only thing making me tough was the trigger laying on my finger.

"I know how that feels man." He looked up at me with sympathizing eyes. Even with a gun barrel staring him in the eyes, he had the audacity to look at me with wittiness. "My family let me go at the age of seventeen. I was still in high school." Taylor talked slowly like he was truly reminiscing about his life. He casually looked at his nails like they reminded him of a memory.

He started pacing around the car with his hands in the air. It bothered me how unfazed he was. I followed his movement with my gun, so he didn't try anything funny. If he got near me, I would back up. I wasn't tired, but my breaths started to get heavier.

"You can probably assume why I was kicked out, but that shit hurts, y'know? I thought I was the most badass, independent kid in the world when I was on my own. But I was just a seventeen-year-old kid. I had no *fuckin* clue what I was doing!" He started to laugh. The fucker laughed. He looked at me and saw how irritable I looked. I couldn't help but seem on-edge. My shoulders stood up on their own.

I wanted to press the trigger so damn badly, but something my body wouldn't let me. It would be so easy. Shoot him while he's distracted, and he dies. Everything is over and done with and I finally get the ending I wanted. "I have a feeling you're experiencing the same thing. It's written all over your face, dude. You and I are not that different."

I loosened my grip on the gun momentarily, along with the muscles needing to hold myself up. His words made me think hard for a second. His 'story' lines up with Lilith's journal pretty well. He was telling the truth. All of that made him seem more human. For a second, he wasn't the monster that he made himself out to be.

"NOW!" Taylor yelled. His expression did a whole 180.

"What?" I heard something from behind run up to me. By the time my ears picked up anything, it was too late. A large man grabbed the front of my neck and tackled me to the floor. I shockingly pulled my trigger. The bullet didn't hit anything, and the recoil from the gun was powerful enough to send the gun flying. The sky was as dark as it could be. There were no stars in sight. I couldn't see a damn thing.

"Taylor! Get out of here!" The man said. From the way he spoke, I could tell it was Lilith's dad, by how she described his voice. He put me in a chokehold.

"Dad? What are you doing? Stop!" Lilith's voice echoed from afar. I was still trying to wrestle Lilith's dad off me. He was bigger and stronger than me, it was like pushing a boulder.

"Lilith, stay out of this! Call the police." Lilith ran over to us and stood above our bodies. The only thing that my eyes allowed me to see was her torso and everything above that. She looked frozen in time. "This is a bad man!"

Trying to think quickly, I bit down on the dad's arm. He let out a loud, painful scream, which prompted me to bite down harder. I gradually sank my teeth deeper into his skin. My jaw was starting to rumble from the pure force I was biting at. I still had no idea where Taylor was or what he was doing. That idea scared me.

Lilith reached down and picked up the gun. She put her arm up and her body stood firm. I couldn't see clearly, but her eyes looked down at us in a certain way.

She slowly aimed the gun at us. I couldn't believe what my eyes were seeing. This time, I was the one looking straight into the gun barrel. I was used to seeing death stare me in the face. But when Lilith played the role of death, it left me terrified, down to my bones.

"SHOOT HIM LILITH!" The dad held me as still as possible. I was frozen from pure shock in the first place, so it didn't take much to hold me still. His tightened chokehold stopped my breathing. I literally wasn't able to breathe, no matter how hard I tried. Yet, the thing I was focused on was the gun.

"... I'm not aiming at him, Dad..." Lilith let out an audible gulp and started tearing up. She shifted the aim away from me and aimed the barrel to my left where the dad was laying.

"Lilith, what are you doing? Fucking shoot him already!" I heard Taylor complain. His voice traveled from outside of his car. He was watching this all unfold and refused to do anything. *Fucking pussy. Can't even protect your own family if your life depended on it, literally.*

"STAY AWAY FROM ME TAYLOR! DON'T YOU *DARE* COME ANY CLOSER!" Lilith screamed out. Her face went wild. She wasn't looking at me, but I felt the energy of her emotions from where I was. She immediately aimed the gun at him. That allowed for the dad and me to loosen up and I was able to breathe again. Lilith was trying to force anger and hate through her words, but her tears acted as an emotional threshold. Tears were racing down her face like they had an agenda of their own.

"Dad, you better get your hands off him or I swear to my mother in heaven I won't hesitate to shoot." Lilith cocked the gun with intent as she looked down at her dad. "I lost a parent already, I'm not afraid to lose another," Lilith commanded, forcing her words through her teeth. Lilith moved her aim to Taylor again. She already put her dad at gunpoint with her words. I looked at the dad, who seemed more scared for his life than I ever could. He fully believed her words, and I did, too. He fully loosened the chokehold on me.

I managed to get to my feet. I was still shaken up from not being able to breathe for a long time. I almost forgot where I was for half a millisecond. When reality came back, I heard Taylor behind me scramble to his car.

"Hey!" Lilith yelled, reaching out her arm. It was too late, though. Taylor revved his engine before taking off. Lilith randomly shot at his car, hoping to hit something. The bullets hopelessly missed, though. At that moment, it was clear to me whose side Lilith was on. That made me smile a bit.

"Lilith, stay here. I'll go after him." My voice had its own form of determination. I didn't want to lose. That feeling of not being afraid to die started to enter my body again.

After being at gunpoint by Lilith, I knew that there was nothing else that could scare me. "Take this, it tracks my car. If you need my location, open it up." I threw my tracker at her and she threw the gun at me. We were eye to eye on what to do. I felt like I could telepathically communicate something and she would get it.

Once again, I could only see Taylor's car by following his tail lights. Whenever I inched closer to him, little doses of dopamine entered my system. It was late at night in Macon, Georgia. There were little to no cars on the road with us. It was just me versus Taylor. But it felt like me versus the world. I bore the weight of everyone on my shoulders. It wasn't just me fighting for myself at this point.

I checked my speedometer: 80 MPH. This was way faster than the last time I was chasing Taylor. The difference between 60 and 80 MPH couldn't be more different. The car was moving so fast that I thought I was going to lose control and crash. I held on to the wheel tightly. My life literally depended on maintaining control of my vehicle.

Taylor took a sharp turn onto the highway. The rubbery part of his tires screeched on the road. The entirety of Macon probably heard them scream.

So, it's this little game again. Taylor races on the highway again, trying to lose me. I've been through this story before. The vivid memory of me deciding to not go on the highway forced itself into my mindscape. It played itself in black and white, like a flashback. I couldn't help but feel regretful in some wicked way.

I made sure this time to follow Taylor onto the highway. My turn was sharper than his, my speed was faster than him, and I had a full head of steam. The highway was completely cleared. The lack of cars and light made the scene almost pitch black.

Since we were driving in a straight line, I took the opportunity to fire at his car. I opened my window and randomly shot at his car. The recoil from the shot was indescribable. All the bullets ended up ricocheting off his car and not doing any damage. It seemed like this chase was never going to end. Whenever I seemed to speed up, he got even faster. My speedometer was reaching its limit. My car was not used to the speed and started to vibrate. Suddenly...

"MARK!" a girl's voice called out. It was a familiar voice. Without even processing who it was, a gram of hope entered my heart. I looked to my left. It was a car. Who was driving the car? Nicole Schmidt. Once again coming to my rescue. I almost shed a tear from the sight of her. "Is that him?" Nicole yelled from her car.

Our cars were parallel to one another, in their own lane. The speed of our cars almost made her voice inaudible. The wind was slicing some of her words out of existence. I could barely hear her.

"Yeah!" I yelled back. Taylor noticed the presence of two cars chasing him, so he slammed on the gas even more. "Where's Sky and Damien?" I yelled into the wind.

"THEY'RE ON THEIR WAY! DON'T WORRY!" Nicole responded, implying that multiple people were coming.

The feeling of abandonment went away quickly. As badass as it felt to be the lone wolf, having people by your side was inexplicably better.

Taylor kept going faster and faster. I gently tried to speed up, but my car started to drive itself out of control momentarily. I bumped Nicole's front tire a bit and the both of us took some knockback. I maintained control after a second, but there was no way I could go any faster than I already was. My car was at its limit.

"Can you catch up to him? My car can't go any faster!" I pleaded with Nicole. I was desperate to make sure he didn't have a chance of getting away. The further he drove out of my sight, the bigger the void in my heart would grow.

"YOU GOT IT!" Nicole confidently said before zooming ahead of me. Her car had further limitations than mine. The engine of her car roared loudly before being parallel with Taylor. I managed to stay behind them enough to be in view of them. I thought about shooting Taylor's car again with the remaining bullets I had, but I didn't want to risk Nicole.

Their cars were neck and neck. If Taylor sped up, so did Nicole. If he slowed down, Nicole made sure to match it. It was like watching two animals of the same species battle it out in the wild. At this point, I was just a spectator.

Nicole managed to inch ahead of Taylor. I could tell both their cars were reaching their limitations. Nicole got overzealous and tried speeding up further. This sent her car into a frenzy and all hell broke loose. Nicole bumped her front into Taylor's and now both of their cars went out of control. Both their cars swerved all over the place, ignoring the lane lines. Both of them kept bumping into each other. *This is bad.*

In the back of my mind, I knew one of their cars had to give up, eventually. No amount of hope could distract me from this reality. I held my breath, knowing that something completely tragic was going to happen.

As a last-ditch attempt, trying to finish what *I* had started, Nicole tried to cut off Taylor in the same lane as him. The sound of her engine roared as loud as ever. Taylor was taken by surprise and back-ended Nicole's car. It wasn't just a bump, this was a collision. Nicole and Taylor both spun out of control and crashed into the side of the road.

A loud *crash* sound filled the chambers of my ears and made my reflexes cringe. A ton of car parts and random rubble flew in every direction. One crash sounded louder than the other, but I couldn't tell whose car took the short end of that stick.

Their cars came to a complete stop. I put an immediate break to my car and jumped out of it with my gun. Smoke came out of their cars, followed by Taylor's car alarm. I bolted my way towards Nicole's car. I held another breath, not ready to see if Nicole survived the crash.

My heart tensed itself up as I put my hand over the door handle. I did a little prayer in my head before checking her door. She might as well have disappeared from my sight because my eyes couldn't believe what they were seeing. Nicole laid limp over her airbag. Her arms drooped below her shoulders, facing away from me. I dropped the gun from pure shock.

"NICOLE! CAN YOU HEAR ME?" I grabbed both her shoulders and made her head face mine. There was blood flowing out of the bottom of her mouth. "NICOLE! PLEASE!" I began to shake her body, trying to force some life into her. Tears immediately ran down my face when I looked into her eyes. Her eyes were slightly open, but they were devoid of all life. I couldn't tell if I was looking at a human being anymore. Her body was lifeless. A body with no host. A soulless character. "PLEASE!" I cried out. My vision began to water up. I continued to shake Nicole's body, but it was no use.

"This is the end of the line pal." I slowly turned around and something sharp jabbed into my stomach. I didn't even feel pain, but a feeling of doom. That was more painful than any stab. My muscles began to give themselves up. My legs collapsed, followed by the rest of my body. I felt my body begin to shut itself down. My vision began to turn black. All I was, at that moment, was a breathing pile of mistakes, waiting for the world to close in on me.

Lilith: My last entry cont.

I didn't have time to explain anything to Dad. My brain was rushing itself while trying to process everything. The way Mark looked me in the eyes, it was nostalgic. Sadly, it wasn't good nostalgia. It was the opposite of good, frankly. The only other time I've seen someone look at me with those eyes was with Taylor. That boy wanted Taylor dead. That was a fact, not wasn't speculation. Something inside of me wanted Taylor dead as well, but that was an internal conflict that I didn't want to have.

I ran inside to grab the keys that were in my room. Dad was still trying to ask me questions and or yell at me. I couldn't tell, to be honest, probably yell at me, since I threatened him at gunpoint. As soon as I grabbed my keys, I made a dashing attempt out of the house. But something looked me in the eyes when I tried to leave my room.

"Lilith..." Mason's eyes somehow met mine. He was sitting in the darkness of his room. The only thing I could see was the whites of his eyes. It got me to freeze in my tracks.

"Yeah, what's up?" I responded as calmly as one could. I was out of fucking breath from everything that just transpired, so it was hard to sound sane.

"Was that Taylor? I heard his voice." Mason's voice went all innocent-like. He was scared of *something*, but there were too many variables to point to one particular thing.

"Uh, yes. That was him." My body was racing to go, but I wasn't physically capable of running away from Mason, no matter how dire everything seemed.

"Are you gonna go protect him from that man?" The whites of Mason's eyes started to glisten.

"I can't ensure anything, Mason," I said in full honesty, which was another way of bending the truth. *I'm sorry, Mason.*

"Promise Lilith. Taylor is going to be okay, right?" His voice started to be enveloped by tears.

Why did Mason suddenly care about Taylor? Taylor has spent more time out of Mason's life than in it. And from what little he knows of Taylor, it isn't very good. I paused for a second, trying to decide if I wanted to make that promise.

"I'm going to try damn hard, Mason." *I'm sorry, Mason.*

I bolted out before he even thought about a response. The instinct to cry again came over me. I told that instinct to fuck off. I told myself there was no time to cry. Mark was either going to kill Taylor or die trying.

I hopped into my car. Before turning it on, I pulled up Mark's tracker. I opened it and it read: 'Mark's car'. I was a bit shocked to see he actually had a name. For the entire time, I referred to him as 'guy' or 'boy' in these diary logs. There was finally a name for the face.

It gave me the option to track Mark's car, and I almost clicked the *no* option because of how much I was freaking out. I put the tracker on my dash and just followed the red dot on the screen that indicated where Mark was.

I've never driven at a speed where I needed to worry about hitting things, so reaching anything above fifty MPH was anxiety-inducing. Although, no matter how quickly I drove, I still couldn't match Mark's speed. I knew he was on the highway, but he was driving at an illegal rate. I was relieved by the idea that he was still alive, driving the car, and not dying to my brother.

I made it to the highway and forced myself to pump the gas as fast as my morals would allow me to. It was about 80 MPH. The faster I got, the more tense my body got. I tried not to think about not crashing this car, but when you tell your brain to *not* think about something, it's obviously going to think about it.

The red dot on the tracker came to a stop. *Fuck*. Either that or the GPS part of its system somehow broke within all that speed. After staring at the phone for five seconds and not looking at the road, I knew the car had come to a stop. I imagined the millions of things that could've happened. None of them we're good. To be frank, it's hard to imagine any of this ending nicely. This was one of those events where you know something is going to go wrong no matter how well executed it could go.

I caught up to Mark's car eventually, which was truly at a stop. That only relieved me slightly. It was stopped on the side of the road. I looked to the left of Mark's car and there were two crashed cars, one of them being Taylor's car. *Spark*.

I ran out of my car to get a better view of the situation. The smell of gasoline, fire, and fresh air punched me in the face. Taylor's car alarm was going off like crazy. Once I got close enough to vividly see the cars, I heard someone say something.

"This is the end of the line pal." It was extremely quiet, but I knew whose voice it was. I walked towards the voice. Once I was twenty feet from one of the crashed cars, I saw Taylor's head looking down at something. His head was smiling at something like he was proud at whatever he was looking at. My brain connected a little of the dots but refused to acknowledge any theory.

"Taylor," I said quietly.

"Lilith-" He immediately heard my voice. I'm surprised he heard me talk over the car alarm. I think he noticed my presence rather than what I said. He started to act very defensive. I couldn't see what was on the other side of the car, but I knew it wasn't good. My leg started to quiver like they knew what was coming.

"Taylor. What the fuck did you do...?" I asked firmly and with tears in my eyes. I know I said I wouldn't cry, but I was petrified to find out what was on the other side.

Taylor paused himself for a second, trying to either regain or lose his sick smile. He then made a hand motion to suggest that I'd come over there myself. It was only like four feet away from me, but I felt like dimensions separated us and we were just somehow communicating through some sort of portal.

I slowly walked over to his side of the dimension. The car alarm was louder over here, the air was thicker and the feeling was dead. I kept peering my eyes away as I walked further into the dimension. I smelled blood, a lot of it. The cold air plus fresh blood did not smell pleasant.

I finally jerked my head to look down at what Taylor was looking at. As soon as my eyes recognized who and what I was looking at, I felt like God himself shot an arrow through my heart.

"YOU KILLED THEM?" I yelled, grabbing Taylor's shirt, and yanking at it. I looked back to make sure I wasn't fucking seeing things. But if my eyes served me correctly. There are two motionless bodies in front of us. There was a familiar-looking girl hanging over the car's airbag and Mark laid flat on stomach, his shirt being dyed in his blood.

"LILITH! THEY WERE GOING TO KILL ME! I HAD NO CHOIC-" Suddenly, I heard the sound of a car coming closer to the scene. Taylor started freaking out. "OH FUCK"

"Taylor, hide in the bushes. I'll distract them!" I quickly yelled.

Taylor proceeded to jump and run into some bushes next to us. Their headlights started to close in on me, illuminating me. I picked up Mark's gun off the floor to use as protection. Two people, a guy, and a girl, came out of the car. I quickly aimed my gun at them. My shoulders were still trembling at the sight of Mark's motionless body.

"YO! Relax! We're not gonna hurt you!" The guy tried to calm me down. It was obvious that I was freaked out about something. The combination of flowing tears and sweat made that apparent. I still held my gun forward at them. It was the only thing that my brain commanded me to do. *Survive, survive, survive.*

Without saying anything, I motioned for the two of them to come next to me. The girl looked terrified at the sight of me. But she immediately ran over beside me to peek over at the dead bodies. I couldn't look at it anymore without wanting to cry even more.

"OH MY GOD!" The girl with the Australian accent quickly looked away, screamed, and immediately started crying. I lowered my gun.

"Sky, what is it?" The guy asked, starting to freak out on his own. The girl continued to bawl her eyes out. The guy went over to peek and his jaw dropped. "H-HOW DID THIS HAPPEN!" The guy said in disbelief. The girl started to cry her own storm.

"I don't know! I was driving by and found them lying here!" I lied.

It was the first thing I thought of to distract them from Taylor. I looked over at the bushes, and Taylor was still hiding for his life.

"You guys need to take them to the ER! NOW!" I commanded.

Both of them immediately went to pick up their bodies. The guy had a look on his face like he was about to cry, but had to power through everything. The girl was already crying. The sound of her crying matched the sound of the beeping car alarms.

It was hard to look at their bodies being carried away like sandbags. The blood from Mark's stomach spilled onto the guy's hands and he started to scream.

"Come on Sky! We need to hurry!" The guy yelled. All of them got in one car with the bodies. The guy started to cry his heart out when he had to carry Mark to the car, seemingly lifeless.

They slammed all the doors and immediately took off in the other direction. The sound of the engine started to dissipate as they got further away from us. I was still trying to catch my breath from the stress.

The reality that Mark might be dead started to settle in. The harsh winds and being surrounded in the dead of night didn't help anything. The weight of that guilt piled onto my shoulders. It made me as stiff as a board. It was hard to stand tall at that moment. My whole body seemed to hurt all over and concentrated in my heart area. All I could do was watch and pray that both of them weren't dead and leave it up to them to get them to the hospital.

"Taylor, they're gone," I said with built-up emotion in my voice.

"Holy fuck, good job." Taylor walked out of the bushes and seemed unfazed by what had just happened.

"A-are you okay? Did they h-hurt you?" I asked, barely able to release the words from my mouth. I felt like there was a weight on the edge of my tongue.

For some reason, even though they were gone, I still held my gun firm. My body didn't loosen up in the slightest. Seeing

Taylor without a scratch of him only made my body tense up more.

`The harsh winter winds continued to cut against us. My hair danced everywhere and Taylor's clothes fluttered in the wind's direction. The more intense the situation grew, the harder the wind blew. It was like nature's way of showing disdain against us.

"No, but that car crash fucked my shoulder up. That girl almost killed both of us, God damn." I heard the sound of him dusting blood off his shirt. It was hard to look at him, let alone in his direction. My eyes were glued to the gun in my left hand. I calmly flailed it around, like it wasn't done being put to use. "Did Dad follow you by any chance? I don't want him to see me like this."

I didn't answer. I bit down on my tongue. The only thing I heard was my own thoughts and the constant sound of car alarms.

"I'm surprised you managed to catch up to us. I thought we were in Alabama by how fast we were driving." Taylor joked. "I'm glad you're okay though." *Shut up, shut the fuck up*. I thought to myself.

He took a step back and encased himself in the environment. He stood in a glorious stance, admiring the work of art that he painted on the world. I held the gun even more firmly. I was squeezing it so hard that I was afraid it would pop out of thin air.

"I'm looking forward to when we can look back on this as adults…" He paused, silencing the world around us. I swear even the winds seemed to cease when he stopped talking. "…and just laugh about it. This can be our little secret, eh?"

My arm started to slowly gravitate upwards. It had a mind of its own. They stopped moving when my arm became the same level as Taylor's head. A feeling of potential regret and unwillingness came over me. It was so strong it made my heart hurt. *Spark.* Except for this time, it wasn't just a spark. The sparks didn't appear. This feeling was too intense for something simple as sparks. It felt a million times more powerful than sparks ever could. I was surprised that I was able to stand on my own two feet.

"Lilith...?" There was an everlasting aura of darkness around him. Instead of looking away, I got the courage to look deep into his character even though he was turned around. The feeling of unwillingness kept coming in waves. It was like a heartbeat that got louder and louder. In fact, it was a heartbeat because it was the sole thing keeping me alive and standing.

Taylor slowly turned around. I haven't moved an inch from where I was standing. When he turned around, he was met with a barrel staring him in the soul. It was satisfying playing the role of death for once, instead of it playing me. But that didn't stop the deadly aura that Taylor gave up. I chose to fight it though. Everything up until now was a fight that I was somehow winning or at least surviving.

"W-what are you doing?" He started to back up slowly. His desperation started to show, mostly in his eyes. I've never seen Taylor's eyes flare like that.

"Give me one *fucking* reason why I shouldn't shoot you in your fucking face," I said with grit in my expression. I made sure to look him dead in the eyes. I wanted both myself and the gun to threaten him. Whenever he took a step back, I took two steps forward.

"Lilith... you can't do this to me. We're family," His voice was mostly air. It blended in with the harsh winds.

"Do you know who else is family? Tess. And look what you did to her?" I said with years of bearing those memories. It was satisfying to release them. "Now that you're on the other side of things, you don't like it, do ya?" I felt powerful knowing my words trumped Taylor's. I wanted Taylor to know how much of a monster he was.

"...." He stood there, trying to process my anger. He's never seen me like this and neither have I. This was a whole new experience for both of us.

"Taylor, I am this close to pulling this trigger, so you better speak the fuck up." I took a big step forward, almost touching his head with the gun. He backed up a few inches.

I remember what it felt like to save Taylor. I couldn't sleep for fucking days after Halloween. I beat myself up for how fucking stupid I was to not give him what he deserved. For the last four years, I wanted to see him dead for what he did to Tess, and I could've done something on Halloween. Now that I had a gun aimed at his face and a finger on the trigger. It was so easy to just press it and be the happiest girl on earth.

"Are you really going to take my life away from our family? How fucking selfish are you, huh?"

He started walking towards me, making me inch backward. The aura followed him as he approached me slowly. My eyes started to replicate his. The world around us flipped.

"If you kill me, do you know how *devastated* Dad would be? What about Mason, huh?" I started to cry profusely. His words felt more abusive than if he hit me. That power I felt started to dissipate.

"Don't you dare bring Mason to this! You damn well know he won't care about you if you die. He's never cared about you and *never will*."

Promise Lilith. Taylor is going to be okay, right? Mason's words started blaring in my head. It became deafening. I tried shaking my head to shake the thought out, but it was latched on. *I lied to Mason's face. So what? Mason doesn't know what Taylor did. Mason doesn't know who*

Taylor is. Mason doesn't know any better. When he grows up, he'll be happy that I killed him.

"Fine then. Shoot me." He opened his arms and waved them. He was asking for it, testing me as a person. "If you think that this world would be better without me in it, and are willing to kill your own brother to protect people that failed to protect themselves, then go ahead."

The sky turned a different color again. Suddenly, my blood felt warm. It soared throughout my body and empowered my every sense. The air I breathed in and out was heavier. This scene felt familiar. *Spark.*

I once again cocked the pistol. I raised my arms one last time and envisioned the bullet going straight through his head. Just envisioning it brought joy to me. Nothing but hate and resent represented my emotions when eyeing down Taylor. It set my heart on fire. The pain was so overwhelming, but so was my desire to kill.

I was fully ready to press the trigger. All it would take was one press of a button and it'll all be over. Taylor was the last beast I needed to conquer in my life. Nothing seemed more satisfying than seeing his head explode from my shot.

"SHOOT ME LILITH! PULL THE TRIGGER!" Taylor screamed, trying to make my ears ring. He embraced the idea of me killing him. He saw all the pent-up rage and bloodlust on my face. His face turned red and his eyes widened. He knew how much I wanted this.

But for some reason, the trigger wouldn't press. My finger muscle refused to press down. It was like there was a wall between my finger and the button. I tried using all the power in my being to press down, but I couldn't. *Spark.*

My heart burned up again. I pressed my other hand against my chest to suppress the pain. It was of no use. Taylor looked at me, still with his open arms, confused at what was happening to me. A ticking clock started to sound in my head.

Each tick resonated in my brain. I didn't know when the clock would stop. It seemed infinite yet limited. I made one last attempt to pull the trigger. Once again, it was of no use. *I'm sorry*. The last tick in my head went off.

"Lilith!" Taylor yelled. My heart gave off one last burn before falling to the floor. My legs gave up... again. Once again, I became entranced by my anger and it brought me to my knees. The world went back to its original color and my blood flowed normally again. I felt like a new person when I transformed back. A better yet worse version of myself.

"Don't touch me, Taylor." I forced through my teeth. I was rushing to get to my feet.

Taylor ran over to me, trying to aid me. With what little strength I had, I aimed the gun at him again. I knew I wasn't able to pull the trigger, but it got him to back off. The muscles in my legs grew non-existent. I had to use my arms to crawl.

"Get away from me Taylor," I said, sounding like I was about to stand up and kill him with my hands.

"Are you oka-"

"I SAID GET AWAY FROM ME TAYLOR!" I screamed. My eyes started to be tinted by my tears. "IF YOU WANT ME TO BE OKAY, THEN GO AWAY! LEAVE GEORGIA! LEAVE THE COUNTRY! IT DOESN'T MATTER! JUST GO BEFORE I CHANGE MY MIND!" I actually felt my life force drain out of my body and lift up into the atmosphere.

My words echoed throughout Taylor's brain, as well as mine. Taylor slowly backed off, then immediately ran to his car. He turned the engine on. I blinked, and he was already on the road. I grabbed the gun again and shot Taylor's car out of hate. The sound of the ricocheting bullet fueled my tears. I shot until there were no more bullets.

I didn't move from the spot I collapsed in. I couldn't get up, nor could I move my legs. I truly hit rock bottom. I was laid down on the side of the road, seemingly trying to drown myself in my own tears. Random cars who acted as passersby probably saw me in my misery and probably thought I was crazy. The sparks went away and Taylor was gone. Once Taylor was out of my sight, I knew he wasn't coming back. If I had the strength or the power, I would chase him using only my legs.

If I somehow went back in time and could relive this whole event again. I knew the result would be the same. Everything inside of me wanted to kill him but didn't know-how.

Mark: December 26: Morning

"NICOLE!" I yelled as I woke up. I jumped up from my bed second I gained consciousness. A team of nurses ran by my side and tried calming me down. All of their words turned into mush, though. My senses were fucked up. I couldn't think clearly. They ended up sounding like aliens. That was enough to convince me that I was in some sort of dream.

"Mark, easy now. Calm down. You're in good hands." Finally, one of the nurses' words made sense to my brain.

I was in a hospital. I realized. Suddenly, a wound on my stomach started to make its painful debut, and it was fucking overwhelming. I writhed in pain all over the place.

"Nancy, get the doctor!" One of the nurses yelled.

This was the most painful thing I ever experienced in my life. It rivaled things like stubbing your toe and getting punched in the dick. I felt like someone was ripping my stomach off by hand.

More medical professionals came in and attempted to calm me down even more. I was freaking out because of my pain, yes, but all the memories started flowing back. Every detail started to pop out at me. The speed of the cars, the temperature of the outside, everything before I blacked out. Nicole's image popped out at me as well. The picture of her lifeless body was as vivid as if she was right in front of me.

Nicole, please hang in there. I prayed, hoping that her life was still hanging by some sort of thread.

After a while, the doctors got me to calm down, and I got injected with a powerful painkiller. It might as well have been anesthetic because it got me to fall asleep almost instantly. Even after I woke up, it still had a strong effect. It basically slowed down all my movement and brain activity. I felt like I was moving and thinking underwater. But I couldn't help but experience a feeling of doom, both incoming and preexisting. This resonated deep within my soul and there was no way I could ignore that, no matter how much or what medicine I took.

"Hey Mark, how are you feeling?" The same doctor from Halloween walked up to my hospital bed. *This was the magical man keeping me alive.* That is what my brain was thinking under heavy medication.

"My wound still hurts a lot. I can't turn my hips without it hurting. Honestly, I'm just surprised that I'm alive." I talked at a fraction of the speed I normally talked at.

"You have your friends to thank. If they arrived even a few minutes later, you had a chance to go into a coma. You would've lost a lot more blood."

He started to write down some stuff on his clipboard. I didn't truly feel the danger of death at that moment since I was medicated, but I definitely felt thankful for the idea of being alive.

"You are a lucky man, you know that? First, you survive a fall, and second, you get stabbed in an area that was the least lethal. The lower quadrant of your abdomen. The blade didn't hit any vital organs."

"Wow really?" I only processed the words: 'lucky man' and 'didn't hit'.

"Yes, that's why we probably don't have to go into surgery, assuming your drainage levels start to go down." At that time, I didn't process any of that, but somehow dopamine got released into my brain.

"Do you know if Nicole is alive?" I interrupted the doctor, explaining my condition.

"Is that your friend that you came with?" The doctor looked up from his clipboard.

"Yeah, is she okay?"

"I don't know Mark. To my knowledge, she was taken to another hospital. You can ask your friends about that one. I hope she's alright though." *I hope so too.*

Mark: December 28

The hospital allowed people to come to see me during visiting hours.

Apparently, both my friends and family have tried visiting me multiple times, even when they knew visiting hours were closed.

My parents came first thing in the morning, even before I woke up. I've been sleeping in three to four-hour intervals because I needed to be woken up to do things like take medicine and do some small tests to make sure I wasn't internally bleeding. But generally, I was always tired no matter what time of the day it was. I think being confined to this one bed and room has contributed to that significantly. I hate to complain, but there really isn't much to do in a hospital. My waking hours consisted of watching whatever was on the TV, which was mostly the news. Other activities included taking twenty minutes to get up to use the bathroom and eating. The constant smell of rubbing alcohol only added to this depressing time.

On the bright side, my doctor assigned me to weaker medicine, since I appeared to be healing pretty quickly and my tests were going well. But that also made it so the wound hurt MUCH more. I wasn't surprised since it was a fucking knife wound, but I never realized how much the earlier medicine was easing the pain.

Anyway, all three of my family came to visit me. They had to sit by my hospital bedside. I felt like the most worthless piece of shit, seeing my mom try not to tear up or say anything egregious in front of my face. They were so distraught that none of them knew what to say.

"So, this is why you needed me, on Christmas night..." my dad uttered.

This whole time I was kind of eyeing my dad to see what he would do. He sat in one of the chairs and seemed like he wasn't able to sit still. I was waiting for him to just explode on me. He was the one person that I didn't need to be around me at that moment.

I didn't know what to say. My jaw kept moving like I was saying something, but no actual words were coming.

"So, this is why you ran away from home!" My dad slammed the table in front of him, spilling my apple sauce. At that point, I was prepared for anything he said. "Why didn't you just tell me? I work for a whole damn police force!" He stood up and got in my face. "You could've died Mark! You could've died!"

"Because y'all weren't doing anything! I'm sorry I had to do the fucking job that you guys get paid to do every day!" I said defensively.

You never get used to swearing at your parents. It didn't feel good, especially since Claire and my mom were here, but it was too late.

"How do you know we aren't doing anything about it? You don't have a clue of what I do at work everyday!" He started waving his hand in multiple places to emphasize his point.

I looked at my mom and Claire and they were tapping him for him to take it down a notch, but my dad forgot they existed.

"And what have you been working on, huh? I've been busting my ass all over Georgia, trying to find this guy. And you have the fucking *audacity* to yell at me!" I was in my dad's face this time. Feeling some sort of power flow in my blood.

"..." His face was turning red by the second.

"Exactly, you haven't been working on it. And you're mad because I wanted to do something about it? Isn't that what you've been teaching me for the past seventeen years?"

"I've had enough of this kid. Babe, I'll be in the car." He stormed out of my hospital room. Apparently, some of the nurses and doctors heard our argument through the wall and their eyes followed my dad as he left.

It was hard to believe this room was quiet one minute prior. Even though the yelling stopped, my ears were ringing with the volume of our argument.

"I should probably check on him." My mom said after a few seconds of silence.

My sister's and my eyes followed her as she left the room. After that, I felt my heart rate go down to normal. I then realized that it wasn't healthy to be in such a state of anger when I'm not far from literally dying.

"I think you did the right thing." Claire blurted. Her eyes were still out the door, even though our mom was out of sight.

"Huh?" I looked at her with one eyebrow raised.

"Sky told me what happened. I really think you should be proud of yourself, Mark." Claire stood up and pushed her hair behind her ear. "I didn't think you'd sacrifice this much for something that seemed impossible."

"He got away though..." I said, monotone.

"Well, be honest, Mark, would you have killed him?" She raised an eyebrow.

I took a few seconds to think, but I slowly nodded, just realizing it myself.

"Then, maybe it's for the best. You would have regretted it for the rest of your life if you killed someone, even if he deserves it."

I thought about that for a minute. Even though what Claire said sounded the most logical, it still didn't feel right. I knew for a fact Taylor deserved death.

"Alright, I have to go to work now and make sure Dad doesn't punch a hole in the car. Hopefully, you two can make up, eventually." Claire patted me on the back. It hurt a bit, but it didn't matter. "Feel better soon, bro."

It made me very happy to see someone, *anyone,* on my side. I know it was just a shitty argument, but it was much more than that for me. I just wanted someone to tell me that I didn't do all of this for no reason. That I wasn't just crazy for wanting to do something right.

I was kind of getting fed up with all my meals having to be in liquid form. I was only allowed to have liquid food. The most solid thing I've eaten were pills and apple sauce if you can even count that as remotely solid.

It was around 7 PM when I woke up from another nap. To be honest, the time of the day didn't matter to me in the slightest. The only thing it affected was how dark or bright it was outside.

As I was being fed my usual dose of applesauce, the group walked in awkwardly. Damien, Sky, and Avery all snuck into my room as quietly as three people could. Damien knocking on the already-open door was the only noise they created.

"Is it a bad time?" Sky asked the nurse who was helping me with my food.

"We were just finishing up. Give me a minute while I clean up." The nurse
responded.

The three of them sat down by my window. Damien looked outside the window, trying to give his eyes something to look at that *wasn't* a boy who was recently stabbed. Sky couldn't help but look at me. Occasionally, our eyes would meet and I would fake a smile at her, but we both knew it was fake. Avery was struggling to sit without having the need to adjust herself every ten seconds.

"We thought you died..." Damien opened up with, the very second the nurse left.

"Damien!" Sky jabbed him in the arm for his blunt opener. I didn't mind all too much, but imagining what they had to go through to save me was intense to think about. I don't blame them for thinking that I died.

"What? I needed to say something. Mark probably knows that better than any of us." Damien defended himself.

"I'm *really* sorry, guys. You don't even know how thankful I feel right now that I'm alive, and all I've done is make things worse." I said softly. It seemed like Sky was about to cry right then and there at my words.

"It's fine Mark. It really is." Avery said with a lump in his throat.

I noticed how differently people talked to you when you're in a hospital bed. They sound like you could just go *poof* any second and disappear out of thin air. I don't blame them, since I would probably do the same thing. Actually, I did the same thing when Avery and Sky were hospitalized. But that whole idea gradually became heavy on my heart.

"You wanted to do the right thing. It's hard to blame you for that." Damien assured me. He was the one who seemed to be the most furious at me a few days ago, so it took me a while to believe him, and he wasn't just saying it for pity.

"We're just glad you're alive mate. If we were just a few minutes late, we could've lost you. I'm glad we showed up when we did." Sky assured.

Sky raised everyone's spirits in the room with that, including herself.

"Have you visited Nicole yet? How is she?" I asked, not even knowing if she was alive or not.

I've been dying to get any information about Nicole. The one thing keeping me awake at night was the memory of her blacked out in her car. That's another image I'll never forget. The lifeless eyes, the motionless body, and the blood coming out of her mouth like a hose.

Damien and Sky awkwardly looked at each other, not responding to my question. The silence sent a doubtful feeling down my spine.

"H-he-h-her-" Sky kept stumbling over her words. Every 'h-' made my doubtfulness multiply by ten.

"Her what?" I interrupted, raising my voice more than I'd like to. The other hospital workers probably heard me yell since the door was wide open. I couldn't handle another second of *not* knowing what was happening to her. My brain has been playing this sick game of theorizing if she was well or not. For fuck's sake, I don't even know if she's alive. Do you know how fucked up that is? I've known her since I was a kindergartener and I don't even know if her soul still resides in her being.

"H-her parents won't allow us to see anything..." Sky finally blurted.

"What? What do you mean?" I leaned up on the edge of my bed.

"We tried visiting her the other night and her parents were in the room with her. They *yelled* at us to get out. We weren't even able to get a look at her." Damien explained.

"I can't believe what I'm hearing right now," I said, speaking out loud.

The pain of Damien's explanation started to overpower the pain of my wound.

"I didn't know they were like *that*," I said with a tone.

"I mean…" Avery paused, trying to review her every word before she said it. "That probably means she's alive, though, right?"

"Yeah Mark, that's probably good news," Damien added.

"I don't know. I just want this sick game to stop. Make it stop, *please!*" I pleaded to *someone*. I don't know who but someone. This felt worse than any wound that could be placed upon my body. I was willing to take another one if that meant Nicole would be alive.

"We're sorry Mark." Sky said, not knowing what else to say.

The two of them embraced me while I sobbed my heart out. I have never cried this profusely in my life. I've seen people cry harder than me, but I never imagined there'd be a low time in my life where I would cry as hopelessly as them.

Mark: January 1

Happy new year! What a year it's been, huh? Let's review the highlights! I graduated junior year, a simpler time, might I add. I almost died three times, almost four times if you count the time Damien kidnapped Sky and me, that was also a simpler time in retrospect.

All of those vivid memories were floating around in my head when the clock struck 12:00. Having so many negative memories in my head at once was unhealthy, and some of the bad ones were *really* bad. I tried to not think about Nicole that much, but her car crash was obviously the most vivid memory by far. It was so vivid that I could paint the scene out exactly if I had any artistic ability.

My family came over for New Year's Eve. The hospital allowed for families to come past visiting hours to spend New Years. It was comforting to see so many smiling faces in the hospital with almost everyone having someone to spend New Years with. Being in here for too long makes you feel isolated from all society, so I knew what they were all feeling.

Claire brought a small, spare TV from the house to set up in my hospital room. My family makes an effort to make sure we're all together to watch the Times Square ball drop on TV.

Of course, my dad didn't come. I asked my mom where he was and she told me that he went to Atlanta to spend New Years with friends. That wasn't exactly an uncommon occurrence, since he's done it twice in my lifetime, but it was pretty apparent why he chose to be away this year. My mom didn't say much about that, but the wide-eyed expression she gave said it all.

Everything pretty much returned to its usual depressing state after everyone left. Claire left the TV here so I could watch more things than just the news. I ended up watching random cartoons from probably the nineties. It gave my eyes something to do while I was constantly being tested. This sounds like the most teenager thing in the world, but not having my phone really sucks in situations like these. I never used it all that much in general, but I felt so bored without it. Sky once again offered me hers to use for the time being, but that's how she talks to her family, so I couldn't take that away from her.

My body was getting a little too used to the routine of waking up every four hours, no matter what time of the day it was. The only reason why I needed to wake up every four hours before was to take medication, but I no longer needed it that often. My doctor gives it every twelve hours. He said the more I get used to not taking it, the faster I'll get used to the pain. Because no matter how much I heal, the wound won't ever stop hurting. Of course, the pain will go down over time, and probably dissipate in the long run, but I had to get used to the feeling of having a ripped open abdomen, basically.

"Hello?" I was about to doze off again (for another four hours) when I heard someone knocking on my door.

"Hi? Sorry, you might have the wrong room." I looked up and a girl with reddish-brown hair walked into my room. I didn't recognize her, so I assumed she stumbled into the wrong room.

"Are you Mark?" She asked.

Her accent was especially southern. I know I live in the south and such, but surprisingly, not a lot of people in this town have heavy southern accents. At least the newer generations don't.

"Yeah, can I help you?" I asked politely. I was trying to dig around in my brain to see if I knew her from somewhere. Nothing was coming to me, though.

"I'm sorry if this'all really sudden, but I'm Tess. Lilith's..." She paused, considering her word choice. The both of us held a breath at the same time in anticipation. "Lilith's cousin."

I've read about you. The first thing I thought.

Every detail that Lilith wrote about Tess was true. The color of her hair, the southern accent, the leather boots. It was all *here.* My eyes widened when she introduced herself as Tess. I've read about her, yes, but seeing her in real life was a completely different experience. I was almost starstruck, like a kid seeing a cartoon character in real life.

"Oh." I reacted seemingly indifferent. Hearing anything relating to Lilith brought mixed feelings. "You must've heard what happened then," I said with the weight of my memories. The room filled itself with sorrow.

"Yeah, unfortunately."

She sat down in a chair that was a notable distance away from my bed.

"*Taylor really hasn't changed, huh?*" Tess said under her breath. My expression widened, but she couldn't see. Her head was parallel to the ground, and she tapped her foot at a slow tempo.

I remembered that she was one of Taylor's victims. If my assumptions are correct, that is. I remember trying to connect the dots when I was first reading Lilith's diary but dropping the thought. But now that she was right in front of me, it made complete sense.

That was harsh to even think about. Taylor and Tess were cousins. This definitely hurt differently than if they weren't family. Tess doesn't know that I know this, so I kept my reactions in check.

"Who told you?" I asked.

"The dad," Tess said with a heavy tongue.

She stood up and started pacing around the room as some sort of coping mechanism. "He ain't taking this well, so he asked me to come 'ere on his behalf." *I can imagine.* Finding out your son is the monster that you hoped that he overcame. I couldn't begin to fathom how broken up he feels.

"Don't you live in Atlanta?" I asked.

"Yeh, how'd you know?" She said, sounding surprised. *Fuck. She's not supposed to know that I know that.*

"Lilith said something about a cousin living in Atlanta some time ago." I lied. She paused her body and awkwardly stared at the ground.

It was weird knowing Tess' entire story relating to Lilith and *also* talking to her *about* Lilith. I probably knew exactly what she was thinking, or at least a vague idea, but she, of course, couldn't say anything.

"Are ya'two friends?" She asked, after what felt like an eternal pause.

"More or less. I met her a few months ago." I admitted.

One night when I was trying to fall asleep, the random flashback of me being pushed off the cliff appeared in my head. It made me shoot up in my bed and I was forced to think for a few moments.

The memory of seeing a girl look me in the eyes as I fell came into my mind. I swear it was like slow motion for those few seconds. I wanted to believe that girl was Lilith at first, but I convinced myself my brain was playing tricks on me. Now that I know everything about Taylor and Lilith is related to him, that theory doesn't sound so far-fetched.

"Weird how the world works, huh? You met someone, ne'xt thing you know, her brother is try'na to kill you and your friends." She scoffed.

It seemed like Tess said that to herself rather than to me. If she said that to my face, I wouldn't know how to react.

"Sorry, I'm takin' too much of your time. Ya probably need to sleep. I should cut to the chase." Tess said out of the blue. Being here was taking a toll on her. It definitely showed in multiple ways.

I noticed she did the same thing that Sky does with her accent. It deepened itself as her emotions grew.

"You're fine," I said nicely.

I honestly didn't mind listening to her random monologues. It was more insight into who Tess was rather than just Lilith's written view of her. Although both were equally complicated.

"I'm here because..." She paused again. She didn't consider her words, rather she didn't want to hear her own words out loud and just wanted to keep them on her tongue. Her lips momentarily quivered as if she was speaking, but the words wouldn't come out. "Lilith's g-gone missing. We don't know where she is." We, including Tess and Lilith's dad. "I was wondering if you happened to know where she went. I'm worried Taylor might've done some'n to her."

"Is Taylor missing too?" I asked, not even knowing if Taylor is even alive or not.

"Yeah, his dad said he wasn't in his dorm room. Even his professors said that they haven't heard of him since the night of the accident."

"Then I don't know where she is. I'm sorry." That pained me to say. "If you ask me, though, I don't think Taylor did anything to Lilith. This might be hard to believe, but I sort of know how Taylor and Lilith's relationship works. I don't think he did anything to her. He wouldn't lay a finger on her.

If anything, it would be Lilith doing something to Taylor." I explained, thinking about certain spots in her diary that led me to that conclusion.

"Y'think so?" She looked at me, not having a conclusion for herself to stand by.

"Almost positive," I said.

Tess left after that, saying not much else besides a goodbye and thank you. She even struggled to say those words. It was nice to know that Tess still cared about Lilith even though Lilith had put her through the wringer. I couldn't imagine what Tess was feeling, knowing that the person she loved could be missing. I was very worried about myself, but I knew I couldn't do much. As much as I knew Lilith and her circumstances, she was battling a lot of things, things I could never begin to understand.

Damien, Sky, and Avery came to visit me for New Years. This time, all of them were in high spirits since I was healing. Seeing them happy brought some normality, which was VERY NEEDED in my life. Damien brought his Lego set that I got him for Christmas to do together. Admittedly, this made me feel like a child, but I would take feeling like a child over feeling like a dying teenager any day.

"Mark, guess what?" Sky asked. I was helping Damien with his build while Sky just watched.

"Damien got a girlfriend!" Sky excitedly said.

"Really?" I responded, also excitedly, but not as much as Sky. "I thought you were still obsessed with Avery?" It's still crazy to me that Damien and Avery used to date. Their personalities couldn't be more different. I looked at Avery and she seemed so relieved. I laughed out loud, knowing that things were becoming somewhat normal again in her life.

"Yeah, still kind of am, but the girl asked me out and my instinct was to say yes. So, I did."

"IT WAS SO ROMANTIC! She asked him out on New Year's Eve. I was there for the whole thing!" Sky radiated that best friend aura that I kind of missed from Nicole lately. My heart started to feel a mix of nostalgia and sadness.

"Oh shush." Damien teased, slightly trying to hide his blush.

"Wait, guys..." Avery called our attention, putting a finger in the air. All three of us instantly turned our heads like a flock of birds. "I got a text back from Manny." Avery's eyes were glued to her phone.

"What does it say?" Damien asked, slightly freaking out. I looked at him and Sky, who had their eyes widened. Their arms slid forward in their chairs.

"Wait Damien, does Mark know about this?" Sky asked. I was so confused.

"Did you tell him...?" Damien asked. I'M SO CONFUSED. I felt like I was a little kid watching the adults talking.

Sky shook her head.

"Avery's friend volunteers at the hospital where Nicole is at." Damien turned his head towards me. "He offered to help us get an insight into Nicole's condition." My eyes also widened, but this was the first time in a while that I widened them out of joy.

"Really?" I almost jumped out of my hospital bed. "Read the text, please!" I was on the edge of my seat, well, bed.

"I tried my best to look at the hospital files, but I couldn't look for long without looking suspicious. It says that she had surgery for something. I don't know what for, but it was a couple of days ago. The surgery was successful, but her recovery time was unknown. If you didn't know, if the recovery time is marked as unknown, there is a chance the patient could die or require other surgeries. Once again, I do not know which one. I hope this helps and tell your friend that I'm praying for him." Sky read aloud.

"THAT MEANS SHE'S ALIVE! OH MY LORD!" I yelled.

Everyone let go of a breath that began when Sky started reading. I was probably the most relieved. Like I said, I've been lying awake at night thinking about if Nicole is alive or not. This lifted a good bit of weight off my shoulders.

"Thank god." Sky said, putting her heart over her chest.

"We still don't know what's wrong with her though..." Damien added, bringing us back down to ground level.

"We just have to hope mate. If Mark can recover, so can Nicole. I believe." Avery said confidently, which gave the rest of us confidence.

The nurse came in and asked them to leave so I could do some tests with the doctor. They ended up just leaving all together since it was getting kind of dark outside. The news about Nicole's life state was the thing I needed to keep me going, at least mentally. I swear I was about to go insane if I didn't have some form of good news.

"Your drainage levels are healing and your tissue is repairing itself pretty fast. That means we can give you some solid food now." My doctor said. He was reading results of his computer from tests he took earlier.

"Oh thank god, I was starting to develop a hate for applesauce," I admitted.

"Sorry kid. I remember when I was hospitalized as a kid and could only eat porridge for a month. So, applesauce doesn't sound all too bad. At least it's sweet." He explained. "How's your pain level? Your wound is closing up a bit, so I assume you're feeling a lot better?" He tried to confirm.

"Yeah, I'm able to move my body a lot more now. I can actually stand up and walk around without much issue." I said as I gently grazed my hand over the wound. It still stung a bit, but the pain was way less than before.

"That's nice to hear."

"Wait, doctor?" He was about to walk out when I wanted to ask for something.

"Yes?" He responded, turning around to face me.

"When do you think I'll be discharged?" I asked.

I've had this question on my mind for some time, but didn't have the guts to ask it until I had some clarity with my health.

"Why? Do you miss your family?" He asked.

"Yeah, and I want to see my friend in the hospital as soon as possible. She was also involved in my accident." I explained.

I really did miss seeing my family and being home and such, but seeing Nicole was my number one priority.

"Well, assuming nothing goes wrong, you ideally should be out in three days, but realistically, you should expect to be here for another week at the least. It's not uncommon for a person's drainage levels to rise even a little after a long time of healing."

"So a week basically?" I asked depressingly.

He slowly nodded. I tried to not sound upset, but my slow exhale gave it away. "Sorry, Mark. Your body is doing a great job of healing and you have people supporting you. You should be out of here in no time." He assured me, although I didn't really feel any better by his words exactly.

As soon as he left, I immediately needed to think of a plan. Some way to get me out of this hospital and a car ride to Nicole's hospital. I already accepted the fact that I couldn't wait a week or potentially more to see if Nicole is healing or dying. Trying to process the fact that she possibly needed multiple surgeries to stay alive was making me go nuts. This was the same girl who was afraid of flu shots, and now her life is in the hands of surgeons and even then, it could still go wrong. I spent all night thinking of a plan. I need to call Damien tomorrow.

How We See The Stars

289

Mark: January 2

"Hello? Sky?"

"*Mark? Is that you?*" Sky asked confusedly since I was using a hospital phone to call her.

"Yeah, I need a favor," I said in a serious tone. I also had to stay quiet, so people outside my room couldn't hear me.

"Anything, what's up?"

"Where are you? Are you in Macon?" I asked, already sounding like sweat was running down my face.

"*No, I'm home in Atlanta. What do you need?*" It was so hard to understand what she was saying, since the phone wasn't exactly of the highest quality.

"Can you come to the hospital with a change of regular clothes?"

There was a long silence between us. The only thing I heard was the cracky static over the phone.

"... Hello-"

"*You're planning to see Nicole, aren't you...?*" Sky suspected. She had a tone in his voice like she knew this sort of thing was coming. I didn't blame her.

"I mean- uh-"

"Mark, stop stutterin."

"You read like me like a book." I spit out.

"Mark, I don't know, mate. Sneaking you out of a hospital? That could get you into some big trouble. I'm being serious."

"Sky, please. We've done things way worse than this. I know *for a fact* you want to see her too." I pleaded. I realize how pathetic it is pleading over the phone.

"...God damn it, Mark. You got me all fucked up doing this shit." Sky said, giving in to my sorrow. "When do you need me to come?"

"As soon as possible, please. The sun's about to go down soon, so please hurry."

"I'll be there in an hour, get ready." Sky aggressively hung up.

I was overjoyed at the fact that I was finally getting out of this hospital. Out of all the plans and crazy things I've done lately, this seemed like the most important. I felt that somehow Nicole's life depended on me seeing her. It was my fault that she ended up like this. That guilt is something I couldn't even begin to describe with words.

"Ready mate?" Sky entered my room without knocking and tossed a pile of clothes on my bed. The amount of joy I experienced when I saw Sky and the smugness on her face was immense. I could've jumped out of my bed and hugged her.

"Jesus, how did you get here so fast? It's a helluva drive here from Atlanta." I said, sounding surprised. I wasn't expecting her to be here for another twenty minutes or so.

"Chasing you and Taylor taught me how to race across the highways, y'know?" Sky laughed audibly.

I imagined Sky zooming across the express lane like she cared about Nicole just as much as I did. I smiled just thinking about it.

"What's the plan? Are we just gonna walk out?" She asked.

"Nah, watch this," I said confidently. "Nurse!" I called out.

"Yeah, Mark?" The front desk was right next to my room, so if I was loud enough, the nurse could hear me.

"My friend is gonna take me to the bathroom. Is that okay?" I asked to confirm.

"Yeah, go ahead. Just don't take too long." She said without thinking too much about it. She turned around after saying that.

"Whoa, that was smooth." Sky complimented, seemingly impressed.

"Okay, let's go."

I took Sky's arm and used it as a crutch to get me to the bathroom. I did my best looking-like-I'm-sickly face to seem more helpless. I wasn't exactly used to moving around, so I didn't have to do *that* much pretending. Every step I took stressed out the wound quite a bit.

"You couldn't bring any better pants?" I complained. Sky leaned up against my stall, waiting for me to change.

"I just grabbed something out of my brother's dresser. There's no way you are fitting in *my* clothes. You'd look like a cross-dresser." The clothes didn't fit the best, but it was convincing enough for me to make a getaway. I forgot what it felt like to wear regular clothes. I've been in a hospital gown for what seemed like forever.

Once we got out of the bathroom, I tried my best to walk out as casually as possible. Sky didn't have to try to look innocent since she wasn't the one escaping the hospital. This was probably the most rebellious thing I've ever done, which is laughable compared to everything I've done up to this point.

That first step outside felt great. I also had forgotten what fresh air smelled like or what the outside temperature felt like. In other words, I was gaining energy by just existing in someplace other than the hospital.

All of that ended pretty quickly once I stepped into Sky's car. It was a little traumatic, to say the least. Being on the road in general brought back some unsolicited memories. Just the image of other cars around us while we were also driving was scary. Every time a car was parallel to us, I tensed up. Also, having the car constantly rock around put a lot of pressure on my wound. Speed bumps were the worst. I felt like someone was manually tearing my stomach open every time there was little consistency in the road.

"We're here." Sky parked in front of the hospital and turned off the car. There was a certain awkwardness in the air. There wasn't much air in this car, to begin with, so every emotion bounced off the walls of the car and back inside ourselves. Sky and I both were trying to prepare to see the worst, without imagining the worst. If I didn't imagine what the worst was, that means that outcome didn't exist or wasn't possible.

I put my hand over the bandage that covered my wound. I tried my best to hide the pain, but being out and about made it hurt like hell. It pained me to the point where I could imagine Taylor's knife going in and out repeatedly, even though it only went in once. It was my body's way of telling me that there was no turning back once I left this car. My first waking moment in the hospital had me thinking about Nicole. I couldn't go to sleep until my brain thought about her for even a few minutes. I couldn't look anyone in the eye without thinking about her.

But what if... not knowing her condition was for the best? I was held innocent of knowing her condition this whole time. *What if that was for the best?* Us being separated into different hospitals. *That's no way that this wasn't fate, right?* If I walked into her hospital and I happened to witness the last of her dying breaths on earth, I wouldn't be able to live with myself.

"Ready mate?" Sky asked, sounding like the truck of reality just hit her.

"Ready as I'll ever be," I said blankly, saying it to myself rather than to anyone else.

Somehow, this hospital was more depressing than mine. That's no fault of the hospital itself. I just had a shitty mindset going into it. Sky tried to stand tall and act as a beacon of hope for me, but her face had doubts written all over it.

"Hi. What room is Nicole Schmidt in?" Sky asked the lady at the front desk.

"Let me check that for you." She started typing on her computer. The woman only took a few seconds to finish typing, but every key she pressed added a level of anxiety to my heart. Time was slowing down and speeding up. "Ms. Schmidt is in room one-two-one-four."

"Thank you." Sky said.

"Have a good day, you two." She mellowly said.

I couldn't wrap my head around how someone could act so calm and normal when people are literally dying in your workspace. The woman was just doing her job, but it angered me how artificially normal she sounded.

"Are you okay?" Sky put her hand over my shoulder. I didn't notice the fact that I was staring deep into the floor tiles, counting each tile that I passed by. My brain wasn't really walking with direction. I just happened to be walking wherever Sky was taking me.

"Could be better," I said blandly. I no longer felt the pain of my wound anymore. My mind was focused on anything but the pain stimulus. "I'm not even sure if I should be here. Now that I'm here, it feels wrong." I was speaking my thoughts, once again, not to anyone in specific.

"You care about your best friend. I don't think you should feel wrong-"

"HELP! DOCTOR! SHE'S DYING!" someone from inside of Nicole's room yelled.

"WE NEED A DOCTOR!" another person yelled; this time a woman's voice.

What?

A few seconds later, a few doctors rushed into her room. Sky and I were forced to step out of the threshold to make room for the doctors. Cold sweat started to creep down my head. I even felt myself start to blackout, but managed to hold on to my consciousness. All I heard was a bunch of doctors yelling commands and the beeping of a heart monitor. It became deafening to hear. It brought me to my knees. It felt like the entire world was crashing down on me at once. The weight of the world was all I could feel. It was so fucking heavy. There wasn't a number in existence that could express the value of how heavy it felt.

"Clear the way!" A doctor yelled.

I looked up and Nicole was being carted off into God knows where. The further she got from my view, the bigger the void in my heart grew. Those same lifeless eyes were all I could see before she disappeared out of my view. I hoped to never see those eyes never again and yet they appeared when I needed them the least.

"WHAT HAPPENED?" Nicole's dad ran into my line of sight. His face turned a bright red.

"I don't know! We came here and her heart rate monitor went off." Sky explained. I opened my mouth to speak at first, but my tears were slowing down my reality.

"*You did this.*" Nicole's dad said under his breath, holding out a fist.

"What?"

"YOU DID THIS!" He grabbed my shirt and pinned me against the wall behind me. My head slammed against the hard surface. "My daughter's life in the fucking balance because of you! How could you let this happen?" I've never seen such pure hatred in someone's eyes.

I deserved every bit of it, though. If he punched me, I wouldn't have minded. Instead, he threw me to the floor and continued to curse me out. While no longer there, the only thing I could hear was the constant beating of the heart rate monitor.

Sky and other people around had to pull him off me, or else he might have actually killed me. It took me a few moments to gather the motivation to get up. If it was up to me, I would've sat on that floor for as long as my bones allowed me to. Sky offered a hand to help me to my feet, but I didn't immediately look up to it. The people around me advised me to leave before things got even uglier. Sky was probably yelling for me to leave, but my mind processed all sounds as gibberish. The yelling soon became inaudible.

I stood outside the hospital entrance and just contemplated life and my current worth. At that moment, I felt like the most worthless thing on earth. *I'm sorry Nicole.* I remember repeating in my head. I could only process the idea that I was destined to fail. *We* were destined to fail. Even if I went back in time and did it all again, the outcome would never change. Taylor would get away, I would wake up in a hospital with a stab wound in me, and Nicole would be fighting an uphill battle for her life. The word regret doesn't even begin to describe how I feel. It goes further beyond that. Your brain tries to convince itself that this is all just a dream or a sick joke, but that's just reality taking its course. All my ideas about getting the ending I wanted sounded stupid. I was so convinced that I was able to bend fate in my favor if I just tried. I thought trying was the difference between life and death, win and lose, good and bad, but it seemed like the ending was already predetermined in a way where I never win.

"I'm sorry Mark. I really am." Sky said, who was on the verge of crying. She was fighting back the tears, knowing that if she cried, I would cry a million times harder.

We hadn't reached the car yet. We were just sitting in the hospital parking lot, trying, and failing, to process the *why* of it all.

"I just," My brain had trouble sending words to my mouth. "I just hope it ends soon." I finally said. There was still the world's weight holding me down. This feeling was usually accompanied by violent tears and sniffles, but I was too distraught to cry. All I could do was laugh. I scoffed, pathetically.

"Do you think she'll make it?" Sky asked. We were both thinking about that question but didn't dare to answer it in our brains.

"It's not what I think. I can think and hope all I want and the outcome won't care about what I have to say." Trying to look for some sort of light, something away from darkness, I looked up at the stars. Normally, I would feel something along the lines of hope, direction, bliss, etc. But that didn't happen today. I just felt numb for the most part.

"All we can do is hope, Mark." She said. I let out a tired laugh.

It sounded useless, but she was right, in a way.

"Mark?" Sky asked, well more like uttered. She sounded as distraught as me.

"What's up?" I slowly responded head parallel to the skyline.

"Do you remember when we first met?" She asked, seemingly out of nowhere.

"Vaguely. It was at school, right? You gave me the note." In my mind, that memory seemed so long ago, even though it was just a couple of months.

"No, it was at the Halloween party."

"What?" I briefly looked down at her to respond. To my surprise, her eyes were also encased in the night sky. "You were there?"

"Yeah, but since you lost your memory, you don't really remember, do you, mate?" Sky's accent thickened a bit.

I slowly shook my head. She saw me in her peripherals.

"Well, I remember seeing you on the roof, staring at the stars. Similar to what you're doing now." In my peripherals, I saw her staring at me with some sort of wonder.

"Ha, sounds like something I would do," I said, laughing at the thought of that scene.

"My first memory of you was watching you stare at the stars and never wanting to look down, ever. I could never wrap my head around it, no matter how much I thought about it. What do you even see up there?" Sometimes I don't even notice myself looking up towards the night sky. For me, it was natural as someone looking forward, or down at the ground.

"I see a lot of things. I see colors, events, memories, personalities, emotions, *people*. I'm still trying to look for things on my own, things that I could never see before." Those are the types of things you say where you don't have to think about the words. It felt like they came from somewhere other than your brain.

"What are you looking for right now?" Sky asked. By this point, both of our heads were parallel towards the stars. I hope somehow Sky was looking for her own meaning from the stars.

"A girl who always looked out for me. A girl who was always at the right place, at the right time. A girl who I..." A shed a tear. I barely felt it coming. "... considered family."

"Do you think you'll find her?"

It was going to take me a while to find that star. It wasn't as simple as a game of Where's Waldo or looking for a place on a map. It was something that I had to do for days, maybe months. I didn't have much left inside of me, but from what little I had left, it was enough to find that star.

"Not a doubt in my mind Sky. Not a doubt in my mind." We both looked at each other and exchanged a smile, a real one, hoping that our smile could somehow change the past.

Lilith: My last entry cont. again

"Hm, I knew you would be here." A strong burst of wind blew between our ears.

"Am I that predictable?" I responded, knowing who was standing behind me.

"No, I just had a hunch, y'know?" I didn't turn around to see him, but his presence was enough to feel connected in a way. "How long have you been out here?" He asked as he kneeled next to me. I was also kneeled. The moisture from the grass was seeping into my jeans, but that was the least of my problems.

"How long ago was the accident?" I asked.

"About a month ago. Thirty-four days ago to be exact." He'd been counting the days. Even though I was on the other side of things, losing track of the days and probably time itself, I knew that feeling of having to count the days.

I let out a heavy yet soft exhale after letting that process itself.

"How's the wound?" I finally turned around and looked at his stomach to see if he had a bandage around it. Turns out he did. A big whitish-brown one.

"Not fully healed, but better, I guess. I was discharged from the hospital around when school started again." He pushed a bit of hair back.

"I uh, heard what happened to Nicole." I struggled to say.

"I know, you don't have to tell me." He interrupted, sounding like he's given up on the world. Something that we now had in common.

"Then why are you here?"

"Her family wants nothing to do with me. I should respect that." He let out a small sigh at the end of his sentence. I could feel the weight of his heart from that one breath. A harsh bit of wind followed.

I wasn't invited to Nicole's funeral, understandably. If I were there, I would burst out crying, knowing the reason why she died.

"That's not fair. She was your best friend, wasn't she?"

"Yeah, she was." He said. I couldn't see him, but I could tell at least a tear or two ran down his face. *"And now she's gone."* He said under his breath. I felt the heaviness of his voice as he traversed through every word. It was enough to make me tear up with him.

"By the way, Tess came to visit me the other day." I heard Mark put his hands in his pockets to keep warm.

"Oh yeah? What did she say?" I said, sounding surprised. I wiped my tears with the sleeve of my shirt.

"Your family is worried about you. Certainly, Tess is. You and Taylor being missing aren't doing them any favors."

"I let Taylor go," I said, trying to remember why I did it. The reason seemed unrealistic, but it was a reason that felt real at the moment. "I could've killed him, but couldn't bring myself to do it. He could be in Italy for all I know." I said with a bunch of emotions in my throat, one of them being regret. That was a sentence no one should ever have to say or even think about.

"I figured. No one should be expected to kill their own brother. I think it might be for the best."

"You think so?"

"I don't think your dad could handle another dead family member, even though most of us would rather have Taylor dead than alive."

It's easy to talk about death when it *didn't* happen. Anyone could wish death upon anyone, but the second the opportunity presents itself, everyone shuts up.

"You read my diary, didn't you?" I barely raised an eyebrow. I honestly couldn't feel my face from how cold it was.

"Was I not supposed to?"

"No, you were. I just didn't expect you to understand it. *I even* forgot what I put in there. If I didn't give it to you, I would've probably burned it."

"I don't think your mom would've wanted that for you."

Mark kneeled down next to me. The wind between my ears became loud when we paused. It wasn't awkward. It was moments where we didn't talk about how empty we'd become.

"She's beautiful."

I looked at Mark and he was staring into the eyes of Mom's tombstone photo. I was admiring Mom's tombstone this whole time and he seemed to understand it with me. Even if that understanding came from written words on a page.

"She looks exactly like me," I said monotonously. I've only come to accept that fact right when I was able to look at her again without the burden of her journals. There was no bitterness anymore that came with her image.

"Do you need more time with her, or are you ready to go home?"

"I think I'm good. I've been with her all this time. She needs a rest."

I stood and looked up at the stars one last time. I knew among the infinite stars in the sky, Mom had to be one of them, looking over me from the heavens. I'd like to think that she shines the brightest out of them all, so I can always see her whenever I need her. *I haven't lived on this earth for that long, but thank you for always being there when I needed you most.*

"Wait, I forgot one last thing," Mark said, stopping in his tracks.

Mark pulled out a backpack, my backpack, and dug around for something. At first, I didn't know what he was doing, but when I realized it, it felt like fate.

Mark pulled out something small. It was small enough for him to hold it with only two fingers. His thumb and pointer finger. In the darkness of night, it was almost impossible to see what he was holding, but as soon as he pulled out my backpack, I knew what it was.

"Is it okay if I leave this here?" He kneeled at Mom's grave again and looked at me. "Or do you want it?"

I stood there in thought for a few seconds, not having an immediate answer come to me. Did I want it? More than anything on earth. Was it right to take it for me? Of course not. I would rather be where Mom is right now than take something from her.

"You can leave it there." I struggled to say it. "*It really is for the best,*" I said under my breath. I think Mark heard it because he turned and smiled at me.

Mark slowly placed the necklace next to the flowers Nonna put on her grave. Both of us looked at it and its rich history. Years of Mom and who she was, confined to one small object. It said more than her journals ever could.

Acknowledgments

I first started writing the world of How We See The Stars back in the summer of 2019. I remember thinking writing that book would only take a few weeks. Gosh, how foolish I was back then. I'm not the best writer my any means, but judging by how sloppy and cringe my first drafts were, I've come a long way. For the past two years, I haven't gone a day without thinking about how I can deepen the world of Mark and Lilith. I know these two characters like the back of my hand. Better yet, I've included them in scenes in my next book, "On Tour".

Before I get to specific people, I want to thank my amazing and most wonderful friends and family for supporting me through this wild journey that is writing and publishing a novel. When times were tough, I realized that I had the support of some of the best friends in the world, and that gave me the motivation to keep going. Some of you are inspirations for some of my characters. Of course I won't name who is who, because that's my little secret. :)

Big thank you to my beta readers for reading all of my work and discussing with me on how I can make my story better. All the feedback I received greatly improved the story and how I write. So thank you to: Era Reid, Luis Rodrigues, Rupsaa Goswami, Kristen Chen, Angeline Yeh, Sireli Sildnik, and Farah Amri.

Also a thank you to Kaitlyn Kitagawa for inspiring the idea of Lilith's necklace and Jada Pineda for bringing the idea to life. I have the real life necklace sitting on my neck as I write this. I consider it one of my most prized possessions and the book wouldn't be the same without it.

Lastly, I'd like to give the HUGEST thank you to my parents for supporting this massive project. You truly are my biggest fans.

About The Author

TYLER BANSIL is a young adult contemporary novelist from the San Francisco Bay Area. Aside from writing his next new novel ideas, he spends a lot of his time in a variety of musical performing arts. He is an avid member of his high school's band and choir programs, but outside of school he is a member of the Kaligayahan Dance Troupe for traditional Filipino folk dancing. He also has an affinity for the color purple.

Visit Tyler Bansil Online!
Instagram: @tylerbansil